# ROCKBUSTER

# ROCKBUSTER

BY GLORIA SKURZYNSKI

Atheneum Books for Young Readers
New York London Toronto Sydney Singapore

Atheneum Books for Yong Readers
An imprint of Simon & Schuster Children's Publishing Division
1230 Avenue of the Americas
New York, New York 10020

Book design by Sonia Chaghatzbanian
The text of this book is set in Sabon.
Printed in the United States of America
2 4 6 8 10 9 7 5 3 1

3002000038371

Library of Congress Cataloging-in-Publication Data
Skurzynski, Gloria.
Rockbuster / by Gloria Skurzynski.
p. cm.
Summary: In 1915, after being asked to sing at the funeral of executed songwriter
and member of the international union, Industrial Workers of the World, Joe Hill,
eighteen-year-old Utah coal miner Tommy Quinlan begins to accept his past and
make decisions about his future.
ISBN 0-689-83991-X
[1. Coal miners—Fiction. 2. Labor unions—Fiction. 3. Identity—Fiction.
4. Prejudices—Fiction. 5. Hill, Joe, 1879–1915—Fiction. 6. Industrial Workers of
the World—Fiction. 7. Utah—Fiction.] I. Title.
PZ7.S6287 Ro 2001
[Fic]—dc21    00-050415

FIRST
**F**
EDITION

For Tom Thliveris, who was born under a lucky star

# And They Obey

Smash down the cities.
Knock the walls to pieces.
Break the factories and cathedrals, warehouses and homes
Into loose piles of stone and lumber and black burnt wood:
You are the soldiers and we command you.
Build up the cities.
Set up the walls again.
Put together once more the factories and cathedrals,
warehouses and homes
Into buildings for life and labor:
You are workmen and citizens all:
We command you.

—*Carl Sandburg, 1916*

# Contents

The interior of the railroad car was dark, mostly. From time to time a passenger would strike a match to light a pipe or a cigar; in the flare of illumination Tommy could glance up to check on his guitar case, rattling on the overhead rack. At first he'd set the guitar upright on the seat beside him, but the conductor had made him move it—because, the man said, a paying passenger might need to sit there.

Fifteen-thousand people were expected to attend the funeral in Chicago. Tommy wondered if any other passengers on this train had been invited, or if he was the only one. Anyway, none of them would get a look at the corpse.

When a man got shot by firing squad, did any one bullet actually kill him, or did all of them kill him equally? The newspapers hadn't said anything about that.

He sighed. The Union Pacific bragged that their trains made it from Salt Lake City to Chicago in forty-two hours. To Tommy, it already seemed like a long train ride, and he still had thirty-four hours to go. A breath of fresh air would be good, but he didn't want to stand on the platform between two moving cars, where flying cinders would dirty the collar of his clean white shirt.

The swaying of the car, the clack of wheels, the smells of stale smoke, damp wool overcoats, sour spilled beer, and train-weary human bodies, all made him sleepy. Leaning his head against the stiff, upright seat back, he remembered the train ride eight years ago, when he was only ten years old. That ride had been his first initiation into violence—the day his uncle Jim got murdered by the railroad detectives.

Now, eight years later, he hoped and prayed that the funeral in Chicago might mark an end to the violence, the agitation, the fury, the hatred. But he doubted that it would.

# PART ONE

# Murders Past and Present

# CHAPTER ONE
## July 26, 1907

They'd ridden the Denver and Rio Grande Western from the coal town of Castle Gate to the growing metropolis of Salt Lake City, arriving at the Union Pacific station well after dark. "Hungry?" Uncle Jim asked, and Tommy nodded.

"No wonder you're hungry, the way you're growin'. You'll be a tall man like your daddy was."

Uncle Jim McInerny wasn't all that tall himself. He would have been, he said, but his growth was stunted during his youth. Once there was a time when the McInerny family had hardly anything to eat—Jim was about Tommy's age then. Since he couldn't stand to hear the hungry whimpering of his little sister, Fiona—who grew up to be Tommy's mother—Jim had taken to giving her half his own food for months on end. That was how Jim McInerny explained his own middling height, but it was hard for Tommy to imagine his uncle Jim ever looking puny and starved. Standing five feet eight in his working-man's boots, Jim was husky, big shouldered, and powerful, with large, strong hands.

Though it was going on midnight, the Union Pacific station

blazed with electric lights and bustled with as many people as if it were daytime. An old woman walked back and forth in front of the station with a basket hanging from her arm. FRESH SAMWICHES 25 CENTS, said a sign stuck on the side of her basket.

"We'll buy two for now and two more for the rest of the train ride," Uncle Jim decided, pulling a silver dollar from the pocket of his trousers.

Tommy was used to the coal trains that dragged full boxcars up the side of the mountain where he lived, so used to them that he hardly paid attention when one tooted past the window of his house. But the locomotive chugging into Salt Lake City's Union Pacific station that night looked different: bigger, and shinier, as though it had been polished. It pulled passenger cars, not coal-loaded freight cars. Tommy stood gape-mouthed, peering at the dimly lighted, curtained windows of the Pullman sleepers—imagine lying down in a train as if you were in your own bed! But that was only for rich people.

The old woman had wrapped the sandwiches in sheets of newspaper. "You want these put in a poke?" she asked, unfolding a paper bag already grease-marked.

"Yes," Jim replied. "And give it to the boy here." Jim's hands were occupied with a box of La Estrallita cigars. Other than that, he carried no luggage, and neither did Tommy. For the trip to Boise they were traveling with nothing more than the two sandwiches that would be left after they'd eaten the first ones, with the cigar box, a few silver dollars jingling in Uncle Jim's pocket, and the clothes they stood in. That was all.

As they passed the train's smoker car Tommy dragged his feet, taking a good look at the inside—or as good a look as he could get, since the interior was thick with smoke. Men stood or sat, puffing cigars and pipes and cigarettes, drinking beer from tall glasses or drinking whiskey from short, stubby ones. Some wore expensive-looking clothes, others dressed plainly, with collarless shirts and ill-fitting jackets. In the heat of the July night a few had taken off their suit coats to sit in shirtsleeves, their wide suspenders stretched across slumped shoulders and bulging bellies.

Then Tommy gasped, because he saw a woman sitting next to the window—*smoking!* None of the proper women in his hometown ever smoked, or if they did, it was in secret where no one could see them; certainly never in a public place. Yet this woman looked proper enough, dressed in a high, feathered hat and a fancy suit. Tommy got a good look at her as they walked along the platform, close enough that he could have reached out and touched the window she peered from—could have touched the woman herself, because her window had been opened partway to let in whatever night breeze wavered around the edges of the hissing, sweating train.

She gave a little smile. At first Tommy thought the smile was meant for him, but then he realized that Uncle Jim, right behind him, had tipped his straw boater hat to the lady.

"Do you know her?" Tommy asked.

"No, but if you weren't with me, Tommy, I'd make it my business to know her before this train ever reached the city of Boise. But," he sighed, "we have a job to do, lad. Can't think about ladies tonight, no matter how—uh—*modern* they appear."

The second-class cars were all the way at the end of the train. "Can you make it up the step?" Jim asked, giving Tommy a boost. Conductors didn't help the second-class passengers to board; they were too busy showing courtesy to the people in first class.

Jim and Tommy found a couple of bench seats side by side at the very back of the last car. Both of them took off their jackets, folded them in a roll, and put them behind their heads to use as lumpy pillows. Jim wedged the cigar box on the seat between the two of them and told Tommy to set the bag of sandwiches on top of that.

"Right on time," Jim said, glancing at the Ingersoll watch he drew from his vest pocket as the train lurched forward. With a squeal of wheels, the groan of couplings, and the hiss of steam, the locomotive hauled its half dozen passenger cars out of the station.

Since his uncle had let him slide into the seat next to the window, Tommy pressed his face against the glass to watch the lights of Salt Lake City pass by, first creeping, then, as the train picked up speed, streaming faster. By the time the locomotive throttled up to full speed, they'd left the city lights behind them and were rattling through the countryside, where all was dark.

"All right, now," Jim began, "we're under way and you haven't a bit of an idea why we're doing this, have you, Tommy?"

Tommy shook his head.

"Well, I'm going to tell you. But no one else can hear. That's why we're sitting way at the back, and here's what I want you to do. Both of us will slump in our seats like we're sleeping. You put your head on my shoulder and close your eyes. Keep them closed. That's right."

Tommy let his eyelids flutter just a bit so he could squint at Uncle Jim, who'd leaned his head against the wall behind them. Jim's straw hat was tilted so far forward that it covered his face down to his mouth. As he spoke softly, the hat's brim shadowed the movement of his lips.

"We're going to Boise, Idaho—that much you know."

"Yes," Tommy agreed.

"You know what's going on in Boise right now? Answer me in a real soft voice, lad."

Tommy knew about it, but only a little. "Big Bill Haywood is being tried for murder."

"Right. The biggest union trial ever held. Haywood is one of the top bosses of the miners' union, and all the rich fellows in Idaho—the mine owners and the elected officials— want to see him hanged."

"Did he do it?" Tommy asked.

"What—commit murder? Naw, a scab named Harry Orchard admitted killing Idaho's ex-governor, and that's what this trial is all about. But Orchard says Bill Haywood ordered him to do it. It's all lies."

Jim lowered his shoulder so that Tommy could fit more comfortably against it before he went on. "The rich men in Idaho promised Orchard they'd set him free if he could pin the rap on Big Bill Haywood. See, the mine owners hate the union worse than death."

Tommy remembered some of it. A year and a half earlier, right after Christmas, there'd been a lot of talk around the Castle Valley coalfields about Frank Steunenberg's death. Idaho's former governor had been walking through the gate to his yard on New Year's Eve when the gate exploded, blowing him to kingdom come.

Tommy didn't like to think about men being blown to bits. His own father had died that way, caught in the Scofield coal mine explosion in 1900. Tommy had been only three years old, too young to understand any of it. But as he grew older he heard the story again and again, about his father, John Quinlan, dying that day along with 199 other miners. Of all of them, John Quinlan's body had been the most shattered. "There weren't enough pieces left of John Quinlan," people used to say, "to fill a peach basket, let alone a coffin."

It was then that Uncle Jim had come from the Pennsylvania coalfields to take care of his sister, Fiona, and her little son, Tommy. He'd moved them away from Scofield, with its awful memories, and into a small house in nearby Castle Gate, Utah. Uncle Jim got a job mining coal there, just as John Quinlan had once mined coal, just as most of the other male inhabitants of the town did every day, six days a week—though to a miner working in the darkness underground, days were no different than nights.

Leaning against Jim's shoulder in the rocking train, Tommy nearly drifted off to sleep, until his uncle said, "Be alert now, lad. We've lots to discuss."

"I'm awake," Tommy said too quickly.

"Well, now, here's the thing. The miners' union got the best lawyer in the land to defend Big Bill Haywood. A lawyer by the name of Clarence Darrow. But such fellows don't come cheap, so union men from all over the country have been pitching in to help with the cost."

Jim turned his head so that his lips were less than an inch from Tommy's ear. "The trial's nearly over, and things look bad for Big Bill. It's almost certain he'll be sentenced to hang. But"—Jim's whisper was hard for Tommy to hear—"even so, prison guards can be bribed."

"Huh?" Tommy raised his head in time to see a finger

cross Jim's lips, a command for silence. Slowly, carefully, Jim drew the cigar box from between them. Without a word he lifted the lid of the box to reveal . . . cigars.

Afraid to make a sound because of the warning pucker of his uncle's eyebrows, Tommy gave the tiniest shrug, as if to ask, *What do cigars have to do with Big Bill Haywood?*

Jim pulled a pocketknife from inside his vest, opened the largest blade, and—deftly for a man with such thick fingers—slid the blade along the inside edge of the box. "False bottom," he whispered. Tommy couldn't even hear the whisper, but he could read the words on his uncle's lips.

"Bend down," Jim whispered next. "Don't want to hold this thing up where anyone else can see it."

50 DARK BROAD-LEAF CIGARS, SWEET AND MELLOW, it said on the inside of the lid, right above a picture of a woman in a long red dress sitting underneath a tree while five sheep grazed in the background. SUN RIPENED FOR MILDNESS. PERFECTO EXTRA—those words shone in gold letters beneath the woman.

As Jim used the knife blade to lift a thin sheet of wood that covered the real bottom of the box, the cigars rolled downhill into his left hand. Tommy got the barest glimpse of green before the panel sank back into place and the cigars covered it again. Money. That's what he'd seen.

With the box safely tucked between them once more, Jim pulled Tommy's head close and murmured, "Twenty fifties. One thousand dollars. For the Haywood defense fund, to pay the lawyers. Or, if Bill Haywood is convicted, it's for the bribe-the-guards-to-break-him-out-of-jail fund. Whichever it turns out to be."

Jim's grip on Tommy's neck was becoming painful. He pulled away enough to ask, "Why am I here?"

"To make me look innocent. Every street in Boise is crawling with detectives—men from the Pinkerton agency who want to see Haywood hanged. I bet there's half a dozen of them right here on this train. They won't suspect a man traveling with a boy your age. We look like father and son going somewhere for a family visit."

A real father couldn't have been kinder to any son than Jim McInerny had always been to Tommy. Jim had never married, even though he was quite a ladies' man. Maybe *because* he was such a ladies' man, he didn't feel the need to marry. At the Irish weddings and wakes in their small coal town he could sing and dance up a storm, even before he'd helped himself to the whiskey that flowed like a fountain into the parched throats of revelers or mourners. No matter how much he drank, Jim McInerny never acted drunk—although he would become increasingly jovial as the evening wore on.

If Jim had an evening or a day off from mining, he would play cards with other miners, or go hunting in the mountains around Castle Gate, or go courting among the local women, whether they were married or not. But the card games and hunting trips might not have been what they seemed to be. Once, when Tommy's mother, Fiona, scalded herself from a cooking pot that burned through, and Tommy had run to look for his uncle, he'd burst into the room where the men were supposedly playing cards. As Tommy threw open the door he found himself looking down the barrel of a revolver that then vanished almost instantly, so fast it might not have been pointed at Tommy at all. But he'd seen it, all right. Young as he was, he knew that he'd busted in on a forbidden union meeting.

"Now, Tommy," Jim was saying, "you know that you and your mother are all the family I've got, so I'd never put you into jeopardy. All you have to do is walk alongside me, innocent like, while I get this cigar box into the proper hands. Of course you're not to say a word about this to anyone, now or ever, understand?"

When Tommy nodded, Jim gave the boy's shoulder a squeeze and said, "You're the best thing in my life, Tom—you and your mother. D'you know that? If I ever had a son, I'd want him to be just like you. So catch a little shut-eye while you can. In an hour or so we have to change trains at Pocatello."

# CHAPTER TWO
## July 27, 1907

Tommy felt hands under his arms, hauling him to his feet. "Come along," Uncle Jim was saying. "This is Pocatello."

Stiff from the hard bench seat, so sleepy he had trouble remembering why he was on a train, Tommy let Jim lead him to the steps. "Look lively, now," Jim told him. "I don't want you tumbling down onto the platform." Jim held Tommy upright with one arm; his other arm stayed clamped around the cigar box and the bag of sandwiches.

The outside air woke Tommy a bit, with its tang of locomotive smoke and the pungent odor of droppings from horses hitched to the hackneys that were waiting for passengers. "Need a ride, mister?" one of the drivers called.

"Nope. Just changing trains," Jim called back. "Come on, Tommy. We'll wait in the station house."

The heat of the July night clung to them. Inside the station house the high ceilings trapped warm air like a lid on a kettle. The Pocatello depot was large, nearly as big as the one in Salt Lake City, but at three in the morning not nearly as crowded. When they chose an unoccupied wooden bench toward the back of the station, Jim opened his shirt collar and used his straw hat to fan both of them. Tommy forced himself to sit upright, although he'd much rather have stretched out on the bench and gone back to sleep.

"Keep an eye on these," Jim said, winking at the cigar box and paper bag. "I'm going to find a newspaper."

That pulled Tommy out of his torpor. Being responsible for a thousand dollars tucked in the bottom of a cigar box was enough to drive away anyone's drowsiness.

Returning with a copy of the *Denver Post,* Jim announced, "Fresh off the press, just now dumped out of a boxcar on a freight from Denver." Tommy could see that the whole front page was taken up with news of the Haywood trial. His uncle immediately grew so absorbed in the stories that Tommy tightened his hold on the cigar box, just in case it should get knocked off the bench.

"Listen to this, Tom," Jim said. "Clarence Darrow gave his closing argument today, and they've printed nearly the whole speech in the paper. I'm gonna read a little bit of it to you, and I want you to let it seep inside your brain and then trickle down to your heart, so when you're a grown man, you'll remember it well."

Folding the paper to the right page, Jim said, "Now, mind you, Tom, this is from the mouth of a man who lawyers for a living, so he's not exactly a working stiff. Clarence Darrow's hands are probably as soft as a woman's. But this will show you that there can be good souls on both sides of the divide." Clearing his throat, Jim began:

> "I don't mean to tell this jury that labor organizations do no wrong. I know them too well for that. They do

wrong often, and sometimes brutally; they are sometimes cruel; they are often unjust; they are frequently
corrupt. . . . But I am here to say that in a great cause
these labor organizations—despised and weak and
outlawed as they generally are—have stood for the
poor, they have stood for the weak, they have stood
for every humane law that was ever placed upon the
statute books. . . . I don't care how many wrongs they
have committed—I don't care how many crimes—
these weak, rugged, unlettered men, who often know
no other power but the brute force of their strong
right arm, who find themselves bound and confined
and impaired whichever way they turn, and who look
up and worship the God of might as the only God
they know. I don't care how often they fail, how many
brutalities they are guilty of. I know their cause is
just."

While he read Clarence Darrow's closing speech, Uncle
Jim kept his voice low, glancing around to make sure no
Pinkerton detective hovered within hearing distance. But he
read it with such emotion, his voice rising and falling not in
the cadence of an educated lawyer like Darrow but with the
inflection of an Irish workingman, that he moved himself to
tears. Unashamed, he wiped the teardrops from his eyes with
a clean white handkerchief and told Tommy, "Engrave those
words on your heart, lad. Aren't they lovely? They should be
known as the Workingman's Creed."

Lovely? Tommy didn't think so. Hadn't Clarence Dar-row
admitted that union men were brutal, cruel, unjust, and corrupt? More than that, he'd called them weak and unlettered.

That sure didn't sound like a lawyer who was trying to get his client off from a murder charge.

That thousand dollars sitting in the box next to Tommy had been collected from the nickels and dimes and hard-earned dollars of coal miners who had little to spare. Why was Uncle Jim taking it to a lawyer who said bad things about the unions, who'd come right out and claimed that union men were criminals?

Or maybe . . . there was that other use for the money that Uncle Jim had talked about. Judging from the speech Darrow had made before the jury, it seemed likely that Haywood would be convicted. And then the thousand dollars could be used to bribe his jailers. Tommy wondered how much money it took to bribe jailers. A thousand dollars was an awful lot. Enough for two jailers? Three?

"Boarding now," a booming voice announced, "train for Burley, Twin Falls, Mountain Home, Boise, Caldwell, and points west."

"That's us," Jim said. "Don't forget the baby." Once again he winked at the cigar box next to the sandwich bag. Tommy picked up both of them.

They settled themselves uncomfortably on the hard seats of the Oregon Short Line passenger car. The Oregon Short Line, like the Union Pacific, Uncle Jim began to explain, was run by rich capitalists from the East. . . . Tommy heard hardly any of it; before the train left the station, he fell asleep again.

He was awakened by his uncle's voice. "I bought these tickets in Salt Lake, mister. One adult and one child."

A conductor with a ticket punch in his hand stood swaying above them. "A child over age twelve needs an adult ticket," he said.

"The boy isn't twelve—he's ten. It's true he's tall for his age, but I give you my word he's only ten. Tell him, Tommy."

"I'm ten. Honest. I was born January eighteenth, 1897." Why was this conductor arguing? Tommy knew his own age. The conductor himself didn't look all that old, not like some of them, whose silvery gray mustaches and sparse gray hair underneath their caps showed they'd worked for the railroad for most of a lifetime. This was a young one. He had no mustache, and his cheeks were pink and smooth. As the argument with Jim escalated, his cheeks got redder.

"Stand up, boy," he ordered tersely.

When Tommy stood, Uncle Jim declared, "He's tall, yes, but you can see the boy's still a child."

"What I can see is that he's too tall for ten," the conductor insisted. "You have to pay me the difference between a child's ticket and an adult's ticket. One dollar and twenty cents."

For some reason, instead of handing over the change in his pocket, Uncle Jim kept arguing. "Oh, come on, man. Don't keep fightin' me when you're wrong. A dollar and twenty cents is hardly enough to cause a disagreement between two reasonable gentlemen like you and me, but it's the principle of the thing. So let's settle it. Here, wet your whistle, have a little nip and we'll talk sense," Jim offered, pulling a thin metal flask from his coat pocket and unscrewing the top. "It's good Irish whiskey inside."

"I don't drink," the conductor answered stiffly.

"Well, then, treat yourself to a fine cigar." Tommy nearly choked when his uncle opened the La Estrallita cigar box and held it up to the conductor.

"I don't smoke."

That was when Uncle Jim made his fatal mistake. "You

don't drink and you don't smoke? Tell me, man, do you sew your own dresses?" Jim let loose his rich, rolling laughter that usually made everyone else in the room laugh right along with him.

The conductor wasn't laughing. A red flush of fury swept from his cheeks all the way up to the brim of his railroad cap. Turning on his heel, he stomped off down the aisle.

"Well, I guess we got rid of that Miss Prissy." Jim chuckled, settling back in his seat. Once again he tipped his straw hat over his eyes to get ready for a little nap.

By then Tommy had become wide awake. He stared out the window, but since it was still pitch-black outside, all he saw was his own pale reflection in the glass. And then he saw other reflections moving across the windowpane.

"Uncle Jim," he whispered, tugging his uncle's coat sleeve. "I think you better wake up."

The young conductor was again striding down the aisle. Following him, looking like they meant business, came two burly men.

"Oh, for—," Jim sputtered. "Here's trouble. Tommy, guard the box." Jim stretched lazily, as though he hadn't a care in the world, as the conductor stopped beside him.

"This is the one," the conductor accused, pointing. "Refused to pay the proper fare."

"Now, that's not really true," Jim said, letting the Irish slide into his voice. "I'm more than willin'. It was just that we had a friendly little difference of opinion about the age of the boy here. But if what I said got your dander up, then I apologize and I'll hand over the money right this very minute."

As Jim tried to reach into his pocket, one of the heavyset men grabbed his arm and twisted it behind him. "If you got a gun in there, you're a dead man," he said.

"Now, what in the world would I be doin' with a gun? I'm on a pleasant little excursion with my son here."

"Search him," the other man said gruffly. Then, in the dim light from the few weak bulbs in the car, he bent over for a better look at Jim's face. "Well, by all that's holy, I do believe we've made ourselves a catch. This here fella is none other than Jimmy Mack."

"Who's Jimmy Mack?" the conductor asked. Frowning, Tommy waited for his uncle to deny that he was anybody named Jimmy Mack.

Still calm, though his arm must have been hurting, bent backward the way it was, Jim asked, "You fellas with the famous Pinkerton Detective Agency?"

"Dead right," the second man said. The two detectives looked a lot alike—middle-aged, paunchy, wearing summer suits and bowler hats. One had a thick mustache and sideburns grown down to meet the edges of it. The other had a bulbous nose lined with spidery red veins.

"He's got no gun," the first man said, and the second one asked, "So, what you been up to, Jimmy?"

"Who's Jimmy Mack?" the conductor asked again.

"Just the main goon for John Mitchell, president of the United Mine Workers union that caused all the ruckus in the Pennsylvania hard-coal mines a while back. Never thought I'd see you again, Jimmy Mack. When you disappeared seven or eight years ago, folks said you musta been shot by a jealous husband who caught you in bed with his wife."

These men had it all wrong. Standing up and clinging to the seat in front of him, Tommy declared, "He's not Jimmy Mack. He's my uncle, James McInerny."

"Uncle? I thought he said he was your father."

Jim slid lower and once again tipped the hat over his eyes.

Leering, the Pinkerton man with the spider-veined nose said, "James McInerny, also known as Jimmy Mack, also known as Lucky Jim because he always gets away when his lady friends' husbands show up. Glad you ain't dead—yet—Jimmy. You and me got a little unfinished business. Let's take a stroll, and you can tell us what you're doin' on this train."

The two Pinkertons dragged Jim out of the seat while the conductor protested, "Don't take him away till he pays a dollar twenty for the ticket."

"Forget the ticket," the larger Pinkerton man growled contemptuously. "We got bigger fish to fry." Keeping Jim's arm clamped behind his back, he shoved him into the aisle.

"Give me just a minute for a bit of talk with my nephew here," Jim pleaded.

"Whatever you got to say, say it out loud," the bigger man insisted.

"Aw, give me a break, man. Just a minute in private with the boy."

"Forget it." Thrusting Jim forward, they hustled him down the aisle, but he turned his head to shout back to Tommy, "Take those sandwiches to Mrs. Gilhooly."

Trembling, Tommy wondered whether he should run after his uncle or wait for him to come back. And what did Jim care about the sandwiches? Glancing down at them, Tommy saw that the paper bag sat on top of his own jacket. For a moment his heart lurched because he couldn't see the cigar box, but when he moved his jacket, there it was. Somehow, during the altercation, Jim had managed to cover the cigar box with the jacket and put the sandwiches on top.

There was no Mrs. Gilhooly that Tommy knew of. Uncle

Jim wouldn't have meant the sandwiches anyway; he meant the cigar box. Take it to—did that mean Uncle Jim wasn't coming back? No, he was just making sure all possibilities were covered. But what if he didn't come back? How was Tommy supposed to stay on the train to Boise all by himself and then deliver the money to—Clarence Darrow? Big Bill Haywood? Which one? And how would he find them?

"Mountain Home!" As the train slowed, the conductor's voice rang out. Tommy didn't know whether to get off and look for his uncle, or stay on and wait for him to come back. It was now past five in the morning, and the sky had begun to show where the sun would rise. He glanced out the window in time to see the two Pinkertons dragging Jim McInerny, his face bloodied, into the station house.

Terrified, too frozen with fear to move, Tommy pressed himself into a corner of the seat.

# CHAPTER THREE
## Still July 27, 1907

This was the third railway station Tommy had entered in the past twelve hours. The little train platform in Castle Gate, Utah—where he and Uncle Jim had boarded for Salt Lake City—didn't count. This Boise depot looked different from the other two because it stood on a hill and it had a tower, but Tommy wasn't interested in his surroundings. All he wanted was for his uncle to appear and tell him what to do.

He sat on a bench and held the cigar box firmly on his knees, noticing as he did so that his socks had fallen down around his ankles, which left his thin legs bare from the cuffs of his knee pants to the tops of his shoes. *Who cares,* he thought.

On a wall in front of him hung a large, round clock, with each jerky movement of its second hand marking the passage of one sixtieth of a minute. Tommy started counting them—counted up to sixty and then started over. Kept doing it, because counting was better than crying. Then he closed his eyes to see whether he could count sixty seconds without watching the thin hand jerk its way across the little black lines on the dial.

Around him, leaning against walls, looking over the magazines on the newsstand, smoking cigars and talking to one another, stood dozens of men who could have been Pinkerton agents—or they could have been just passengers. Women strolled past dressed in lightweight, light-colored dresses and broad-brimmed, summer straw hats. What if the women were Pinkerton detectives too? In school one of Tommy's classmates had shown him a dime novel about a lady detective.

When the paper bag slid off his lap, it reminded him that he was hungry. He guessed it would be all right to eat one of the sandwiches. He pulled it out to find that the newspaper wrapping had turned soggy. After picking bits of damp paper off the bread, he took a small bite, not even caring whether it tasted good, because his mind was filled with a much bigger worry—about Uncle Jim. More than an hour had passed, and Jim hadn't shown up.

Tommy had to go to the bathroom. The sign that said MEN was all the way around on the other side of the depot. Looking right and left to keep an eye out for Uncle Jim, Tommy walked to the men's room and went inside, where a few grown-up fellows stood in front of the urinals.

The remaining sandwich he could tuck under his arm, but what to do with the cigar box? Squeezing it between his chin and his chest, he tried to unbutton the fly of his knee pants—which took two hands because the buttonholes were tight. But the box kept him from seeing what he was doing. A man who'd just finished using the urinal next to him started to laugh and said, "Want me to hold that for you, kid?"

Tommy couldn't shake his head no, or the box would fall down for sure. He pushed his chin harder against it while he mumbled, "No, thanks." By then other men in the restroom had started to laugh at him, and the laughter built up louder and louder, making Tommy's face burn bright with embarrassment. If he hadn't had to go so bad, he'd have fled. Somehow he managed to unfasten his pants, do what he had to do, and run out of the restroom clutching the box in one hand and the waistband of his pants in the other, with the sandwich still tucked in his armpit. Once outside, he stood against a wall, his back turned toward the big waiting room, while he buttoned himself up again.

Wandering around the high-ceilinged depot, he stopped in front of the newsstand to stare at the headline of the *Idaho Statesman*. It read HAYWOOD TRIAL NEARS END. He peered at the front page, moving closer and closer, until the man behind the counter snarled around the cigar in his mouth, "You wanna read the paper, kid? Then buy it."

Buy it! With what? Tommy didn't have as much as a penny in his pocket. If he hadn't felt so shaky over all the things that were happening to him, he might have laughed out loud. There he was, carrying a thousand dollars cash, and he couldn't buy a two-cent newspaper.

As he backed off from the newsstand he bumped into a man standing behind him. "Here, son, you can have my paper," the man said, handing it to him. "I'm done with it." Before Tommy could thank him properly, the man walked away.

Finding a bench that faced the back of the building, where the trains came in—so Uncle Jim would have no trouble spotting him when he arrived—Tommy sat down and began to read. The paper was so fresh that the ink smeared; it blackened his fingers. Column after column reported the goings-on in the Boise courthouse. One column caught Tommy's attention with its headline PROSECUTOR'S CLOSING REMARKS.

Printed in full was the final argument of William Borah, a U.S. senator from Idaho who'd taken on the job of prosecutor because Frank Steunenberg had been his friend, the article said. And, as Borah claimed, friend to everyone in Idaho, except to those venomous, barbaric miners in Coeur d'Alene who'd dynamited and murdered and committed such brutal atrocities that Frank Steunenberg, when governor, had called out the National Guard to arrest them. And for this, Borah declared, the very same Frank Steunenberg, former governor of Idaho, friend to so many people in the courtroom, had been viciously executed. Yes, Harry Orchard might have admitted planting the bomb that blew up Frank Steunenberg while this wonderful man was entering his own garden gate. But it was Bill Haywood and the other union leaders who'd ordered the execution.

The paper quoted Borah:

> I remembered again the awful night of December 30, 1905. . . . I felt again its cold and icy chill, faced the drifting snow and peered at last into the darkness for the sacred spot where last lay the body of my dead friend, and saw true, only too true, the stain of his life's blood upon the whitened earth. I saw Idaho dishonored and disgraced. I saw murder—no, not murder, a thousand times worse than murder—I saw anarchy wave its first bloody triumph in Idaho.

Tommy didn't know what *anarchy* meant, but it must be something awful if it was a thousand times worse than murder. He tried to keep reading, but the station house was warm and his eyelids grew heavier every minute. He'd jerk himself awake, glance at the doors to look for Uncle Jim, read some more, and find that his mind was playing with him, changing the words in the newspaper into nonsense phrases inside his head while he drifted off once again. Nonsense and then strange dreams. Calling out to him was the lady in the red dress, the lady with flowers in her hair who paid no attention to the sheep grazing behind her. She kept reaching for Tommy—she was La Estrallita! The lady of the cigars! Convulsively, Tommy clutched the box.

The dream, and the rumbling of his stomach, woke him. Two in the afternoon and he felt hungry again. He decided he'd better save the last sandwich until he was really hungry, in case Uncle Jim—who had enough money in his pocket to buy them a dinner—would be stalled even longer, wherever he was.

By four o'clock Tommy had convinced himself that Uncle Jim must have come looking for him while he was in the men's room. Not finding him, Jim had probably gone straight to the courthouse. Tommy didn't know where that might be, but everyone in Boise—except the newsstand man—seemed friendly enough that he was sure he could ask for directions.

In front of the depot a railroad porter pointed and said, "Easy! You just walk up Capitol Street."

"And then what?"

"And then nothin'. You just keep on walking, and when there ain't no more Capitol Street, you're there."

"You mean Capitol Street goes all the way to the courthouse and then stops?"

"Uh-huh."

"Thank you."

"Welcome."

That sounded easy enough. He started out, walking downhill. After about a mile he came to a river, crossed the bridge, and found that the other side of it was still called Capitol Street.

He passed houses where the smell of fried onions and beef drifted out of open windows—it was suppertime in Boise. Tommy kept on walking, and walking. Suppertime ended, and people came out on their front porches to escape the heat of their kitchens, fanning themselves with palm-leaf fans.

His feet were burning. He hadn't taken off his shoes for more than twenty-four hours, and the paved sidewalks felt hot underfoot. The whole town was hot. It must have been ninety-five in the shade, and he was wearing his jacket because he didn't want to carry it—his hands were already full. The sleeve of his shirt, hanging below the too-short sleeve of his jacket, grew damp where he'd used it to wipe sweat from his upper lip. His shirtfront had been blackened by the print on the newspaper. But coming from a coal town, he was used to looking dirty. Even the few wealthy people in Castle Gate, Utah, got grimy around the edges.

A dandy-looking young man wearing a straw hat and carrying a bouquet of flowers came toward him, probably on his way to see his sweetheart. It was Saturday evening, the best time for courting. "You're on the right street, buddy," he told Tommy. "It's only about another half mile and you'll run into it. See that dome up ahead? That's the capitol building. The courthouse is right next to it."

When Tommy looked, the capitol dome was so obvious that he didn't know why he hadn't seen it before. The closer he got, the larger the dome loomed above the red brick walls beneath it. The whole block next to the statehouse was torn up with construction—huge, high cranes looming over the skeleton of a new building. The courthouse must be on the other side, Tommy figured.

Here and there groups of people stood together talking, gesturing, pointing to the top of a square three-story building, also redbrick, with a wooden cupola on top and striped awnings hanging like half-closed eyes over the windows. Tommy walked all the way around it until he came to a steep flight of steps that led to the entrance, where he saw the sign: ADA COUNTY COURTHOUSE.

Could Uncle Jim be inside? Tommy climbed the stairs but was met at the top by a guard. "What do you want, kid?" the man asked.

"Is there a bathroom in there?" Tommy figured that might be the best excuse to get inside.

"Yes, but you can't come in," the man told him. "The Haywood jury is sequestered on the top floor, so no one's allowed in this building now except deputies, attorneys, and reporters. If you need to pee, there's an outhouse down the block, right beside where the new statehouse is getting built."

"Thanks," Tommy said.

He prowled around the outside of the courthouse, looking for his uncle and lingering near bystanders to pick up bits of their talk. Men stood in small groups with their jackets slung through the crooks of their arms, their vests unbuttoned, and their hats shoved back so they could mop their sweating foreheads with wrinkled handkerchiefs. "He's gonna hang for sure," one insisted, "and I'd like to be the one to tie the noose."

"One of them reporters told the bartender down at the Ore House that it's ten to two for conviction."

"Wonder which two jurors are against."

"You been to the trial every day, Jake. I'll take your bet which two it is."

A group of shabbier-looking men at the bottom of the stairway railed against "that handpicked jury of Idaho farmers that don't care beans about miners like us."

"It's gotta be hot where they are up there in that jury room, Eli. A tin roof'll sweat your brains out."

"Hot! Not hot enough. Hope they all fry!" Eli spat.

As the evening wore on, Tommy heard saloons mentioned often—the Ore House, the Silver Bell, the Golden Slipper. Before long most of the small groups had melted away, no doubt to find those saloons and soothe throats strained from loud arguing.

As the sun set he finished the last sandwich, at the same time saying a prayer that Uncle Jim would soon come to find him. Tommy was alone in a strange place with not a cent to his name, with night coming on and the growing fear that some thug might try to steal the cigar box in the dark.

At the edge of the courthouse lawn grew a tall, thick spruce tree, its bottom branches close to the ground. Tommy slithered his way under those branches and pulled off his shoes and socks, wiggling his toes in the now cooler evening air. Through the branches he could see the top floor of the courthouse, where lights blazed far into the night. That was the jury room. Twelve men were in there deciding whether Bill Haywood would hang.

At last, lying facedown with the cigar box beneath him, he slept fitfully, awakened every hour by the chiming of a clock in a bell tower somewhere nearby.

# CHAPTER FOUR
July 28, 1907

When the clock struck seven, Tommy crawled out from under the tree and brushed spruce needles from his shirt and pants. He'd just finished tying his shoes when he noticed men running toward the courthouse. The guard was letting them in.

Tommy ran after the men and managed to slip in between them, following as they climbed a flight of stairs. No one stopped him when he trailed after the crowd through a pair of open doors.

The room was as big as a barn. At one end stood a high, wooden, thronelike chair with a tall desk in front of it. Rows of wooden benches filled the room. Along another wall sat twelve high-backed chairs. As soon as Tommy saw those twelve chairs, he knew they were for the jurors. This was the courtroom.

Since the benches were filling up fast, he slid into a space near the back just as the judge entered, stern in his black robe. "I don't want any reporters from the Socialist newspapers in this courtroom," he called out to the guards flanking the doors.

A man in a rumpled suit, his hair falling over his fore-head, challenged, "Your Honor, you are denying entry to a legitimate segment of the press. How do you justify that?"

The judge looked haggard, but his voice rang out strongly. "Mr. Darrow, this is not a propitious time for you to argue with me. I suggest that you take your seat and let the matter rest, just as I am about to take my seat to begin these proceedings."

So the man with the lank hair and pale face was Clarence Darrow! Tommy strained to get a better look and noticed Darrow drape his arm around someone sitting next to him, giving the man's shoulder a pat as if to encourage him. That had to be the accused, Big Bill Haywood. Tommy stood up to see, but a woman sitting behind him hissed at him to get down.

Twelve men entered the room and slowly, solemnly took their places in the jurors' box. The night before Tommy had heard them called a bunch of Idaho farmers, and that's exactly what they looked like. Three of them had white beards, and the other nine wore thick, drooping mustaches. To Tommy, they all looked old.

He didn't care if the woman behind him hissed again, he had to stand up to find his Uncle Jim. Since Tommy was in the back, he could only see people from behind. Out of deference to the court all the men had removed their hats; since Uncle Jim's hair was such a bright mixture of blond and orange, and was so curly, in that hatless crowd he'd be sure to stand out. But he wasn't there.

"Sit *down!*" the woman said again, out loud this time. Placing both her heavy hands on his shoulders, she shoved him back onto his seat.

"Gentlemen of the jury," the judge was asking, "have you reached a verdict?"

"We have, Your Honor." The man in the first chair of the jurors' box handed over an envelope.

Trying to stay rooted in his seat so the woman wouldn't yell at him again, Tommy stretched to see. The famous lawyer, Clarence Darrow, sat holding his head in his hands, as though he expected the worst. The about-to-be-hanged Big Bill Haywood stayed unmoving, his back rigid, staring straight ahead.

Fumbling with the envelope, the judge opened it and then turned it upside down to shake it. "There's nothing in here!" he sputtered.

One of the jurors nudged the foreman and said, loud enough for everyone to hear, "I think you must have given him the wrong envelope, Mr. Gess. The real one's right there in your coat pocket."

Sheepishly the foreman handed another envelope to the judge, mumbling, "Sorry." This time the judge found a piece of paper inside. He read the note silently. Without a word he handed it to the court clerk.

Every person in the courtroom seemed to be holding his breath. Or her breath, because a number of women were present. Since the court clerk was standing, Tommy could see him well enough, could notice that the man's face was expressionless and his hands stayed steady. He cleared his throat, then said in a voice without emotion, separating each word from the next, "The state of Idaho against William D. Haywood. We the jury in the above-entitled cause find the defendant, William D. Haywood, not guilty."

For a moment all was silent as death. Then the courtroom erupted as though the bomb that killed Frank Steunenberg had gone off right in the middle of the room. Some men shouted angrily; others sat stunned and mute. Bill Haywood jumped to his feet to hug Clarence Darrow. Cheering supporters surrounded Haywood, each trying to slap his back or grab his hand, but Big Bill pushed his way to the jurors' box and shook hands with every one of the twelve Idaho farmers who'd voted to acquit him.

Slowly the mob around Haywood moved him through the doors and into the corridor. "I'm going straight downstairs to the jail and tell those fellows down there what happened," he shouted as he fought his way through the well-wishers. "Where's a telephone? I have to call my wife."

When the stairs had cleared enough for Tommy to get down them, he hurried outside into the bright sunshine to look for Uncle Jim. In the excitement of the verdict he'd almost forgotten the most important thing: finding his uncle to ask what he was supposed to do now with the cigar box. The crowd from the courthouse—including dozens of newspaper reporters heading for telephones and the telegraph office—jammed the street, getting in the way of men and women dressed in their best; they must be on their way to church, because it was Sunday, Tommy realized. He should be in church too; as a Catholic, he was obligated to attend Mass. He'd never missed Sunday Mass, except for the few times he was sick, but here in Boise he didn't know where a Catholic church might be, and if he did find one and went inside it, he'd be giving up his chance to connect with Uncle Jim.

When Big Bill Haywood and Clarence Darrow came out of the courthouse, still surrounded by an excited mob, Tommy thought he'd better follow them. He needed to get rid of the cigar box, which wasn't heavy to carry but had grown increasingly weighty, burdening him, as it did, with unwanted responsibility. Uncle Jim's last instructions—though he'd spoken the name of Mrs. Gilhooly—had been for Tommy to get that box to either Clarence Darrow or Big Bill Haywood.

The crowd made its way slowly and noisily along several city blocks until it approached a redbrick and sandstone building six stories high. Above the entryway a porchlike steel canopy thrust out over the sidewalk; on it stood several men holding rifles.

"What's that place?" Tommy asked out loud, and a man answered, "The Idanha Hotel."

So many people pushed through the brass doors of the hotel that even if Tommy hadn't wanted to be swept inside, he couldn't have stopped himself. "Don't wait for the elevator," men were shouting. "There's too many of us. Take the stairs."

Tommy ducked into an alcove, hanging back until most of the crowd had gone up the stairs, although a few waited in the lobby for the elevator. He really wanted to ride that elevator. Uncle Jim had told him how they worked, but Tommy had never been on one—in fact, had never even seen one before. He thought better of it, though, and climbed the stairs, reaching the top just behind a few paunchy, heavyset middle-aged men who panted as they made their way into the hotel corridor.

It was easy to see where everyone was going. Through an open door shouts and laughter and cheers spilled into the corridor, where uniformed bellhops wheeled carts full of bottles, glasses, and ice. Moving uncertainly, Tommy crept toward the door, but a bellhop stopped him.

"Do you belong here?" the bellhop asked.

Tommy held out the cigar box. "I have to give this to Mr. Haywood."

"Are you a delivery boy?"

Tommy guessed he was, in a way, so he nodded.

"Well, don't expect any tip," the bellhop told him. "Those Socialists are tighter than my granny's corset."

He might be tall for a ten-year-old, but he wasn't tall enough to see over the broad backs of the men who jostled one another in the crowded, smoke-filled room. Several women were in the room too, one holding a lit cigar in her gloved fingers—Tommy stared at that, until she noticed and gave him a haughty frown. These women weren't as well dressed as the lady in the smoker car of the train; they wore plain shirtwaists and skirts, or tailored suits not much fancier than the clothes his mother wore to church.

Skinny enough to slip through the crush of bodies, Tommy caught sight of Clarence Darrow, who was laughing and trying to drink from a tall glass, although so many men kept slapping him on the back that he couldn't get his mouth near the rim. As Tommy was pushing his way to hand the cigar box to Mr. Darrow the crowd happened to part a bit, right in front of Big Bill Haywood.

That gave him his chance. He went right up to Mr. Haywood, held out the box, and said, "This is for you."

"Get out of the way!" a man yelled. "Don't touch it! It might be a bomb!"

Women screamed. Pandemonium broke out as people tried to duck out of the way, almost trampling one another in their rush toward the door, but the throng was too dense. Suddenly a fist reached out to knock the box out of Tommy's hand, away from Bill Haywood. It flew nearly to the ceiling, where it arced and fell back down, spilling cigars and fifty-dollar bills all over the place.

"What the—" Haywood gasped. "Pick them up! How much was in there, boy?"

"A thousand dollars," Tommy answered, his voice shaking as hard as he was.

"All fifties?"

"Yes, sir."

"Count it," Haywood barked to men who were scrambling around picking money up off the floor. Then he leaned down, his face close to Tommy's, and asked, "Who are you?"

Tommy wanted to run from the room. He wanted to scream, the way those women had screamed. Because Big Bill Haywood was staring straight at him, and the man's right eye—was dead! Scarred, milky white, grotesque, it bored into Tommy, sending daggers of shock and fear into him. "T-Thomas Quinlan," he stammered.

"Who gave you this money?"

"My Uncle Jim."

"Does your Uncle Jim have a last name?"

"He's James McInerny."

"My God," Haywood whispered. "It's Jimmy Mack." Murmurs rose from the men around him, then Haywood said, "Thomas, I thank you for delivering these . . . cigars to me. You're a brave boy. Uh . . . would you happen to be hungry?"

Tommy admitted that he was.

"Take him downstairs to the café," Haywood told the man who was handing him the money, "and buy him some breakfast. Keep him there till we figure this out."

The crowd, now silent, parted before them like the biblical seas as Tommy and the man went into the corridor. "We'll use the elevator," the man told him. "My name's Henry."

It was like stepping into a brass cage. The floor beneath

their feet lurched as the elevator began its descent, but it wasn't the sudden movement that made Tommy's heart pound—he was still scared from having that box knocked out of his hand and from the glare of Mr. Haywood's lifeless eye.

"What happened to his eye?" he asked, his voice small.

"Whittling with a knife when he was about your age. The knife slipped. Here we are in the lobby. Come on, Thomas, I'll get you something to eat."

The marble floor looked so clean and polished that Tommy took cautious steps, not wanting to scuff the surface. Henry led him to a green-and-yellow room where diners sat at cloth-covered tables set with bright glasses and shining silverware. Suddenly Tommy realized that his hands were empty. He'd carried the cigar box for so long, clutching it, guarding it, fussing over it, that his hands now felt oddly useless. Useless and dirty.

"You can order anything you want," Henry was telling him.

"Could I wash my hands first?"

Snapping his fingers, Henry called out, "Boy!" At first Tommy thought he was the boy Henry meant, but almost immediately a colored waiter reached their table. "Take this kid to the men's room," Henry told him.

Tommy followed the waiter, who stopped at the door to ask, "Can you find your way back?"

"Sure." The café was just around the corner, after all.

He'd never seen sinks and toilets so shiny and white. Polished mirrors hung above the sinks; with dismay Tommy saw how grubby he looked. He turned the gold-plated faucets and felt warm water on his hands. For a few seconds he played with the faucets, enjoying the splash of first warm, then cold, water. Nearby waited soap and real towels, soft and white. He guessed it was all right to use them. Working up a lather, he scrubbed his face and hands and even his hair, rubbing it dry on the towels, then smoothing it with his fingers because he didn't have a comb. He pulled up his socks to tuck them under the cuffs of his knee pants, pushed his shirttail into his pants, and buttoned his jacket to hide his dirty shirtfront. Then he went back to the table where Henry waited.

Fried eggs, sausage, pancakes and syrup—as much as he could hold, all of it tasting better than anything his mother had ever cooked. By the time Tommy finished his meal, Henry was acting fidgety. "Look, kid," he said, "I'm gonna go back upstairs and see what's going on. Will you be all right by yourself for a few minutes? Don't leave here. Just wait."

Promising he would, Tommy leaned back in his chair to look around. If only his uncle would show up, he'd feel quite content—no longer hungry, and sitting in the fanciest place he'd ever seen in his whole life.

Gold leaf was everywhere. Tall windows with thick velvet drapes. In one corner of the room stood a mahogany upright piano. All during the meal Tommy had heard music coming from that corner, soft tunes he didn't recognize. Just then the piano player—a black man—started to play a different kind of music. Faster. Bouncier. It made Tommy's feet twitch, pulled him right across the café toward the piano, where he crept up to stand just behind the man's shoulder.

The man turned and smiled at him. "You like this?"

Tommy nodded.

"It's ragtime."

"I like it a lot," Tommy told him.

"'Maple Leaf Rag.' Do you play music?"

"No. I wish I knew how. But sometimes I sing. My uncle Jim can sing."

"Ragtime doesn't have any words," the man told him. "Just the beat that gets into your feet." His smile grew wider. "Want to hear another ragtime tune?"

"Yes, please." Lost in the music, unaware how much time had passed, Tommy jumped when he felt a hand on his arm. It was Henry, saying, "Come on over here, Thomas. Mr. Haywood wants to talk to you."

This time when Big Bill Haywood bent toward Tommy, the dead eye wasn't as frightening. He was truly a big man, taller than six feet, barrel-chested and broad-faced. His touch felt heavy, but not threatening, on Tommy's shoulders. "Upstairs I said you were a brave boy," he began. "Now you've got to be even braver. Your uncle Jimmy Mack was found dead yesterday in the woods behind the Mountain Home train station."

Tommy just stared, unwilling to comprehend.

"Do you know who did it?" Haywood asked him.

"The Pinkerton men," Tommy whispered. "They took him away."

"You're probably right, but we'll never be able to prove it. We've been in touch with our people by telegraph—they say those two detectives who hauled Jimmy off the train are claiming they just questioned him and then let him go. The conductor swears Jimmy got right back on the train before it pulled out of Mountain Home."

"He's lying. He's a *liar!*" The conductor might not smoke or drink, but he was telling filthy, rotten lies.

"Look here, see this?" Haywood asked, holding a fifty-dollar bill in front of Tommy's face. "I'm going to pin it inside your shirt. You take this home to your mother." He turned and gestured for Henry, saying, "Put Thomas in a first-class car on the train." And then, to Tommy, "We'll have someone meet you in Salt Lake City to make sure you and the casket get transported to Castle Gate."

"How did you know we lived in Castle Gate?" Tommy asked.

With his large, awkward hands Haywood pinned the money to the inside of Tommy's shirt using a safety pin. "We were always in touch," he murmured, "Jimmy Mack and the Western Federation of Miners. He was a good union man. I hope you grow up to be half the man he was."

Another one of Haywood's supporters—he didn't bother to tell Tommy his name—drove him to the railroad station in a livery carriage. After the man bought him a first-class ticket, he instructed the conductor to make sure Tommy got on the right train in Pocatello. The conductor wasn't the nonsmoking, non-drinking, lie-telling scab from the earlier train. Tommy was glad of that.

Too dazed to thank Haywood's man, he found himself shoved aboard a mahogany-and-plush railroad car filled with well-dressed ladies and gentlemen. He had a padded and upholstered seat all to himself.

In the swaying train the truth he'd blocked from his consciousness seeped into him, slowly at first, and then, like the speeding locomotive, faster and faster until it drove itself into every bit of his brain. Uncle Jim was dead! His body lay inside a coffin in the baggage car. Never again would he sing rollicking Irish songs, or flirt with the ladies, or pour the money from his pay envelope into Tommy's mother's hands. Never again would he tousle Tommy's hair in affection, or ask Tommy to read aloud from one of his schoolbooks. Jim was dead. His rough good looks, his strong, broad hands, his easy smile, all were gone forever.

Grief filled Tommy until he thought his heart would burst

with it. Then, slowly, the creeping realization of what he'd done began to crowd out the grief. And when that realization set in, harsh and undeniable, Tommy wanted to scream out in horror.

He'd murdered his own uncle!

The words rang in his head as if he were inside a giant bell that wouldn't stop its pealing. "He's not Jimmy Mack. He's my uncle, James McInerny." That simple, foolish statement had condemned his uncle to death.

The shock of what he'd done dried up his tears. Furtively he glanced at the other passengers, as if expecting them to point fingers at him, accusing him, damning him as the boy who'd betrayed his loving uncle.

But no one had to know about it. How would anyone else find out? The only others who knew were the Pinkerton men and the railway conductor, and Tommy would never see them again. His secret was safe. He would keep the terrible truth locked inside himself until the day they lowered him into his own grave.

Wretched, he sat with his arms covering his eyes all the way to Pocatello.

The train ride to Chicago was much longer in miles than the one from Boise to Castle Gate, Utah, but thinking back on it, that ride eight years ago had seemed as long as a trip to the moon. And at the end of it he'd had to confront the anguish of his mother.

Jim had been so brutally beaten that the undertaker gave up on making him look presentable in his coffin. The women who crowded around it had tried to comfort Fiona, telling her, "It's a deplorable thing you have to endure, dearie, seein' your own brother lyin' here dead. But the coal mines are full of men who'd be willin' to marry you and support both you and the boy."

"Never, never will I marry another miner," Tom's mother had shrieked. "If they don't get killed one way, they get killed some other way, like my brother here. I'll take in washing; I'll scrub my fingers to the bone to support my son, but I'll never again marry a miner." At that she'd burst into great, desperate wails of grief, which was expected at an Irish wake, but which tormented Tommy like the flames of hell, since he knew he was to blame.

At night he'd slept with a work shirt of Jim's wrapped in his arms and Jim's boots under his bed. He'd tried to imitate Jim's hearty laugh, but Tommy had a boy's voice, not a man's, and the laugh came out forced and unnatural, nothing at all like Jim's.

Later, when Fiona started sorting through Jim's things to get rid of them, she'd called Tommy and showed him a guitar in its case, the same guitar that now rode on the rack above his head on this speeding train to Chicago. "Jim won it in a poker game," she'd explained. "He always said he was going to learn to play so he could entertain at the Irish parties, but he never did. I couldn't get more than a couple of dollars for it now, so you may have it if you like. But mind that you don't neglect your schoolwork if you start fooling around with music."

The schoolwork hadn't been neglected; it had been terminated. Since the fifty dollars from Bill Haywood couldn't last forever, and taking in washing didn't earn much, in spite of all Fiona's wild talk about miners, she had been forced to let her son become one.

At age eleven Tommy went to work in the coal mine.

PART TWO

# He Descended into Hell

# CHAPTER FIVE
## Groundhog Day, 1911

It was Peter Connolly who'd arranged to have Tommy hired as a trapper boy. "The job isn't hard at all, Fiona," Peter had told Tommy's mother. "I was a friend of your late husband John and I thought the world of your brother Jim, so I'm making sure your son Tommy will be safe in the mine. He'll be right close to the mine portal. If there's any rockfall from blasting, he can run like the devil and get out."

"No one's safe in the mine," Fiona had answered, speaking low.

"As safe as possible. All he has to do is open and close doors so the ventilators keep pumping air into the right tunnels, where the men are working."

"All alone in the dark."

"I don't mind that, Mom." Alone, in the dark, no one would come to him, asking to hear the story of Uncle Jim's death last summer. "Can I bring my guitar into the mine?" he'd asked. He hardly ever had time to play it. Each day when he got home from school, his mother needed his help. It was his job to keep the coal fires burning to heat the water to wash the laundry she did for unmarried miners like Peter Connolly. And lately she'd begun to wash and iron for the wealthier households, where the Castle Gate mine bosses lived.

In the window of the Quinlans' small frame house hung a sign, FINE LAUNDERING AND INVISIBLE MENDING. The sign was hardly necessary. Everyone recognized Fiona Quinlan as the best laundress in Castle Gate. The dress shirts she laundered were the whitest in town, the shirtfronts showed not the tiniest wrinkle, and the cuffs stayed stiff with starch.

It was Tommy's job—one of many—to keep two flatirons heated properly on top of the kitchen stove: not too cold, and never so hot they would scorch. And then, when the laundry was finished and the shirts and underdrawers had been neatly folded and wrapped with brown paper, it was Tommy's job, too, to deliver them to the wealthier homes. Most of the ordinary miners, like Peter Connolly, came to the house to pick up their own laundry. And since most of their laundry consisted of work shirts and bib overalls, it didn't need to be carefully wrapped.

"I hate to think of Tommy spending long hours in that pit," Fiona'd objected.

"What long hours?" Peter had answered. "In Utah the law says no more than eight hours a day, six days a week. It's like heaven compared to the way it used to be."

"Heaven! Mines aren't heaven. Mines are hell."

Peter lowered his eyes, took a deep breath, and tried again. "You've told me, Fiona, that you can't manage on what you earn. If Tommy must work, this is the best job for him."

"I know, I know," she cried. "But he's only eleven!"

"I was nine when I started," Peter declared, "and I worked a lot harder then, and a lot longer hours, than Tommy will work now."

Through the whole argument Tommy had sat silent, look-ing from one to the other, not knowing whether he wanted his mother to win or Peter Connolly. It was true his mother could barely earn enough to feed herself and Tommy, even though she worked far into the night. It was just as true that Tommy didn't want to leave school. During the once-a-week music classes, he excelled. What's more, he was the best reader in his class and the swiftest pupil at arithmetic, even though since the death of his uncle he'd stayed quiet and rarely volunteered an answer. But he realized that a dollar and a quarter a day times six days a week came to seven dollars and fifty cents. That would make a big difference in their life.

And so he'd gone to work at the age of eleven. For three years now he'd been a trapper boy in the Castle Gate Coal Mine, where he'd learned that isolation suited him. Deep in the bowels of the earth, caught in the gloom of perpetual night, entombed in the blind, shapeless realm where eyes became useless and only fingers could see through blackness, Tommy had taught himself to play the guitar.

Other men labored together with picks and shovels; Tommy sat by himself on a bench, picking out tunes. Every hour or so he'd open a door for a mule-drawn coal cart to be driven through by a boy bigger than he was, or by one of the greenhorns who kept arriving from Europe by the boat-load—Italians, Greeks, Slovenians. After the cart moved through, Tommy would shut the door again. And for this he got paid a dollar and a quarter a day.

Over time he'd begun to guess when a cart would be coming through, and he'd light his carbide lantern to see the door better. On the rare occasions that he fell asleep on the job, the cursing of the mule driver on the other side of the door would wake him, and he'd lunge for the door handle in the dark. Most of the mule drivers liked him well enough. "Hey, trapper boy. You!" they'd shout. "Make songs for us at dinner break."

"I'll be there," he'd promise, and when the dinner pails had been emptied and there was still time before the whistle blew to call the miners back to work, those immigrants would teach him songs from their native lands. Sad, plaintive songs or wild shrill songs or melting songs of love, Tommy had such a good ear for music that he could pick up the foreign melodies after he'd heard only a verse or two. Since few of those men could speak English, they never talked much, and that suited Tommy too.

Back on his bench he preferred to stay in darkness in order to save on the carbide the lantern burned, because money was so scarce for the Quinlans. Since he couldn't see anything—not even a sliver of light penetrated the passage-way—his hearing sharpened. He learned to slide the fingers of his left hand up and down the neck of the guitar to land on exactly the right spot on the frets. And since he was alone, he could sing while he played and no one would hear him. If he didn't know the words to a song, he made up his own words. When he first went into the Castle Gate mine, he'd sung with the high voice of a boy; now, at the age of fourteen, his voice was not quite as deep as a man's, but was getting there.

After the shrill closing whistle blew on Groundhog Day of 1911, Tommy lowered his guitar into its case and walked down the tunnel to the outside world. That was always star-tling: the first taste of real air, no matter how tainted it was with coal smoke from locomotives. By four o'clock the sky had turned gray and the snow looked even grayer, dirtied from coal dust and smoke. Freshly fallen snow never stayed white for very long in Castle Gate.

"Tommy, wait a bit," Peter Connolly called out. "I'll walk home with you. I need to talk to you and maybe your mother too."

"Did the groundhog see its shadow today, do you think?" Tommy asked, shivering in the icy air, which was fifty degrees colder than the temperature inside the mine.

"Now, how would I know? How would either of us know, since we work in a place where the only shadows are cast by carbide lamps? But slow down a bit and I'll tell you something I think you'll want to hear."

Tommy did tend to walk fast, since he was now approaching six feet tall and his legs were long.

"Last night in the saloon," Peter began, "I was talking to a fellow from the Kenilworth mine. He told me they're having a grand party there next Sunday evening, with Irish music and all. So I was telling him how good you are with your guitar and your singing, and the upshot is—if you go over there and play for their party, they'll give you two dollars."

"Two dollars!" His mind darted ahead. If his mother could lend him a dollar tonight, he'd go to the company store and buy new guitar strings, because it wouldn't do to have a string break during his first music job for pay. Then he could give her the two dollars he earned at Kenilworth.

"Is two dollars enough?" Peter asked.

"Yes! Mom ought to let me go for that."

"Ah . . . but there might be a problem, and I wanted to ask you whether I should even bring it up with Fiona. Today the Greek miners at Kenilworth went out on strike."

Tommy frowned. "Why would that be a problem?"

"Oh, you know those Greeks. They're a wild bunch. If they're not working, they'll probably be drinking and carousing and maybe cause trouble. But then . . ." When Peter

Connolly laughed, it was as though Tommy could hear his Uncle Jim all over again—the same rich, rolling laughter that filled Tommy with longing and remorse. "But then . . . the *Irishers* at the party will be drinking and carousing too, now, won't they? And who knows what's worse—a bunch of drunken Irishmen or a bunch of drunken Greeks! So if they mix it up and start a bit of a riot—"

Tommy decided quickly. "Don't mention anything about that to my mother."

Seven miles of snow-packed road wound between Castle Gate and Kenilworth. On either side snow lay deep enough to cover the fence posts of the intermittent farms. As the sleigh sped along, Peter Connolly cracked a whip in the air above Johnny Bull.

"Why'd you name your horse Johnny Bull?" Tommy asked, his breath rising like steam in the icy air.

"Well, we Irish call the English folk Johnny Bulls. And I figured it would always give me great pleasure to smack the rump of a Johnny Bull with a whip." Peter laughed his great, buoyant laugh as he cracked the whip again. "He's a good horse, in spite of his name. He was a wild mustang, you know. I trapped him on the rangeland quite a ways south of the Book Cliffs."

"When you were working on a ranch." Tommy knew that much about Peter's life.

Peter grinned, remembering. "He sure gave me a hard time breaking him. Finally I said to him, 'You have two choices, horse. You either get broke, or you get gelded. If you want to keep on being a stallion, you better start minding me.' That's what I told him."

"What happened then?"

"Well, old Johnny Bull took a long look at all those pretty little mares and decided to remain a stud." Peter's laughter sent vapor into the frigid, darkening sky.

Tommy had heard other men talk about Peter Connolly's skill as a rider. And as a shooter. It was said Peter could slide down the side of Johnny Bull, aim a revolver from beneath the mustang's belly, and shoot to smithereens, one after the other, six bottles lined up on a fence.

"But that was in my younger days," Peter admitted, "when I was twenty-five or so. I'm forty-two now, Tommy. That's why I turned to mining instead of cowboying. As a miner you get blown to bits, as a cowboy you get your neck broke, but at least miners don't have to round up smelly old cows."

When they arrived, the inside of the Kenilworth Amusement Hall felt warm from its coal fire blazing on the hearth. But Tommy kept his coat on for a good ten minutes, holding his mittened hands under his armpits. His fingers needed to warm up so he could make a good impression when he played for these people, the first real audience of his life. After the mittens came off, he spread his hands over the fire until they became flexible. Then he turned to take a look at the crowd.

Twice as many men as women filled the room, the women laying dishes on a long table, the men crowding against a makeshift bar, already drinking. Little kids chased one another around the edges of the room. The few young people Tommy's age sat apart from one another, darting sidelong glances and whispering to their friends.

Tommy was startled when Peter Connolly banged a spoon against a glass to get everyone's attention. Did that mean Tommy was supposed to start performing? Hurriedly, he opened the guitar case and took out the guitar.

Peter cleared his throat. "We're most of us miners here," he began, "and wives and children of miners. And we're most of us Irish."

"That's right," a few people agreed, but Peter didn't have the crowd's full attention. They were still milling about and talking. Once again he banged on the glass.

"As I was saying, we're Irish. We emigrated to this country just like the Slavs and the Greeks and Italians did. So you could say we're foreigners like they are."

A man shouted, "Only, we speak the language that's spoken in the United States of America. And we plan on stayin' right here. We don't save up our money so we can go back to the old country and lord it over the peasants, like them foreigners want to do. And we don't go around causin' trouble in the mines."

At this the murmuring grew louder, mostly in agreement with the speaker.

"Now, hold it a minute, Clarence Kelly," Peter said, still calm. "These Greek miners went on strike here because they claim the weighmaster shorted them. It's important for the scales to be honest. And the man who does the weighing needs to be honest too."

"The mine superintendent said he'd balance the scales," a woman called out, wiping her hands on her apron. "Even when he promised that, the Greeks wouldn't go back to work."

Peter was shouting now. "They wanted to. But the fifteen men who went on strike in the first place got fired, so the others stayed out in a show of solidarity. Look, one of those Greek miners is right here with us in this hall. Let's give him a chance to talk, all right? His name is Theos Kambanakis."

The dark-haired Greek miner, standing there in his worn

work clothes, appeared nervous. He squeezed his hat in his hands as he tried to speak. "The boss say he not cheat us. We know he cheats—alla time. So we ask boss for one of our own men to be weighmaster."

"Is that supposed to mean," Clarence Kelly yelled out, "that every bunch of dagos and Hunkies and greasers in the mines gets to have their own weighmaster?" The muttering from the crowd grew louder. Not everyone was against the Greek strikers though; someone called out, "Why don't you shut your yap, Kelly, and let the Greek talk?"

"Right!" Peter agreed. "These men just want to talk to you about their grievances, and they want you fellows to support them in their strike. They're asking you to stay out of the mines while they—"

"Hold it!" Clarence Kelly was on his feet, walking toward the front of the room. "What gives you the right to butt in here, Connolly? You work at Castle Gate, not Kenilworth. So you ought to keep your nose out of our business and not be taking sides with these anarchists." Kelly pushed himself right in front of Tommy, who backed up quickly to keep from getting stepped on.

Turning toward the Greek man, Kelly said, "So your name is Theos?"

The man nodded.

"One of my pals back there told me that *Theos* is supposed to mean 'God.' That right?"

"Yes." Sensing a threat, the Greek's dark eyebrows lowered in a frown, his shoulders hunched and his fists clenched.

"Well," Kelly said, sneering, "you may think you're a Greek god, but to me you're nothin' but a goddamn Greek. Now get out of here and let us enjoy our party."

*Bam!* As the Greek's fist smashed into Kelly's face, Kelly

reeled backward, grabbing Tommy's guitar to keep his balance. Indignantly Tommy yanked his guitar away and shoved Kelly, pushing him right back into the waiting fist of the Greek. Men rushed forward to join the fight. The first in line took a swing at Peter, right in the middle of Peter's plea that everyone calm down and act sensible. So of course Peter had to hit back.

Within seconds, the brawl was in full swing—Irishman against Irishman—while the Greek named Theos beat a hasty retreat out the door. Trying to protect his guitar, Tommy jumped up onto the boards that had been set up for a bar. Glasses smashed onto the floor, and blood—mostly from noses and cut lips—dripped on top of the broken glass. It looked like rioting would destroy the party before it even got started. Fists swung, connecting with noses and chins and midriffs—men spit out grunts and curses and blood and an occasional tooth.

In the melee of swinging arms, wild punches, and loud yelps it was hard to tell who was fighting whom, or why. Peter held his own, with only a lump on his cheek and no blood on his face. Tommy was afraid the battle might go on all night. To the brawny young Irishmen, a good free-for-all was recreation, like dessert after a week's diet of hard labor in the mines. To the older, weaker men, it was spectator sport. They crowded around the combatants, cheering, yelling, urging on their favorites: "Thump his sniffer, Michael," "Bloody his conk, Patrick."

Tommy had promised his mother two dollars for this night's work. If he sang, even just a single song, maybe they'd still pay him at least a little for coming all the way to Kenilworth. Standing there on the table boards, his legs planted far apart and his guitar clutched against his chest, he figured it was worth a try. At the top of his lungs he began to belt out:

"If . . . I . . . knock the *L* out of Kelly,
  It would still be Kelly to me.
  Oh, a single *L-Y* or a double *L-Y,*
  It looks just the same to an Irishman's eye. . . ."

It was a song he'd heard for the first time at a vaudeville show in Castle Gate only a month before, a perfect song to accompany this riot, since a man named Clarence Kelly had started it.

"Knock off an *L* from Killarney,
  Sure, Killarney it always would be,
  But if I knock the *L* out of Kelly,
  He will knock the *L* out of me."

Hearing the song, the rest of the people in the room began to laugh, appreciating how Tommy had turned the ruckus into a farce, since Irish brawls didn't usually come with musical accompaniment. "Again!" they shouted, and when Tommy sang the chorus a second time, many of the crowd joined in, yelling, "Knock the *L* out of Kelly! That's you, Clarence. You're getting the *L* knocked out of you, all right." A few of the combatants even started to laugh through their bloodied lips.

Peter jumped onto the makeshift table beside Tommy and shouted, "Let's stop this! The Greek has gone, and all of us came here to have a good time. You've heard this lad sing—he's first-rate, don't you think?"

"Yes!" they yelled.

"So give him a chance to entertain us. Drinks are on me, fellows. I'm buying."

As broken glass crunched beneath their thick boots, the men crowded the bar to get their free whiskey. Rubbing the bruise that darkened his cheekbone, Peter muttered, "You did great, Tommy. Now, sing another song right away, before rioting breaks out again, and stay up here on the table where everyone can see you."

Exhilarated over the crowd's response, Tommy shouted out, "Here's a number by that great Irish American song-and-dance man, George M. Cohan:

"You're a grand old flag, you're a high-flying flag,
    And forever in peace may you wave.
    You're the emblem of the land I love,
    The home of the free and the brave."

He had them in the palm of his hand. The combination of George M. Cohan, free whisky, and the American flag proved too great to resist. Everyone knew the words and music, and they all got caught up in the thumping, patriotic rhythm. Little boys started to march in step, and a boy about Tommy's age jumped up to tap-dance, imitating the great George M. Cohan.

When that song was over—three choruses of it—Peter flung his arm around Tommy's shoulder and shouted, "Did I tell you this boy was good? And he can play any song you ask for." In Tommy's ear he murmured, "Be ready to run for it if that Theos goes to Greek Town and comes back with a gang of his countrymen. If we're caught in a brawl, your mother will kill me for sure."

Tommy brushed that worry away. He didn't want to

leave; he wanted to keep standing there, playing and singing, leading everyone in the lively music. To him, the singing and dancing and laughing and clapping were like water to a parched man in the desert. People kept asking for one Irish tune after another, and Tommy knew them all—"The Fine Ould Irish Gentleman," "Larry O'Gaff," "The Wake of Teddy Roe," "McSorley's Twins," "O'Dooley's Five O'clock Tea." As he played and sang, the approving shouts of the crowd went to his head; dizzy with success, he hardly took a breath from one piece to the next.

Luckily all those hours of practice in the mines had developed good, hard calluses on his fingertips; otherwise they'd have bled, because he kept playing the guitar and singing until he could barely croak out the words. But it didn't matter, because everyone else knew the words too. Twice he had to stop to replace strings: His vigorous strumming broke first an E string and then a G string. During the pause for repairs someone brought him food, which he ate fast so he could play again.

And luckily the Greek miners never came back.

"We'll spend the night here," Peter announced around midnight. "I told your mother we might stay, if it got too late. We can start back to Castle Gate as soon as it's light in the morning."

Tommy was relieved to spend the night in Kenilworth. Once the party was over and the excitement of performing began to seep out of him, he realized how dog-tired he felt. A seven-mile sleigh ride in twenty-below weather was just too brutal to contemplate.

They slept on the floor in front of the banked coal fire in the Kenilworth Amusement Hall. Peter woke first, when the panes of glass in the windows had barely changed from black to gray. "Let's go, lad," he said. "We can get home in time for some breakfast before work. I'll harness Johnny Bull."

Carrying his guitar case, Tommy walked outside to look for an outhouse. Blood from the fight the night before stained the snow—some of the combatants had battled their way outside. He'd heard that Clarence Kelly had suffered a broken nose, and he was glad, because that insulting, boorish loudmouth was the sort of ruffian his mother called Pig Irish, the ones that let pigs sleep with them inside their shanties in the old country.

In the near darkness of the bitter-cold morning Tommy couldn't locate the outhouse—wind from the mountains had swept so much snow over the path that a person had to know exactly where to look for it. He walked around to the front of the building, stopping in puzzlement when he heard a loud *ping*. Something had cracked one of the building blocks in the amusement hall. The terrible cold maybe.

On the hills surrounding Kenilworth, fires blazed. What could that mean? Tommy wondered. Who would be up there building open fires at this time of morning in that empty land no one owned? Then he heard a sound he had no trouble recognizing. A rifle shot! Instinctively he held his guitar case in front of him. The impact of the next bullet, when it hit, slammed him against the wall.

Tommy burst away from the wall, not sure which way to go. More shots peppered the snow around him. His breath came in hard gasps. Should he stay where the snow was flattened, or risk getting mired in deep drifts? He didn't ask it in words inside his head, because words were too slow: He acted on instinct. The only cleared place was the railroad track, where locomotives with snowplows attached in front pushed snow off the tracks several times a day. Once Tommy reached the tracks, the bullets stopped, perhaps because the snow on each side of the tracks stood far higher than his head, hiding him.

Panting, sweating, he dropped to his knees, checking to see whether he was bleeding anywhere, but he wasn't. Peter was back there with the horse and sleigh, but maybe Peter had been shot by now. It had to be the Greeks; Tommy knew it. Since the other miners refused to strike, the Greeks considered them strike-breaking scabs, and scabs were fair game for vengeance. The Greek strikers must have mistaken Tommy for a scab on his way to work. But where was Peter? Did he get caught in the ambush?

In the distance Tommy heard the sound of the coal train coming toward him. The tunnel of snow was so narrow that if he stayed where he was, the train would hit him. Yet if he ran back to the amusement hall, he'd be a sure target for the marauders in the hills. The sky was lightening now, making him easier to see.

Bullets or a locomotive—not much of a choice. If he hadn't been in so much danger, he might have likened it to a melodrama where the heroine, tied to the railroad tracks, either gives in to the villain or gets run over by a train.

He knew that trains toiling up an incline, heavily laden with coal, moved slowly, so he had time to work it out. He began frantically digging into the snowbank with his hands, pulling out frozen snow in great, thick clods. The train was coming closer, its whistle blasting shrilly. No time to dig deeper—he'd made an upright trench shaped like a sarcophagus, barely tall and wide enough for him to fit into. Sucking in his breath, he backed into it and clutched the guitar case to his chest.

Never again would he want to be that close to a moving locomotive. The smell of it, the sparks, the thunder of the wheels as the great steel body roared past within inches of him—all that would stay in his nightmares forever, like the sight of his uncle Jim's battered body. The locomotive went by, pulling the first coal car. Then the second car. Then the third. Timing it to the split second, Tommy leaped for the coupling between the third and fourth cars.

He made it. Hanging on with one nearly frozen hand to the rodlike steps that ran from the bottom to the top of the car, he huddled there, making himself as small a target as his height would allow, for fear that the striking miners would fire at the train. If they tried to stop it, they would find him. Or maybe they'd blow it up; dynamite was as easy to buy as candy, and anarchists liked explosions—in the years since his trip to Boise, Tommy had learned what *anarchist* meant. But nothing happened. The train chugged peaceably from Kenilworth to Castle Gate, the place where it would turn north for the trip to Salt Lake City.

At Castle Gate he yelled to a man walking next to the tracks, "Catch this!" then threw his guitar case at the man. Though startled, the man caught it neatly. Tommy jumped from the train, tumbling in the filthy, cinder-laden mix of ice and snow beside the tracks. Righting himself, he grabbed the case, said "Thanks" to the bewildered man, and ran toward the office of the mine owner.

It was only seven in the morning, but Ellis Farnham was already seated at his heavy oak desk when Tommy burst into his office, followed by a male secretary shouting, "You can't go in there!"

"There's trouble at Kenilworth!" Tommy cried to Mr. Farnham.

Ellis Farnham, a balding man wearing a high starched collar that Tommy's mother had ironed, took one look at Tommy's smoke-stained face and dirty clothes and said, "Tell me."

Even before Tommy had spilled out the whole story, Mr. Farnham was on the telephone, talking fast to someone at the other end. After a minute he glanced up and said, "You can go now, young man. Oh, and what's your name?"

"Thomas Quinlan, sir."

"Good work, Thomas." Mr. Farnham waved him away. After a minute he looked up again and said, "I told you to go, Thomas."

"I can't, sir! I need to find out about my friend Peter Connolly."

Frowning, Mr. Farnham said into the telephone mouthpiece, "The two men who were shot—who were they?"

Tommy couldn't breathe, couldn't hear anything except the pounding in his ears, until Farnham spoke to him. "One of them was a Greek miner named Theos Kambanakis. The other was a company guard named Virgil Dewey." Setting the phone's receiver into its hook, he added, "No one else has been hurt. There's a posse leaving here for Kenilworth right now, and a larger contingent of armed men will be on their way soon from Salt Lake City. The strike will be quelled quickly."

All of it had been too much, and Tommy felt tears well up in his eyes. Peter was safe, at least so far. But Theos Kambanakis had died. If it hadn't been for that lowlife Clarence Kelly, none of this would have started.

"Thomas, is that your guitar case?" Mr. Farnham asked. "It looks like there's a bullet hole in the top."

"Yes, sir, I was playing at a party in Kenilworth last night. And yes, sir, that's a bullet hole."

Mr. Farnham took off his glasses and rubbed the bridge of his nose. "Do you work here at Castle Gate, Thomas?"

"Yes, sir. I'm a trapper boy."

"Very good. You can take the day off. With pay."

Just then the door burst open and Peter rushed inside, followed by the blustering secretary. "Tommy!" he cried, grabbing him and hugging him. "I got here as fast as I could. I rode Johnny Bull bareback all the way."

Pulling away, Tommy asked, "How'd you know I'd be here?"

"One of the Greeks on the hill yelled down, 'The boy is on the coal train.' It must have been Theos Kambanakis."

"Before he was shot," Tommy said.

"What!"

Mr. Farnham broke in, "There have been two killings at Kenilworth so far. Thanks to the boy Thomas here, who alerted me, I've been able to call the state militia. They should stop the trouble before it goes any further."

"Oh, God!" Peter cried. "Poor Theos. All because of me."

Tommy's head jerked up. Was Peter, too, feeling responsible for a man's death? But that was foolish. Peter hadn't sent Theos up into the hills with a rifle. "No, if it was because of anyone, it was Clarence Kelly," Tommy declared. "Not you."

"Connolly," Mr. Farnham said, "I've told the boy he can take the day off with pay. From the looks of you, you'd better do the same."

# CHAPTER SIX
### St. Patrick's Day, 1912

"Do you think you'll ever stop growing?" Tommy's mother asked him. "I don't know how much farther I can let down the legs of these trousers."

Tommy mumbled around a mouthful of potatoes, "Why do you have to work on that during supper, Mom? I don't like to sit here eating all by myself while you sew my pants."

"It's because I want you to look nice tonight." Fiona bit the thread with her teeth and told him, "I want to feel proud of you. Oh, I don't mean that I'm not proud of you all the time, Tommy, but tonight is special. Saint Paddy's Day. To your dad, March seventeenth was a bigger holiday than Christmas even."

Mopping up the rest of the gravy with his bread, Tommy answered, "Well, I guess he'll be with us in spirit at the party, since I'm gonna wear his suit coat and his pants." His father hadn't been buried in the suit the mine owners had provided, because after the mine exploded, not enough of John Quinlan's body had remained to put a suit on it.

Sighing, Fiona answered, "You won't wear his clothes

much longer. Only fifteen and you're already taller than your dad ever was, God rest his soul. Now, finish up quick so you have time to shine your shoes."

Catching her hand, he said, "We have plenty of time before Peter comes with the sleigh. Sit down and have a cup of tea with me. There's something I want to talk about."

Fiona took Tommy's plate to the sink, then wiped the oilcloth with a dishrag. Each week she washed and ironed seven long white linen tablecloths for mine owner Ellis Farnham's dining room. That was more than enough fussing over fancy table coverings, she said; oilcloth would do just fine for her own kitchen table, which was where they always ate anyway, since they didn't have a dining room. Oilcloth never had to be laundered, only wiped clean after every meal.

"All right, what is it you want to tell me?" she asked after she'd settled herself with a teacup in front of her.

Nervous about how to proceed, Tommy drummed his fingers on the table. Then he announced, "A couple of weeks after Christmas I'll be sixteen."

"Christmas! It's only Saint Patrick's Day. Why are you thinking so far ahead? You just turned fifteen two months ago."

She wasn't making this easy for him, and he wanted her to take it seriously. Defensively he answered, "You're the one who always says if you want to get ahead, you've got to think ahead."

"All right, I'm listening." She folded her hands in her lap and gave him the kind of look she'd given him when he was small and wanted to share something with her—an exaggerated attention.

"Mom, I'd like to start working as a laborer in the mine. I think Peter can set it up for me, once I'm sixteen." He'd blurted the words, knowing how much his mother hated the dangerous jobs inside the mine; in fact, she still fretted over his being a trapper boy.

"Why would you want to do such a thing?" she asked.

He'd rehearsed this, so in a rush he began to put forth his argument. "Think about this, Mom. As a laborer I'll get paid three dollars a day. That's eighteen dollars a week."

"I can do sums," she said.

"Money wouldn't be so tight then, and you wouldn't have to stay up late at night mending and ironing."

"Have you heard me complaining?" she asked him. Then she fell silent. Frowning, weaving her fingers together, resting her elbows on the table, she sat there and thought. Soon she got up and began to pace.

In the silence the wall clock ticked loudly. Tommy counted the seconds, until he could no longer tolerate the sound of them. Still she paced, until he asked, "So, what do you say, Mom?"

Stopping in front of him, she answered, "This is what I say. It's funny that you should want to earn more so I can work less, Tommy. You've got it quite backward. I'll explain, and then I'll make a bargain with you."

"Go ahead," he said. "What is it?"

"Just this—that I work more and you work less." Suddenly the words came pouring out of her. "If you should get this job when you're sixteen, I could buy a washing machine with your extra wages. I've seen them in the Sears catalog. You pour hot water and soap into them, and there's a lever you push back and forth, and it moves paddles inside the tub so the paddles loosen the dirt. No more scrubbing on a washboard, unless the clothes are really filthy—so of course I wouldn't get rid of my washboard, because some of those miners' socks really stink."

Taken aback, Tommy asked, "But why would you want to do more laundry?"

"To get you out of the mine!" she cried. "I've been struggling to put a bit of cash aside for a washing machine, but it's too hard, considering the little that you and I earn. With a machine I could take in more laundry and earn more money. What I'd really like is to hire a girl to help with the laundry so that I could concentrate more on the fine mending." Pushing back the strands of dark hair that had come loose from the bun on top of her head, she demanded, "Do you know how few women can mend and alter clothes as well as I can? Nobody else here in Castle Gate, I can tell you that."

Tommy argued, "You already do too much work. I don't know why you'd want to do more." This wasn't going the way he wanted it to.

"Oh, pish! Look at me. I have two people to cook and keep house for—you and me. Now think about the other women around here. The Slavs, the Italians, the Mormon women out there on the farms. They have eight, nine, ten, twelve children to care for, and some of them take in boarders too. They do almost as much laundry as I do, and twenty times more cooking, and besides that they grow their own vegetables. Which they bottle and preserve. And then in the fall they butcher pigs. Am I not as strong as any of them?" She lifted her arms like a prizefighter showing off his biceps. "Or am I any better than any of those women, so that I'm entitled to an easier life? The answer to that one is no!"

"That's *your* answer. Maybe it's not *my* answer."

"Wait! I haven't finished. I haven't told you about the bargain part of it. So this is what I propose: You work just as long as it takes for me to get a really good start on this business, and then you quit the mines."

"And do what?" Now he was standing too.

"Oh, I don't know." She wrapped her arms around him in a fervent hug. "Oh, Tommy darlin', it's not that I'm ungrateful for what you're trying to do for me. It's just that I want you to get out of the mines alive. You could get another kind of job, or go back to school."

"School? After all this time?" He'd left school at the end of sixth grade. All his classmates, at least the ones who hadn't gone into the mines, were now in high school. What was he supposed to do—sit in a classroom full of twelve-year-olds? Anyway, he liked working in a coal mine, liked the importance of coal. It ran railroads and steel mills and steamships. "I won't promise anything," he said. "Anyway, I haven't even got the job yet. Like you said, it's a long way off."

She tightened her arms around him, saying, "The reason I'd even consider it is—I'd like to run my own business, even if it's just a laundry. I want to be independent. Someday you'll go off and get married, and I'll need something to keep me going in my old age. I'd never want to be a burden on you and your wife."

"Wife! What wife? Mom, I'm only fifteen!" Marrying was the last thing in the world Tommy had on his mind. With his job in the mine and helping out his mother after work, he never even had time to meet any girls.

"That's all for now," she said. "We'll both think about this. You'd better get ready for the party."

As he blacked his shoes Tommy went over everything she'd said. At least his mother hadn't forbidden him to work as a laborer. The surprise was that she had ambitions of her own. She was a hard worker, that he knew, but then, nearly everyone in Castle Gate worked hard. The highest accolade one person could give another was to call that person a good worker. A man could be a drinker, stay out late carousing, never go to church, and ignore his children, but if he was a "good worker," he would be admired.

Looking over to where his mother again sat at the table with a needle in her hand, he said, "You're after me to get ready for the party. What about you?"

"I can comb my hair and change my dress in ten minutes. I promised Mrs. Farnham I'd get this chemise returned by tomorrow. That daughter of theirs keeps bursting out of her chemises, one after the other. She must be growing remarkable bosoms."

"Mom!"

"What? Is it that you don't want me to talk about girls' figures, or is it that you think rich girls are too high and mighty to develop bosoms like the rest of us? Ooh, look at you, Tommy! I made you blush." She jumped up and danced the chemise in front of him, teasing him with the lacy, frilly thing until he ran to his room to change clothes.

When Peter arrived with his sleigh, Fiona was ready but Tommy wasn't. His hair kept sticking up the wrong way. Even when he doused it with water, it rebelled. He opened his bedroom door to ask if Peter minded waiting for a few minutes longer but quickly closed it again, though not all the way.

Peter had been talking about him. Pressing his ear into the space between the door's edge and the door frame, Tommy heard him say, "He does his job the way he's supposed to, but he never talks to anyone."

"How can he talk to anyone when he sits by himself all day long?" Fiona asked.

"At the dinner break. There are boys his own age in the mine, but he never hangs around with them. He keeps to himself. In a fifteen-year-old that's not natural. As his mother, you should be aware of that."

"How would you know anything about raising a boy?" Fiona asked, scorn in her voice.

"I don't," Peter admitted. "But I know about *being* a boy. No matter what long hours they work, boys always find time to be with their friends. Tommy has no friends."

"No friends!" Fiona laughed out loud. "Have you seen him at parties? People love him! He's the most popular boy in Castle Gate."

In the moment of silence that followed, Tommy was tempted to open the door wider so he could watch Peter's face when he answered that, but he didn't want to get caught eavesdropping.

"Fiona," Peter said softly, and Tommy had to strain to hear. "Those people aren't Tommy's friends—they're his audience. There's a big difference. Tommy's a fine performer, and yes, people love him for that, but when the performance is over, he separates himself from everyone again. There's a darkness inside him that he keeps locked up."

"Nonsense!" Fiona spat.

Silence again, and then Peter asked, "Fiona, do you remember a saying from the old country: 'An Irishman has an abiding sense of tragedy that sustains him through temporary periods of joy'?"

"Yes, and I never understood the saying then and I still don't, and it has nothing at all to do with Tommy."

Quietly Tommy closed the door. If Peter only understood the guilt Tommy carried inside him. . . . Well, if he did, he'd no longer want to be Tommy's friend. And Peter was right: Tommy had no other friends.

When Tommy came out of his room, Fiona's lips were

pressed tightly in irritation, and Peter's greeting to Tommy sounded restrained. Tommy was just as restrained. He couldn't meet Peter's eyes.

Outside, Peter helped Fiona into her seat in the sleigh and tucked a blanket around her. "Back in Ireland," Fiona commented as the sleigh moved smoothly over the icy road, "my mother always planted her peas on Saint Patrick's Day. Here in Castle Gate we can't even see any earth to plant anything into it. All this snow covers the ground well into spring." She shivered under the blanket.

The hint of longing in her voice made Tommy wish he could send his mother to Ireland for a visit. As a laundress, even with her own washing machine, she'd never earn more than the bare necessities. But if Tommy stayed in the mines, and times were good, and he earned more by working a lot of overtime, he might be able to swing it—in five or six years, if he was lucky.

Driving under the full moon, they passed the towering monoliths the town was named after: two wide, enormously tall pillars of sandstone that looked for all the world like the turrets of a castle. The columns stood guard on either side of the road. Now the moon balanced itself on one of the turrets, but before they reached the amusement hall in the nearby town of Helper, the moon had broken free to climb, solitary and regal, into the clear sky.

"We're a bit early," Peter said as he helped Fiona alight from the sleigh.

"That's good," she answered. "I brought deviled eggs, and I want to find a nice spot for them on the table before all the other women arrive with their dishes."

"Tommy, you come with me, then, to the livery stable to take care of Johnny Bull, will you?" Peter asked.

"Sure. Glad to." He jumped at the chance to talk to Peter about the job, although he still felt uncomfortable about what he'd overheard.

They busied themselves unhitching the horse and instructing the livery boy to make sure Johnny Bull was covered with a blanket. As they tramped back toward the hall, Tommy brought up the subject of the job. Right away Peter agreed.

"It's a grand idea," Peter announced. "When you're old enough, I'll see if you can work with me. A laborer is only supposed to shovel coal into the coal carts, but I can start teaching you the job of mining, so you'll be ready when the chance comes to better yourself."

They stomped the snow off their rubber boots and left them outside the door. Peter's dress shoes were fancier than Tommy's, but Tommy never got to dance much anyway, since he was always playing music. "Old Tim Shaughnessy is going to play with me tonight," he said. "We make a good team, Tim on his fiddle and me on the guitar. This will be the third time we've played together." The two of them would split the four-dollar pay, which was a dollar less than Tommy earned now when he played solo, but that didn't matter. He liked making music with Tim.

"Why don't you bring your guitar and come with me for a bit?" Peter invited. "There are a few fellows in the back room I want you to meet."

Surprised, wondering if he was supposed to play for the "few fellows" before the real party started, Tommy followed Peter to a small room thick with smoke. Half a dozen men sat around a square table, drinking beer and puffing their pipes. Tommy knew two of them, but the others were strangers.

"Pull up a chair," Peter said after he'd introduced Tommy. "I brought the boy with me because he wants to be a laborer when he turns sixteen next year." When Peter added, "He's Jimmy Mack's nephew," Tommy cringed inside.

Peter pulled a small, folded newspaper out of his pocket and asked, "Fellow workers, have you heard what Big Bill Haywood pulled off?"

At the sound of "Haywood," Tommy glanced quickly toward the paper. The masthead read, SOLIDARITY, THE NEWS-PAPER OF THE IWW. IWW, Tommy knew, stood for Industrial Workers of the World. The Wobblies.

Peter told them, "Haywood got twenty-three thousand textile workers to strike for nine whole weeks in Lawrence, Massachusetts. And they won! The bosses gave in!"

The other men looked unimpressed.

Growing excited, holding up *Solidarity,* Peter went on, "Listen to what Bill Haywood said to the workers in a speech after they won the strike: 'Passive, with folded arms, without violence, the strikers of Lawrence triumphed. You have demonstrated the common interest of the working class in bringing all nationalities together.'"

An Englishman named Monty—Tommy hadn't caught whether that was his first name or last name—said, "If that's what they want to do up there in Massachusetts, fine. But I don't want to be in any union with foreigners." Then he coughed. Small and gaunt, Monty appeared to be ravaged by the coal miners' curse, black lung disease. Yet he never stopped puffing his pipe.

Another man, whose pale complexion contrasted with his long, dark mustache, declared, "I'm like Evans here—I don't like them Wobblies. The Western Federation of Miners is good enough for me. I'll work in the mines with the foreign laborers, but outside the mines I don't want nothin' to do with them."

Running his fingers through his hair, Peter said, "All right. I just want you to think about this. Who do we have here in this room right now? A German, two Irishmen, two Welshmen, a Dane, and an Englishman. We're the ones favored by the mine bosses. But is that fair? The IWW wants one big union for everybody, including Italians, Poles, Slavs, Greeks, and all the rest."

"The offscourings of southern Europe," commented one of the Welshmen.

Monty agreed, adding, "Look what the Greeks did last year in Kenilworth."

Tommy had become so absorbed in the argument that he forgot to wonder why he was there. He was startled when Peter announced, "I'm glad you brought that up. Tommy, hold up your guitar case and tell these fellows about it."

All eyes turned to Tommy as Peter urged, "Show them the bullet hole and tell them what you told me."

Standing up, Tommy set his guitar case on a chair and pointed to the cavity in the neck of it. "See," he began, "when I heard the shots, I held the guitar case in front of me, like this, with the wide part covering my chest." He demonstrated. "The narrow end was resting on the ground."

"Go on," Peter said.

"The Greeks were up in the mountains, so when the rifle shot came, the bullet traveled downward, at this angle." He pointed his finger down. "It just barely nicked the headstock of the guitar inside the case." When the men looked blank, he said, "You know, the place at the top of the guitar's neck. Where the pegs are, to tighten the strings."

The German declared, "They were trying to kill you."

"I don't think so," Tommy answered. "I was standing right in front of a stone wall. If they'd wanted to kill me, they'd have aimed for my head. Instead they aimed between my feet."

"*Gott!* How could you believe that?" the man scoffed.

"They were just lousy marksmen," one of the Welshmen said. "So they missed your brains and nearly shot you in the foot. I'd say that's pretty poor shootin'."

After that terrible morning Tommy'd had plenty of time to relive the memory and try to sort it out. He told the men, "I think they were only trying to scare me."

To back up Tommy, Peter broke in, "Warning shots— that's all they were. It was only after the Americans started shooting back that it turned into a real war."

"You're both crazy." The Dane, named Thorvald, got to his feet, declaring, "This meeting's going nowhere, and my wife's waiting supper for me. You Micks go on and celebrate your potato famine, or whatever it is that Saint Patrick's is supposed to be about."

Though Peter tried to get the rest of the men to stay and talk, they just shrugged, pulled on their overcoats, and walked away. Tommy couldn't help feeling sorry for Peter, yet he was glad to get out of there. The unions held no interest for him, not the IWW or the Western Federation of Miners or the United Mine Workers of America or any others, if there were any others. He had his job, he was going to get a better job next year, and the last thing he wanted was to join a union. Men who belonged to unions, like Jim McInerny and Theos Kambanakis, too often got killed.

The main hall was full when Tommy and Peter walked

into it. "There he is!" some of the revelers shouted. "We're waiting for you, Tommy! Start the music!"

Almost everybody knew him by now. They no longer said, "There's Tommy Quinlan, Jim McInerny's nephew." Now they said, "That's Tommy, the lad who plays and sings for our celebrations." And not just at the Irish parties. He kept getting invited to all kinds of parties—in Castle Gate, in nearby Helper, and in the larger town of Price. And his mother was right. Everybody loved Tommy Quinlan the singer.

Old Tim Shaughnessy waited for him, fiddle at the ready, all tuned up. Tim had very few teeth, so he always smiled with his mouth closed and never spoke unless he had to.

"Look what Peter brought me from Salt Lake City, Tim," Tommy said, holding out sheet music so Tim could see it, although he knew Tim couldn't read music. "It's a new song. I'll play the first chorus, and you can pick it up from there."

Tim smiled and nodded.

"Here we go, folks," Tommy called out. Completely at ease now in front of a gathering, he liked the way an audience quieted down and waited, smiling and expectant, for him to begin. He had a special treat for these people tonight—a Saint Patrick's Day joke he'd been working on all week. "Thanks to Peter Connolly," he told them, "and his mysterious weekly trips to Salt Lake City . . ."

Most everybody laughed. They knew Peter caught the earliest train every Sunday morning and came back late at night.

"Thanks to our friend Peter, we have a brand-new song, a sweetheart of a song, one that was just published this month. I guarantee you'll love it."

Strumming a few chords on his guitar, he began to sing:

"When Irish eyes are smiling,
 Sure it's like a morn in spring.
 In the lilt of Irish laughter
 You can hear the angels sing.


 When Irish hearts are happy . . ."

He was right, they loved it. They yelled and cheered and insisted that Tommy sing it over again, and then a third time, and by then they all knew the words and tune and sang along, while Old Tim, wearing a sunken, approving smile, stood there bowing away on his violin.

That he could command a crowd this way filled Tommy with a sense of power and wonder. Now he was ready to spring his joke. He told them, "Here it is Saint Patrick's Day, as if you didn't know."

"As if we didn't!" Cheers erupted, and applause.

"And something very strange happened. A little Irish leprechaun named Tiny Tom got into this sheet music." He held up "When Irish Eyes Are Smiling." "And this little leprechaun erased the real words and put different words to the music."

They were all watching him, anticipating whatever he was leading to. "Same tune, different words," Tommy said. "But don't blame me—it's all the fault of the leprechaun. Let's go, Tim." And Tommy sang,

"The dirty, dirty Irish,
 Sure they never wash their clothes,

For there are no Chinese laundries
Where the River Shannon flows.

They put them on in springtime,
And they wear them till it snows,
For there—"

"Thomas Quinlan, you stop that this very instant," Fiona shouted, storming up to the front of the room. "It's a disgrace," she cried, pulling the guitar from his hands. "How dare you insult your own people!"

"It was only a joke, Mom," he protested. "I wasn't trying to insult anybody."

"What would your poor, dead father have thought?" she cried.

Peter appeared, retrieving the guitar from Fiona and saying, "I don't know what his father would have said, but I know for sure that his uncle, Jim McInerny, would have laughed himself fit to bustin'. Don't get yourself all in a twitter, Fiona. The boy was just having a bit of fun."

Caught in the middle, Tommy hesitated, uncertain what to do. He could see the anger building in his mother's eyes as Peter tried to smooth things.

"Don't you go butting in where you're not wanted, Peter Connolly, when I'm dealing with Tommy," Fiona warned. "He's not your son, he's mine, and he's never going to be your son, because I wouldn't marry you if you asked me a thousand times."

Peter began to laugh, making half the people in the hall laugh with him, while some of the others stayed as indignant as Fiona. "But Fiona," he said, "I've never asked you even once to marry me. And what a terrible oversight that was. So I'll ask you now."

Right in front of the hundred or so people at the party, Irish folks from Castle Gate and Kenilworth and Sunnyside and Scofield, Peter Connolly dropped to his knees, threw his arms wide, and said, "Fiona darlin', will you marry me?"

Laughter, cheers, and applause filled the room—this was better entertainment than the melodrama theater that came through Helper every few months. Tommy saw not a hint of amusement in his mother's face. Quite the contrary. He thought he'd better get to her quick, but he felt Old Tim's clawlike hand on his arm, restraining him.

Fiona's eyes shot fire. Her voice seemed to pour forth from the depth of some wrathful Celtic warrior woman. "Never!" she cried. "Never would I marry the likes of you, Peter Connolly. I'm taking my son and we're going home right now."

A groan rose from the crowd. "Fiona, it's only the shank of the evening," someone protested. "We need Tommy here. The party will be all spoiled if you take him."

Tim's hand still held Tommy's arm, but Tommy no longer needed to be held. It was time to start speaking up for himself, or his mother would forever make his choices for him. He hated to defy her in front of all these people, but he'd hate it worse if he left the hall when the party had barely begun. People were counting on him. Flat out he told her, "I'm not leaving, Mom. I was hired to play, and I intend to go ahead with it."

Fiona gasped. Her face flamed. Forced to retreat, she had nowhere to take refuge; she stood there, embarrassed and vulnerable in front of everyone. Tim nodded and winked at

Tommy, then raised his fiddle to play "My Wild Irish Rose." At the first bar of music Peter climbed to his feet.

*Now,* Tommy thought, *Peter will make things right.* But Peter walked right past Fiona and went straight to Meg Rourke, a pretty, young widow whose husband had died in a rockfall in the mine less than a year before. He held out his arms to her, and they began to waltz.

"Git to your mam," the old fiddler told Tommy, prodding him with the tip of the violin bow. But Tommy was already on his way.

When he put his arm around his mother she felt stiff as a board and her cheeks still burned, yet what could she do other than dance with her son, since everyone was watching? Her eyes glittered, not with anger, but from unshed tears of humiliation.

"Smile. Hold your head up high," he told her. "I'm sorry I made you upset. Pretend you like dancing with me."

"I'd like to dance at Peter Connolly's funeral," Fiona muttered. "I'd like to dance on his grave." After a few minutes she declared, "And if you think I've forgiven you, Tommy, about that song, you're wrong. Where did you get those awful words?"

"I made them up, Mom. It's a parody—I make up words all the time. It was supposed to be funny. I never thought it would start a ruckus. But at least it got Peter to declare his intentions in public."

"Hmph," she snorted.

"And I learned something tonight," he said.

She was loosening up in his arms, getting into the spirit of the waltz. "What did you learn?"

He spun her around. Tommy wasn't the greatest dancer;

he never got to dance much, since he was always making the music. He was thankful Fiona was so light on her feet.

"So what did you learn?" she asked him again.

"That all this time I thought Peter was being kind to me, he was doing it just to get close to you. It wasn't me he cared about, it was you."

She was silent as Old Tim swung into still another chorus of "My Wild Irish Rose." Half the people in the hall sang along, while the other half waltzed. "I don't think you're being fair," she told him. "Peter does care about you, a great deal. He's a very caring person."

That surprised Tommy. "Caring? I thought you wanted to dance on his grave. Does that mean you might marry him?"

"Did I say that?" The fire was back in her eyes. "You know how I feel about miners."

"I'm almost a miner, Mom. I will be by the beginning of next year, I hope."

"You're my son. I didn't choose you, although every day I thank God that I have you. Husbands are different. A woman gets to choose a husband. And I thank God for that too. For giving us the choice."

He glanced up at the guitar case rattling on the train rack overhead. His first major lie to his mother had been about the hole in the neck of that case. He'd told her it had come from a live coal that flew out of the fire grate in Kenilworth. The coal had burned through the case, he'd said, and even damaged a bit of the guitar's headstock. If Fiona had known it was really a bullet hole, that would have been the end of Peter, for sure—from then on Tommy wouldn't have been allowed near the man. Fiona was a strong, stubborn woman.

Tommy was strong too. He'd had to be, to become his own man. If he spent his life trying to please his mother, he'd turn into one of those pitiable Irishmen who never marry, who stay at home all their lives, being catered to by an aging mam. That was why he sometimes deceived her, so he could choose what was right for himself.

For months after that Saint Patrick's night more than three years ago he'd worried because he'd told the true story of the bullet hole, at Peter's urging, to those six men. Worried that they'd go home and repeat it to their wives. Since women gossiped among themselves, the truth might have reached Fiona. But it hadn't, and for that Tommy was everlastingly grateful.

Outside now it was growing light. He got up to stretch, then sat back down to look out the train window. Never had he seen land so flat. Born and raised in Utah's high mountains, where even the valley he lived in stood at an altitude of six thousand feet, he found this flat prairie unappealing. Yet the snow here was white, not gray like Castle Gate's. With a few distant farmhouses showing lights in the windows and smoke from the chimneys, it did look like a peaceful Christmas scene.

Christmas. It would soon be Christmas, 1915. He leaned back in the seat and smiled, remembering the Christmas midnight mass two years ago that had changed his life.

# CHAPTER SEVEN
## Christmas Eve, 1913

One day of shoveling coal was all it had taken, and Tommy understood why the men were called laborers. He'd spent the fourth hour praying for the dinner break. By the sixth hour he doubted he'd make it to the closing whistle. When the whistle blew, he could barely move his feet along the tunnels to the mine portal.

"You'll get used to it," Peter had told him on the way out. "Truth to tell, I took it easy on you today; when you were looking like you'd keel over, I threw in a few shovelfuls for you."

If it hadn't been for his own stubborn pride, Tommy might have asked for a different job, but it had taken him too long to get this one, and he didn't want to lose it. During most of 1913 there'd been a slump in the coal industry—instead of being hired, miners were getting laid off. It wasn't until October that the demand for miners had risen once again, when the need for fuel to heat homes had made its usual seasonal upswing. Not till then could Peter get Tommy on as a laborer.

As days turned into weeks he'd kept waiting for the job to get easier, but it didn't.

"You've got to build up those muscles," Peter had told him. "You might have strong fingers from plucking that guitar of yours, but it does nothing to strengthen your shoulders. Eat hearty every meal."

Some evenings Tommy was so tired he could barely force himself to eat at all. He tried to hide his weariness from his mother—if she'd known how fatigued he really felt, she'd have made him look for another job. Nothing else he could find would have paid the three dollars a day he earned in the mines, even though most of it came in the form of scrip that could be spent only at the company store. They used it to buy all their groceries and supplies for Fiona's laundering, then tried to put into savings at least some of the cash she earned.

Tommy had hoped they could order the washing machine this Christmas, but at the rate they were saving, they'd be lucky to afford it by next Christmas.

After the quitting whistle blew on December 24, he arrived home so dog-tired he wanted to throw himself onto his bed in his filthy work clothes and sleep the whole night and all through Christmas Day. But he couldn't. The priest had asked him to play and sing for midnight mass.

"I've got a washtub full of hot water waiting for you in the kitchen," his mother announced as he came through the door. "Take a good bath, and be sure to wash your hair nice and clean so I can give it a trim before we go."

Tommy set his dinner pail down hard on the kitchen table, irritated that his mother kept treating him like a little kid. In another month he'd be seventeen. He was a laborer in the mines, earning the three dollars a day. Did she think he didn't know enough to wash his hair?

The hot water soothed the aches out of his muscles, and the

supper she'd prepared—meatless, of course, because Christmas Eve was a fast day—soothed his hunger.

"Take a nap now," she told him, again treating him like a three-year-old. "I'll wake you in plenty of time to get ready."

For the next few hours he was dead to the world. When he felt his mother's hand shaking his shoulder, he thought it was time to get up and go to work in the mine. Not until she said, "Come on, now. I need to cut your hair," did he realize it was ten o'clock on Christmas Eve, not the crack of dawn, when he'd have to face another day of shoveling coal.

Snipping with the scissors as she circled him, she commented, "You're lucky to have a washerwoman for a mother."

"Why?"

"Take a look at that shirt hanging over there. Did you ever see anything so white, or ironed so perfectly? That's for you to wear tonight. And I pressed your suit too."

"I don't know why you bothered," he told her. "Father Mike says I have to wear a surplice and cassock over my suit."

"Oh." For a moment she looked disappointed, but then she brightened. "Afterward you can take off the surplice and cassock, and everyone will see how nice you look. Mr. and Mrs. Farnham will be there with their family."

"Is that right?" That surprised Tommy. Mr. Farnham wasn't Catholic.

"His wife told me about it when I delivered her mending today," Fiona went on. "It's because their daughter, Eugenie, goes to a Catholic boarding school in Salt Lake City. Eugenie talked them into attending midnight mass at our church."

"Has the daughter turned Catholic or something?" Tommy wondered.

"Oh, no. She just likes the music."

Tommy had grown up listening to the music of the mass

and had never thought about it much. What was there about it that this Eugenie, whoever she was, should like? He'd never seen her. Because the Farnhams had moved to Castle Gate just three years earlier, when Mr. Farnham became part owner of the mine, the daughter wouldn't have been in school when Tommy was. He knew he'd have remembered any girl with such an odd name.

It had surprised him that Father Mike wanted him to sing "Silent Night" and play it on his guitar, when all the rest of the mass would be sung in Latin to organ accompaniment. But the priest had told him that "Silent Night" was originally sung to the music of a guitar, almost a hundred years earlier.

At first, when Father Mike asked him, Tommy had refused. "I—I'm really not worthy to sing at Christmas mass, Father," he'd stammered.

"Dear boy," the priest had answered, "if every priest, altar boy, organist, and choir member had to be worthy, Mass would never get sung anywhere in the world. All of us are unworthy, you know. It's part of being human. But God loves us anyway. Just make a good confession and you'll be entirely worthy."

A good confession. How could he confess his enormous offense? He knew from catechism class that it wasn't really a sin, because to sin a person had to deliberately choose evil over good. Yet his terrible . . . blunder—even if it wasn't a sin—had caused Uncle Jim's death, and it made Tommy unworthy to stand up in church on the holiest of nights to sing about God's birth. Even though, finally, he did agree to it.

His mother kept snipping at him with the scissors, making smidgens of his dark hair fall to the ground. Strange, Uncle Jim's hair had been strawberry blond, but Fiona's was dark brown, and Tommy took after her. He couldn't remember his father enough to know what color his hair had been. He'd have to ask.

"There!" Fiona said, shaking out the towel. "You look as handsome as the Prince of Killarney. Sweep up the bits of hair, will you, while I go and change my dress."

A quarter hour later, as Tommy was placing studs through the tiny holes in his shirtfront, a knock came at the kitchen door. He wondered who it might be, since Peter wasn't expected to pick them up for a while. After opening the door, Tommy stood there, unmoving, astonished into silence. "Mom, you'd better come," he called.

"Not now, Tommy. I don't have the pins in my hair yet."

"Mom, come!" he yelled, insisting.

"What in the world could be so important?" She walked out of her bedroom with her long, dark hair streaming around her shoulders, a pretty woman, he had to admit, even if she was his own mother.

There, in the snow on their kitchen doorstep, stood a washing machine. Like Tommy, his mother was dumbstruck, until Peter, grinning foolishly, poked his head around the door frame and said, "Merry Christmas, Fiona. Tommy, help me bring it inside. I had a devil of a time getting it out of the sleigh."

His mother had gone white as a sheet, except for the red spots high on her cheeks. "Don't bring that thing in here!" she cried.

Undaunted, Peter answered, "It isn't a *thing,* Fiona, it's a Hired Girl."

"What!"

"Look at the brand-name label on the front. It says, 'The Hired Girl Washer.' Give me a hand, Tommy."

"Don't you dare, Tommy! I don't want that . . . *thing* in my house."

This was one of the times Tommy chose to ignore his mother's orders. As he helped Peter carry it in he was impressed by the weight of it. This machine was built to last. Copper bands circled the wooden slats of the tub, and the legs it rested on were sturdy, with crosspiece reinforcements. A metal lid with a handle in the center fitted snugly onto the tub. Best of all, a set of wringers sat, gleaming and white, on the top edge.

"What do you think, Tommy?" Peter asked, ignoring Fiona.

Tommy thought it was great. He took off the lid to inspect the paddles. Instead of a wooden lever, as his mother had described, this one had shiny metal rods on the outside that moved the gears that worked the paddles inside. This machine must have cost plenty.

Fiona stood there in her stocking feet, with her hair all loose, trying to look dignified. "You understand that I cannot accept this," she said stiffly to Peter.

"Of course you can, Fiona," he answered.

"I meant I *will* not accept it from you," she declared, stretching herself as tall as she could.

Peter pulled himself up to his own full height, which was much more imposing than hers. "Well, you'd better," he told her. "I brought this all the way from Salt Lake City, and I sure as hell don't intend to take it all the way back."

Changing emotions played across her features like the scenery inside a kaleidoscope: firm resolve, slightly less firm denial, followed by craving, and then covetousness. Tommy realized how much she wanted that magnificent piece of machinery.

Her fingers twitched with the desire to touch it, but still she refused to look at Peter. The two of them had been on precarious terms ever since the debacle of that Saint Paddy's evening a whole year and a half before. She hadn't forgiven Peter until last Labor Day, although she'd pardoned Tommy much sooner.

Clasping her hands tightly to keep from reaching out to the Hired Girl, she began to pace. Tommy knew what the pacing meant: She was trying hard to work out a plan that would let her keep the washer and still keep to her high-minded resolve. Raising his eyebrows, Tommy shot Peter a look that meant, *Wait and see.*

Finally Fiona stopped pacing and allowed herself to touch, gingerly, the lid of the machine. "I'll accept this," she declared. "On one condition."

"Name it," Peter said.

"Whatever this cost you, you must allow me to pay it back, as much as I can afford at a time, till I've paid the full amount."

Peter hesitated, squinting and scratching the side of his face, which was clean shaven for the Christmas mass. "You know how to take the joy out of gift giving, Fiona," he told her.

"Do you accept my terms or not?"

"As long as you promise you'll never do without anything just so you can pay me back money that I don't need."

"Agreed." Awkwardly they shook hands.

*Oh, Mother, can't you at least give this good man a hug?* Tommy thought. She was so generous with her warmth to everyone else, and so stingy to poor old Peter.

At least she had to sit next to him in the church that night, since Tommy had been told to stand in front of the altar, facing the congregation. Before the mass began, he should have asked Father Mike whether he was supposed to stand there during the *whole* mass, but he'd been too busy getting into his surplice and cassock, and so had Father Mike. Then, after mass began, he saw that there was no place for him to sit, because when Mr. Farnham and his family had filed into the church, they had been led by an usher to the very first pew, right in front of where Tommy stood.

He'd seen Mrs. Farnham around town once or twice, but he'd never before seen the Farnham children, a boy a couple of years older than Tommy—and Eugenie.

She was the only one of the Farnhams who bothered to kneel. Since the space between the altar rail and the first pew was rather narrow, when Eugenie knelt, she was no more than two feet away from Tommy. Then she slid back into the pew and slipped out of her coat.

He nearly gasped. In her deep red dress Eugenie looked like La Estrallita, the lady on the cigar box who still haunted his dreams. He attempted to concentrate on the words of the mass being sung right behind him by the priest on the altar, but the likeness was striking: the dress; her hair, just a little darker than blond, piled in soft waves low on her neck; her full red lips. . . . He tried not to stare, but his eyes kept drifting to the girl. After his first few glances she looked at him inquiringly, as if wondering whether they'd met before.

How old was she? Tommy's age? A year younger? A year older? Whatever her real age, she seemed far beyond him in sophistication, not to mention wealth. Her dress must have cost more than he earned in a month.

He was so distracted that he missed his cue during the Offertory—one of the altar boys had to nudge him and whisper that Tommy was supposed to sing now.

His guitar, with its bullet-hole nick in the headstock,

sounded mellow after all that organ music. His voice, after a
wavering start, caught firm and worked well enough. Proud
that he was now a true baritone, he'd pitched the song lower
than normal.

After the four traditional verses of "Silent Night" he hesitated, playing a little riff while he decided whether he had
enough courage to sing a verse he'd composed for this mass.
Probably no one would notice, he thought, so he began, softly:

> "Silent night, Child of Light,
>   Rescue me from my plight.
>   Lift my burden of sorrow and pain,
>   Only you can redeem me again.
>   Bring me peace and forgiveness
>   On . . . this night of your birth."

Eugenie's head tilted slightly. She raised her eyes, question-
ing, and as he sang each additional line her gaze grew more
intense. Then it was time to go to Communion, and he was
wondering what he should do with his guitar, when Eugenie
reached out to take it. After Communion she handed it back to
him. Softly he whispered, "Thank you."

When the mass had ended, Mr. Farnham said to Tommy,
"Do I recognize you? Aren't you the lad who barged into my
office—let's see, it was almost three years ago—about the
trouble in Kenilworth?"

"Yes, sir," Tommy answered, worried because Mr. Farnham
had used the term *barged in*. That's what he'd done, all right,
without permission, practically demanding that Mr. Farnham
find out whether Peter was safe.

"What's your name again, young man?"

"Thomas Quinlan, sir."

"Ah, yes, Thomas. Nice singing tonight. This is my son, Glenn," he said.

Glenn smiled and nodded, looking anxious to be out of there.

"And my wife, Mrs. Farnham, and my daughter, Eugenie."

Eugenie, the last to leave the pew, murmured, "That verse . . . the last one you sang . . . I've never heard it before."

"It's mine," he answered.

"Yours? Are you saying you composed it? When?"

"Just before mass."

"You mean you wrote those words tonight?"

"Well, I didn't exactly write them . . . ," he hedged.

A smile twisted her full lips; Tommy could tell what she was thinking, as surely as if she'd spoken it aloud—that he was fibbing to impress her.

"I mean," he explained, "I couldn't write them down because I didn't have a pencil or paper. I just made them up inside my head as we were riding here in Peter Connolly's sleigh."

She studied him for a long moment. Her eyes were green, her lashes long and dark.

"Truly?" she asked.

"It's Christmas and I just received Communion—I wouldn't lie to you."

Again she smiled, and this time it was accepting. She was just about to say more, when her father called to her. "I have to go," she said. With a slight brush of her fingers against Tommy's hand, she turned and disappeared into the crowd of churchgoers.

PART THREE

# He Ascended into Heaven

# CHAPTER EIGHT
## Valentine's Day Eve, 1914

If he'd dreamed of La Estrallita occasionally before Christmas, after Christmas he'd dreamed of her often. In his dreams La Estrallita became Eugenie Farnham, or Eugenie became La Estrallita; they were one and the same. When the pale light of dawn showed that it was time for him to get up and go to work, Tommy would try to hold on to the final wisps of his dreams before they disappeared like vapor into the cold morning. Once, La Estrallita had been woven into terrible memories of Uncle Jim's death. Now the dreams brought Tommy pleasure as well as pain.

At the beginning of February, Peter had handed Tommy a pamphlet-sized leaflet titled *The Little Red Songbook*. "They were selling these in Salt Lake City for the Joe Hill Defense Fund," he said. "You'll find great union songs inside—in fact, Joe Hill himself wrote most of them. I hope you learn some, Tommy, so if we ever have a big union rally here in Castle Gate, you can play them."

Tommy doubted he'd ever sing for a union rally, but he'd looked over the words. They were clever, all right—parodies set to well-known popular songs. "What's the Joe Hill Defense Fund?" he'd asked.

Resting his pick on his shoulder as they walked toward the mine, Peter answered, "Well, I told you this fellow Joe Hill was arrested for the murder of two grocers in Salt Lake City a couple of weeks ago. Not much evidence against him, but when they found out he was a Wobbly from the IWW, they slammed him in the hoosegow and threw the book at him. Not the songbook," Peter added wryly, "though I'm sure when they read his words about overthrowing the capitalists, it didn't help his case much."

Tommy had tucked the booklet into his coat pocket and pretty much forgot about it. Coal production was at its usual winter high, with long hours of work from dawn to dusk. They were assigned to a "room," a square chamber where the walls and ceiling showed nothing but thick seams of coal; light from the carbide lamps hooked onto the miners' caps reflected dimly on the shiny surfaces. With his pick Peter would undermine the seams, then use his drill to make holes, where he placed the dynamite charges to be set off at the end of the shift. After the blasts had knocked tons of coal onto the floor—and after everyone had finished coughing and choking on the black coal dust that invaded their lungs like a phantom of death—they would leave the mines to let the dust settle. The next morning, at the start of the new shift, Tommy would shovel up the massive chunks and dump them into the carts. Lately he'd begun to develop decent muscles, which made the work easier, but at the end of each long day he still felt bone weary.

Cutting coal in the same room with Tommy and Peter was a Welshman, Morgan Jones, the man who'd once called foreigners the "offscourings of southern Europe." Ironically, the laborer assigned to work with Morgan Jones happened to be one of those "off-scourings," a Slovenian by the name of Edo Cvetek. Though his hair was blond, everyone called the man Black Edo, since his face was permanently spotted, from forehead to chin, with big round splotches of coal dust. A couple of years earlier Edo had got caught in a mine explosion. It was minor enough that he didn't get killed, yet powerful enough to blow coal dust right through his skin like a tattoo. With all those permanent black spots on his face Edo looked pretty strange, but Tommy got used to him quickly enough.

During the dinner breaks, since both Tommy and Edo were laborers, they usually sat together. Outside the mine Peter was Tommy's friend, but during working hours Peter ate with the other, older, experienced miners, men higher up in the coal-mining hierarchy. That didn't bother Tommy, at least not a lot.

"What did you bring today?" Tommy always asked Black Edo.

"Good stuff!" came the usual reply. Since Edo lived in a boardinghouse run by a Slovenian woman who also cooked for him, his dinner pail held interesting oddities—like bread layered thickly with lard and salt.

"I'm tell you—is good," Edo would say when Tommy looked disdainfully at the food. "At home on farm in Slovenia we have not too much meat, but lots of cream and milk and bacon. My mother always have girls at home for cook, you know. They take potatoes, boil 'em with pig fat—tree or four inch thick. Smear 'em on bread like this. You want try some, hokay?" And Edo would hold the greasy concoction so close to Tommy's lips it almost touched them, laughing hard and loud when Tommy wrinkled his nose and turned away.

"You can afford meat now, Edo," Tommy said once. "So why are you still eating lard?"

"My boarding missus—she don't know how to cook nothing but Slovenian. Anyway, I send all my money back to Slovenia. For dowries. For my sisters. I have six sisters. Six! Count 'em"—he held up his fingers to count—"One, two, tree, four, five—that how many dowries I send back already. One more to go."

The idea of dowries seemed foreign to Tommy, but after all, Black Edo *was* a foreigner. Edo explained that in Slovenia the men in a family had to provide dowries for all the unmarried daughters, no matter how many, even if a family had six daughters and only one son, like Edo's family. It was a matter of honor, Edo said. If the father or brother couldn't do that, the whole family would be disgraced in the eyes of the villagers.

By working hard and scrimping, Edo had managed to provide enough money for dowries for five of his sisters so far. "Just one more to go," he said again. "And then—they send me a bride."

"A bride? You mean they'll pick out a girl for you to marry, even if you never met her?"

"Sure! Pick her out, then they send her over to United States—a good Slovenian girl from my village. Don't worry," he said, seeing the doubt on Tommy's face. "My family gonna send me a nice girl—pretty one, a good, hard worker."

When Edo talked about his future wife—this unknown girl he would never meet until she arrived in Castle Gate to marry him—his blue eyes lit up in his black-spotted face. Tommy wondered how a young, unsuspecting Slovenian girl might react when she got a look at the discolored skin of this man she was obliged to marry. Maybe, Tommy thought wryly, Edo should just stop washing his face—at the end of a day shoveling coal, his black spots always disappeared into the layer of coal dust that coated every mine worker's face. By the time the quitting whistle blew, Edo looked just like everyone else, including Tommy: coal-blackened.

Tommy had taken to soaking his hands in the soapiest, hottest water he could stand at night, trying to work the coal dust out of his fingernails and the cracks in his skin. When he pictured Eugenie Farnham with her smooth, pale arms, he couldn't imagine taking her hand to dance if his own hands were begrimed from hard labor in a coal mine. But how else should he expect them to look? And except in his dreams, when would he ever in his hardscrabble life dance with the likes of Eugenie Farnham?

On Saturday evening, February 13, he soaked his hands twice as long as usual, almost getting them clean. Since he didn't want his mother to know what he was planning to do, he carried an old ironing board into his room and set it up next to his bed. On top of it he laid the board from the middle of the kitchen table, the one they put in to extend the length of the table on the rare occasions when they had company. Then, handling it carefully by the edges, he placed the single sheet of thick white paper onto the board, the paper he'd bought that afternoon, after work, at the company store.

The bottle of ink he borrowed from the kitchen cupboard; his mother used it to write up the accounts from her laundry business. Cautiously, sliding himself onto the edge of his bed, careful not to knock over the ironing board or the table board and especially not the bottle of ink, he sat down and picked up his pen.

*A Valentine For Eugenie Farnham From An Admirer,* he wrote in his most painstaking script, and underneath that,

*To Be Sung To The Tune Of "Jeanie With The Light Brown Hair," A Song Composed By Stephen Collins Foster.*

At the Christmas mass Eugenie had asked him about the verse he'd composed for "Silent Night." That gave him the courage to write a verse just for her. Although he wouldn't sign it, he hoped she'd know it was his.

He took a deep breath, dipped the pen point into the ink bottle, and put down the words he'd written in his head before he slept last night:

> *I dream of Genie with the light brown hair;*
> *Only by dreaming can I ever dare*
> *To see Eugenie and to sing her my song,*
> *Since I know to her world I can never belong.*
> *If she ever spoke to me, how would I behave?*
> *She's a lofty princess, while I'm a mere slave.*
> *Yet in my dreams we walk together at dawn;*
> *Then when I awaken, sweet Eugenie is gone.*

His fingers were cramped from holding the pen extra tight to make sure it didn't scratch or splatter. The inside of his third finger was stained from ink, as was the tip of his index finger. Setting down the pen, he carefully extricated himself from behind the ironing board, then went to the kitchen to scrub the ink from his fingers with a stiff scrub brush. He still had to address the envelope. Ink-stained fingers could smudge that extra-thick white envelope that had cost him a quarter—just for the envelope! The paper was a dime. Since thirty-five cents was the cost of a pound of steak, his mother would never have approved such extravagance, especially if he'd told her what he was using it for.

Back in his room he wrote on the envelope, *To Eugenie Farnham. Happy Valentine's Day, 1914.*

Then he sat and looked at it. Sealing wax would be a romantic touch. He'd read about sealing wax in a book somewhere, but he certainly didn't have any, and he didn't even know anyone who'd ever used it. What was the difference, he wondered, between sealing wax and regular candle wax? Back he went to the kitchen cupboard, where they kept candles for the frequent times the electric power went out. Luckily his mother was too absorbed in reweaving a customer's torn coat to pay any attention to him.

In his room once again, he lit the candle with a wooden match, wondering what the best way would be to drip wax on the envelope. Should he wait till the wax ran down the side of the candle, or tip the candle sideways over the envelope? While he thought it over, some wax spilled down the candle and burned his fingers. "Ow!" he muttered, quickly checking to make sure none of it had fallen onto the wrong place on the envelope.

Tilting the candle, he let the drops fall. They splashed, and what was worse, the red wax turned a sickly pink, laced with black soot from the wick. It didn't look at all romantic. It looked pretty silly. He groaned.

It was too late to run back to the company store for another envelope, even if he could have justified the extra expense. The kitchen clock said seven.

"Where's the Farnhams' laundry, Mom?" he asked. "I'll deliver it tonight so they'll have it for tomorrow when they go to church."

"Thank you, Tommy," she said, looking up from her mending. "Just take it to their back door and give it to Dorothy."

Dorothy was the girl who worked in the Farnhams' kitchen.

She and Tommy had gone to school together. "Is Dorothy supposed to pay me tonight?" he asked.

"It doesn't matter. Sometimes Mrs. Farnham makes me wait a week or two for the money, and sometimes I get it right away. I never complain, because she always pays sooner or later." Fiona bent over her work again. "I wonder if my eyes are going bad, Tommy. Maybe I'll need glasses one of these days to make it easier when I do the fine stitching."

Tommy slipped out of the house with the package of laundry in his arms and with the envelope tucked into the inside pocket of his heavy overcoat, the coat that had belonged to Uncle Jim. He was feeling more than a little nervous because the next part—which would have to take place inside Superintendent Farnham's house—was going to be tricky.

"How do, Dorothy," he said when she opened the Farnhams' back door. "How 'bout inviting me into the warm kitchen? It's freezing out here. I brought the laundry."

"Hello, Tommy," she said. Her cheeks, already rosy from the warmth, seemed to grow a little more flushed as she took the package of laundry from his hands.

"Do you need to be paid right now?" she asked. "The Farnhams are still at dinner."

"Well, we sure could use the money tonight," Tommy answered. "Maybe I could just wait here until they're finished eating." Would he need to tell that tiny lie in confession, or was it too small to count as even a venial sin?

"All right." Dorothy brushed some unnoticeable crumbs from her apron. "Would you like a glass of water or something, Tommy?"

"I know what!" he answered, teasing her. "Let's both you and me have a cup of tea together, Dorothy. It's such a

cold night, a cup of really hot tea would taste wonderful."
Tommy knew perfectly well that Dorothy was a Mormon,
and Mormons never drank tea. Or coffee. Or wine or beer or
hard liquor.

Dorothy seemed surprised that he was acting so friendly,
since he usually dropped off the laundry with no more than a
brief "hello" and "good-bye." "Oh, Tommy," she sighed,
"you know I can't drink tea with you." One of thirteen children of a Mormon farmer and his wife, Dorothy had been
born somewhere in the middle of that great big family. The
oldest of them now worked on the farm or helped in the
house, cooking and washing and tending the young ones.
Since Dorothy wasn't really needed for any of those jobs at
home, she'd hired out to work for the Farnhams.

"How much do they pay you here?" Tommy asked, a
little ashamed that he'd teased her about the tea.

"Two dollars a week. That really helps out at home."

Two dollars a week. Tommy earned three dollars a day,
yet the Quinlans still had trouble making ends meet. "And
you stay here all week long?" he asked her. "You sleep here?"

"I get to be home on Sundays. I'll be leaving tonight as
soon as I finish the dinner dishes, because our church starts
very early in the morning." She looked up sharply. "They're
ringing the bell for me to come clear the plates. I'll be right
back."

That was the moment Tommy had been waiting for. As
Dorothy pushed through the swinging door that connected
the dining room to the kitchen, he moved quickly toward an
adjacent door, hoping that one would lead to the hall.
Fortune smiled on him. He found himself in the dimly lit
hall, where a small square table held a vase filled with dried
flowers. Pulling the envelope from his pocket, he propped it

against the vase, then dashed back into the kitchen to sit innocently at the table before Dorothy returned, her hands and arms filled with dirty dinner plates.

"Listen, we don't really need the money tonight," he told her. "I'm not going to bother waiting. We'll just pick it up the next time."

"Oh." Dorothy looked a little disappointed. "All right."

On his way home he walked fast, wondering when Eugenie would see his valentine. Would she be the one to find it before anyone else did? If her mother or father found it, would they open it before giving it to her? This was the first time he'd actually written down the words to one of his parodies, the first time he'd ever given something he'd created to someone else.

No matter which Farnham—other than Eugenie—picked up the envelope first, they'd never guess who it came from. Even though he'd stood right in front of them all through the Christmas mass, they wouldn't connect Tommy's singing to the written valentine. But Eugenie might. Maybe not. It could be that she'd already forgotten him.

As he stomped the snow off his boots before entering his own kitchen door he thought about poor Dorothy, who would have to walk two miles through this frigid night to her family's farm. Too bad she couldn't have a nice cup of tea to warm her insides.

# CHAPTER NINE
### Decoration Day, 1914

His mother had said it casually, without a hint of suspicion that her words would transform Tommy's world. "There's a letter for you from the Farnhams."

"For *me!*" Tommy's voice squeaked in a way it hadn't since he'd become a permanent baritone.

"Yes. Their maid dropped it off with the dirty laundry."

"Did you open it?" he demanded.

"No. I was a little curious, but I've been too busy to take a look. It's on the kitchen table."

Tommy saw the square envelope with his name on it. So white! And his hands were so black. He lifted the lid of the washing machine and plunged his hands right into the hot suds.

"Tommy! That's my wash water for the white shirts! You'll get them all grimy."

He didn't care. After he dried his hands on a dishrag, he used a table knife to carefully pry up the envelope's flap, not wanting to tear it, since he might never again receive anything so extraordinary. Could it be from Eugenie?

It read, "To Thomas Quinlan from Enid Farnham (Mrs.):

On Decoration Day, May 30, we will entertain friends at a farewell party for our son, Glenn, who will sail to England, where he will study at Oxford University. We would like you to sing and play for our guests for a period of fifteen minutes to a half hour during the evening. For that we will pay you your usual fee—you must let us know what that would be. Please arrive at seven in the evening."

Too dumbfounded to speak, Tommy passed the note to his mother.

"Dear heaven!" Fiona said. "You've received a summons from the queen. What in the world are you going to wear?"

"Wear? My suit, I guess."

"On Decoration Day? You can't be seen in a winter wool suit by all those elegant people. The rules of high society say that from May thirtieth to Labor Day people wear summer clothes, not winter clothes. If you're going to be with people like that, even if you're only part of the entertainment, you have to look proper."

Tommy stared woefully at the piece of paper his mother had handed back to him and said, "Then I guess I can't go."

"Nonsense!" Fiona came out from behind her ironing board and declared, "I just need time to think." As always when she had to think deeply about something, she began to pace.

Tommy waited, his hopes soaring and then dashing, while Fiona paced, wearing a furrowed brow matched by the one on Tommy's face. Suddenly she stopped and said, "I have it!"

"What? Tell me."

"Be right back," she said, and hurried into her tiny bedroom, emerging minutes later with a man's linen suit that had once been white but was now faded to a soft cream.

"Do you remember Sven Allgren?" she asked. "He used to be a big, strapping Swede, but when he came down with black lung disease, he got thinner and thinner, so he brought this suit to me and asked me to alter it to fit him. Before I could even start on it, he died." For a moment she stopped, remembering not only the dead Swede but her own dead husband, Tommy suspected. Then Fiona continued, "Since the mine owners always donate a black suit for a miner to be buried in when he dies of something related to the mines, no one ever came to claim *this* suit." She picked it up and shook out the folds.

"Didn't he have any relatives?" Tommy asked.

"No. He was all alone. He lived in Mrs. Rhenquist's boardinghouse. He may have had family back in Sweden, but if he did, I never heard about it. I kept the suit, thinking that maybe someday someone might come for it, but no one has."

She held the jacket in front of Tommy. "It's a nice piece of cloth. Much too wide for you, but I can take it in to fit. It's good that Sven was so tall."

Was he going to spend his life wearing dead men's clothes? Tommy wondered. In this case it would be worth it: He could sing at the Farnhams' party. Undoubtedly Eugenie Farnham would be there. For the chance to see her again he'd gladly have shown up wearing a shroud pulled off a fresh corpse.

"Wait!" he cried, getting worried all over again. "Deco-ration Day is Saturday, and it's already Wednesday—will you have time to fix it?"

Fiona shrugged. "I'll give up sleeping. But you'll have to go out into the hills and find some wildflowers to deco-rate your father's and your uncle Jimmy's graves. I know Deco-ration Day is supposed to be a memorial for men who died in the Civil War and the Spanish-American War, but nobody . . ."—she paused for emphasis—"had better try to tell me that dead miners don't deserve a memorial day too."

Grinning, Tommy said, "You drive a hard bargain, Mom.

You'll redo this suit, but I have to pay you back by picking flowers." He rushed to give her a hug to show how grateful he felt. "I'll bring back bushels of flowers for the graves. Only, you'll have to take them to the cemetery yourself, because by the time I get off work on Saturday, I'll barely be able to scrub off the filth before I need to get dressed to go."

Fiona told him, "There's one more part to the bargain. You must promise to remember every single detail of the party so you can tell me all about it when you get home. I mean *every* detail! I want to know what all the ladies wore, down to the color of their shoes."

"I'll try."

"And the food! I want to know what the Farnhams served, and how the table looked. Oh, I hope they feed you some of whatever they serve their guests, so you can describe it to me, even though you'll have to eat in the kitchen."

That brought him back to Earth. He would not be a guest at the Farnhams' party; he'd be a paid employee, no different from Dorothy in the kitchen, although he wouldn't have to work as hard as Dorothy and he'd be paid a lot more.

Noticing his expression, Fiona said, "Don't you worry, son. You'll look as good as—or better than—any of those rich men with their fancy vests and gold watch chains. I'll see to that!"

For the next two evenings he made lists of all the songs he knew, trying to figure out what Mrs. Farnham might like. No Irish songs, certainly; Irish songs were considered even more low-class than Irish people. Stephen Collins Foster—Mrs. Farnham would be sure to like those songs, but what if she asked for "Jeanie with the Light Brown Hair"? Could he sing it in front of Eugenie without his face betraying him? Impossible! If he had to sing it, Eugenie would know for sure that he was the one who'd sent the valentine.

Would they want popular tunes, such as "By the Beautiful Sea" or "Abba-Dabba Honeymoon"? On his weekly trips to and from Salt Lake City, Peter always brought back sheet music of all the latest songs. No, Tommy couldn't picture stodgy mine officials such as Ellis Farnham, and their stiff, proper wives, requesting songs like "Snookey Ookums."

So, what should he plan to sing? Maybe he'd have to wait till he got there, get a sense of what the guests would like, and then—fake it.

Front door or back door? Hesitant, Tommy stood at the Farnhams' gate, holding his guitar case, with its bullet hole pointing toward the large brick house. The only other times he'd gone there had been to deliver laundry at the back door. But now he was dressed immaculately, wearing a high, starched collar, a new necktie Peter had contributed, and the remade linen suit, which fit him like the handiwork of a fine tailor from an elegant, big-city shop.

He took a deep breath and marched toward the front door. Before he reached it, the door swung open. Glenn Farnham stood there—ready to tell Tommy to go around the other way? No; Glenn smiled and said, "Come on in. Your name's Tom, right? I heard you sing at Christmastime at that Catholic church." Glenn offered his hand to shake, but before Tommy could transfer his guitar case from his right hand to his left, Glenn gestured and said, "Come on, follow me. The guests won't be coming for a half hour, so I'll show you where you're supposed to sing. You work in the mine, right? You were some sort of boy hero—my dad said you warned him about the uprising at Kenilworth in time to save some lives."

Glenn Farnham was shorter and stockier than Tommy, and also a little older—at least eighteen, or maybe nineteen. He had the same dark blond hair as his sister, Eugenie, who was nowhere in sight. Tommy tried to glance around, but Glenn was moving so fast, and the hall was so crowded with small tables holding bric-a-brac, along with umbrella stands, upright lamps under large, fringed shades, and a few Greek statues, that he had to be careful not to let his guitar case bump against any of them.

"I think this is the plan," Glenn announced, leading Tommy into a wide room with a large fireplace. "You're supposed to stand here, in front of the mantel, and the guests will sit looking at you." Rows of chairs were already in place—Tommy made a quick count. Forty chairs. Forty guests. He'd have no trouble being heard with so few people, since he was used to performing for a hundred or more.

The French windows stood open; a sweet-smelling breeze lifted the filmy underdrapes without ruffling the heavier, pulled-back draperies. "You know, this party is for me," Glenn confided. "But I'd rather be just about anywhere else. There's no one coming but old fuddies. So—do you have to tune up or something?"

It was the first time Glenn had given Tommy a chance to speak. "It would be a good idea," he admitted.

"Need a piano?" Glenn asked. "I don't know anything about musical instruments, but my sister Eugenie is always plinking notes on the piano for my dad to tune his violin."

*Your sister Eugenie plays the piano?* Tommy wanted to ask. And Mr. Farnham, that stuffy-looking mine owner, played the violin? His stomach tightened. It was one thing to perform in front of a bunch of partygoers who wouldn't notice if Tommy hit a wrong chord, but if Eugenie and Mr. Farnham knew music . . .

"The piano's over there in the library," Glenn was saying, walking rapidly again, so that Tommy had no choice but to follow him. Glenn swung wide a set of double doors, and there, at the piano, sat Eugenie.

"Help Tom tune up, will you, sis?" Glenn asked. Then he was gone.

Tommy stood frozen just inside the doorway, unable to move or talk. His mother had told him to notice everything that everyone was wearing; he might not remember anyone else, but the image of Eugenie at the piano would forever be seared onto his brain. Her dress was pink—a kind of shimmery material—with a square neck trimmed in fancy white something-or-other. Its short sleeves revealed her smooth arms. Around her wrist hung a chain that linked together tiny pearls; her earrings held the same small pearls. The dark blond hair had been piled high on her head, but tendrils escaped around her ears and onto her smooth neck. She was the loveliest thing he'd ever seen in his whole life.

"Do you play the piano?" she asked him.

He shook his head.

"I do," she said. "Close the door and come inside, and I'll play for you. My mother hates the kind of music I want to play, but I bet you'll like it the way I do."

As Tommy drew closer she began to play softly. Blues! "Do you know this one?" she asked him. "It's called 'I Wonder Where My Lovin' Man Has Gone.'"

"I know 'Saint Louis Blues,'" he told her, and without missing a beat, she swung into that song.

Fumbling to get his guitar out of the case so he could play along with her, Tommy was electrified when she began singing:

"Saint Louis woman, with her diamon' rings,
  Pulls dat man roun' by her apron strings."

Her voice was much huskier than he would have expected, though she sang very softly, as though she didn't want to be overheard.

"Twant for powder an' for store-bought hair,
  De man ah love, would not gone nowhere, nowhere."

By the time she reached the chorus, Tommy had his guitar ready. He joined her with, "Got de Saint Louis Blues, jes as blue as ah can be, O Lord!" He struck the C7 chord six times, fast and hard—and then once again, really powerful, like percussion!

Suddenly the door flew open and Mrs. Farnham stood there frowning. "What are you doing, Eugenie?" she demanded.

"Helping Thomas tune his guitar, Mother," she answered pleasantly.

"Well, tune it with a Chopin waltz or something, rather than that . . . that . . . darky music! And come out here quickly, because the guests are beginning to arrive."

Rising from the piano stool, Eugenie asked Tommy, "Can you finish tuning it without the piano? I have to go."

"Yes," he assured her. "You . . . your playing . . . it's wonderful!"

"Thanks!" Smiling, she said quietly, "Mother will probably want me to play the Chopin stuff for the guests before the evening's over." Leaning closer, she whispered, "She thinks Chopin was French, but he was really Polish." Laughing softly, Eugenie moved out of the room and closed the door behind her.

Tommy collapsed onto the piano stool, trying to catch his breath. Gently he touched the keys her fingers had rested on only a moment before. He could hear conversations in the hall and beyond—deep, booming male voices peppered with laughter, and more muted female voices. The smell of cigar smoke drifted beneath the door and into the room where he sat.

Good thing he didn't have to perform immediately. He was too disconcerted even to tune his guitar right; he'd twist one peg and then stop, remembering her throaty voice. He'd heard she went to a convent school; when had she had a chance to learn the blues in a convent school? The nuns would have squelched it faster and even more vehemently than Mrs. Farnham.

Finally he got himself pulled together and his guitar tuned, and then he waited. A large pendulum clock on the wall ticked out the seconds. Eugenie didn't come back. No one came. Tommy imagined the Farnhams and their guests eating—where? They must be out at tables on the lawn, because the Farnham dining room couldn't hold all that many people. At least they'd left him sitting in the library rather than sending him to the kitchen, but in the kitchen Dorothy might have given him something to eat. He was hungry. Yet it might be better that he didn't eat—he wouldn't want to spill anything on this latest of his dead-men's suits.

At twenty minutes to nine Glenn opened the library door and asked, "You still in here, Tom? Mother sent me to fetch you. I guess everyone's ready for you now. Do you need anything? A glass of water?"

"That would be real good," Tommy answered.

"I'll go get it. You know where you're supposed to be," Glenn said, pointing. "Right through the hall."

Alone, Tommy crept across the hallway into the back of the large room, where no one noticed him; since everyone sat facing forward, he saw only their backs. Should he make his way through the seated guests to the front of the room? Was anyone going to introduce him, or was he supposed to start singing without any preliminaries? In any one of the string of coal-town amusement halls where all the people knew him, he wouldn't have hesitated for a second; he'd have barged right in and started jollying up the crowd. Here, he hung back, uncertain.

At last Mrs. Farnham stood up, turned around, and saw him. "There you are, Thomas," she said. "Come up front, please."

Awkwardly Tommy pushed through the chairs, trying not to step on anyone's feet or bump them with his guitar. When he reached the fireplace, Mrs. Farnham announced, "This young man is Thomas Quinlan, one of the employees at Castle Gate Mine. He's going to sing for us." She took her seat again just as Glenn appeared with the glass of water. Eugenie hadn't arrived.

Tommy took a deep breath and asked, "Is there anything in particular you'd like to hear, Mrs. Farnham?"

At that moment Eugenie entered the room, and Tommy's voice faltered enough that he had to repeat the question. Since all the chairs were filled, one of the men stood up to offer Eugenie his seat, but she murmured, "That's all right. There's a little stool right up front; I'll use that."

"And I'll be right here beside you, sitting on the floor because you're going to take my stool," her brother announced, settling himself cross-legged near Tommy. "So get up here, Genie, and let's let Tom get started."

Genie! So her family really did call her Genie, just as Tommy had in the first line of the verse he'd written for her. In the confusion while the brother and sister arranged themselves Mrs. Farnham asked, "Thomas, would you happen to know 'I Love You Truly'? That's a favorite of mine."

"Yes, ma'am, I do." Very sedately Tommy began the song, and was surprised to hear Mrs. Farnham sing along with him. Soon others in the room joined in. He relaxed. This wasn't going to be too different from the kind of performing he was used to. They began to call out requests—"The Merry Widow Waltz" and "By the Light of the Silvery Moon" and more. He played and sang them all, with almost everyone joining in. But with every note that came out of his mouth, with every chord his fingers struck, he was intensely aware of Eugenie sitting almost at his feet.

It was going well, Tommy thought. The half hour that Mrs. Farnham had mentioned in her letter was nearly over. He'd made it through without mishap. Then Mrs. Farnham asked, "Thomas, do you know 'Jeanie with the Light Brown Hair'?"

As soon as she requested it, he felt the heat rush to his cheeks. Glancing quickly at the woman, he wondered if she was deliberately trying to test him—after all, he'd stolen into her house and left a valentine for her daughter. But Mrs. Farnham looked innocent, waiting for his answer.

Glenn, however, who was sitting on the floor not three feet in front of Tommy, nudged Eugenie with his elbow and started to chuckle. So Glenn knew. But did he realize it was Tommy who'd sent the valentine? More important, did *Eugenie* know?

Almost afraid to look at her, Tommy let his eyes dart past. Unlike her brother, Eugenie wasn't laughing—if she had been, Tommy would have felt ridiculed. Quite the contrary; Eugenie's cheeks were flushed as red as his. With downcast eyes and a blush that wouldn't go away, she stared at the fringe of rug underneath her feet.

"I'm sorry, Mrs. Farnham, I don't know that song," Tommy lied.

"Oh, well . . ." She turned to ask Mr. Farnham, seated next to her in the third row, "Is there any song you'd especially like, dear?"

Offhand, as though it didn't much matter, Mr. Farnham remarked, "I suppose I like hymns as well as anything. How about 'In the Sweet Bye and Bye'?"

Now Tommy was in trouble. He couldn't say no two times in a row, but since he'd never even set foot inside a Protestant church, he didn't know any Protestant hymns at all. Blessedly Eugenie came to his rescue: In her full, vibrant voice she began to sing, "In the sweet bye and bye . . ."

Right away Tommy recognized the tune enough to play it—it was one of Joe Hill's parodies from *The Little Red Songbook*. He didn't know the words the people were singing, but he knew Joe Hill's words, and everyone else was singing loud enough that they'd never catch on that Tommy was faking it.

"You will eat, bye and bye," he sang, using Joe Hill's words.

"In that beautiful land in the sky, way up high,
 Work and pray, live on hay,
 You'll get pie in the sky when you die."

Nobody heard him—except Eugenie and Glenn. Eugenie clapped her hand over her mouth; Glenn snorted with laughter, then took out a handkerchief and pretended to blow his nose.

After a few more verses, mercifully, it was all over and the guests applauded politely, signaling that Tommy could leave. He felt as drained as if he'd worked two days back-to-back shoveling coal.

While Glenn helped Eugenie to her feet, he muttered to Tommy, "You've gotta come into the library. Right now!"

As the room emptied, Tommy followed the brother and sister across the hall and through the double doors. Once inside, Glenn closed the doors, leaned back against them, and broke into loud guffaws. "What a howl!" he cried. "A real cockeyed howl! Where'd you get those words to that song? 'Live on hay'—that's rich! Did you make it up?"

"Joe Hill wrote it," Tommy answered.

"You mean Joe Hill the murderer?" Eugenie asked.

Tommy hesitated. "He hasn't been tried yet—he's still in jail. I don't know if he's a murderer. He writes songs for the union."

"Well, murderer or not," Glenn said, "I want to hear the rest of the song. Sing it for us, will you? Not too loud, because Father would have a fit if he heard you."

"Sure," Tommy agreed. Strumming his guitar, he began to sing "The Preacher and the Slave," Joe Hill's spoof about poor workingmen trying to get a handout from storefront-church ministers, who send the bums packing without so much as a crumb.

"Look," Glenn announced after Tommy had gone through all the verses, "I better get out there and keep Mother happy, since this is supposed to be my farewell party. You two can stay here for a while. Maybe you have something to say to each other." Waving his fingers at them, Glenn made his escape.

Tommy and Eugenie glanced at one another, then glanced away. After a heavy silence he figured he'd take the plunge and bring things out into the open. Might as well since he'd probably never see her again. "What did Glenn mean, that we have something to say to each other? About what?" he began, already knowing the answer.

"The valentine," she said softly.

No sense pretending. "Glenn knows about it?" he asked.

"Yes. But only Glenn. Mother and Father never saw it. You wrote it to me, didn't you?" Now she looked up at him, her eyes huge in the dimming light, the pupils wide and dark.

He nodded. "Yeah, I did."

"I liked it." Hesitantly she reached out for his hand, but Tommy pulled it away. Surprised and hurt, Eugenie stared up at him. He was a good eight inches taller than she.

"I'm sorry. It's just . . . my hands are all rough and callused," he explained.

With a little laugh she told him, "When I was very small, I remember my daddy's hands feeling rough too. 'These are the hands of a good workingman,' he used to tell me. He was a miner, you know."

"You mean it? Mr. Farnham dug coal?" That was such startling news, Tommy found it hard to envision. He had to hold back a chuckle when he pictured Ellis Farnham, with his high, starched collars and gold-rimmed eyeglasses, swinging a pick.

"Really. He worked in the mines and studied at night and kept getting better and better jobs until he got to be a superintendent. Then when we came here, he became part owner of Castle Gate."

It was as though a dam broke then, as she started to spill things about herself and her family. "People think Eugenie is such a highfalutin name, but we don't come from high-society people. It's just that when Mother was expecting me, she read every French novel she could get her hands on. Glenn and I laugh about it now; we call it Mother's French Period. She decided to name me after the empress Eugénie, Napoléon III's wife, even though Dad had hardly begun to work his way up in the mines. When I was little, Dad used to call me Empress. He still does sometimes."

So Mrs. Farnham loved French novels. And French composers. Maybe she wasn't as stiff and proper as Tommy had thought.

Eugenie went on, "All the heroines in those novels went to convent schools, so Mother decided to send me to Saint Mary's of the Wasatch Academy in Salt Lake City, although we aren't Catholic. And since we're not, I don't have to attend Sunday Mass like the other girls in the school. The nuns let me go to Saint Mark's Episcopal Cathedral on Sunday mornings."

All that was very interesting, but—

"So, what I'm getting at," Eugenie said, "is . . . " This time the pause was longer. For a moment she looked uncertain, then she seemed to make up her mind. "Thomas Quinlan, would you care to meet me next Sunday morning at ten o'clock at Saint Mark's Cathedral? Not to go to church! Just to . . . meet."

So thunderstruck that the answer got stuck in his throat, Tommy blurted, "Th-there . . . is nothing, in the entire world, I would like better than to meet you next Sunday." He didn't know where Saint Mark's was, didn't know how he'd explain to his mother why he was going to miss Sunday mass in Castle Gate, didn't know how he'd even get to Salt Lake City. But if he had to walk every step of the way, beginning right after work next Saturday, he would be at Saint Mark's Cathedral on Sunday morning, June 7.

That is, if all this wasn't a dream.

# CHAPTER TEN
## June 7, 1914

"So, now, tell me all about the party yesterday. How was it?" his mother asked him.

"Fine."

"What did they have to eat?"

"I don't know."

"What do you mean you don't know?"

"They didn't give me anything."

Her voice rising indignantly, Fiona demanded, "You mean you spent all those hours at the Farnhams' and no one offered you a bite to eat? What kind of manners do those people have? I wouldn't send a dog into the night without at least a bone."

Tommy wanted to sound loyal to the Farnhams, even though at the party he'd thought they were kind of rude to starve him. He told Fiona, "I wasn't very hungry, Mom. Anyway, it's not a good idea to eat right before you sing."

Muttering, "At least they could have fixed you a plate to bring home," Fiona set down her flatiron on the stove, crossed her arms, and gave him her undivided attention. "All right, now tell me what everyone was wearing."

"Uh . . . Eugenie had a pink dress with white stuff around the neck," he began.

"White lace?" Fiona prompted.

"No . . . uh . . . like cloth with little holes in it."

"You mean eyelet. How long was it? The dress, I mean. Did it come to just above her ankles, or higher than that?"

Racking his memory, Tommy said, "Higher."

"And what about Mrs. Farnham? When Dorothy dropped off the laundry last week, she said Mrs. Farnham had ordered a new dress from a seamstress in Salt Lake City. How high was that hemline?"

"Mom!" Tommy cried, stretching the word into two syllables. "How am I supposed to notice stuff like that?"

"Well, what color was it? At least tell me that much."

"Blue. Green. I don't know. I'm going out."

The evening sun hung close above the mountains, casting an alpenglow on snow that still lingered on the high peaks, even near the beginning of June. Tommy had changed out of his church clothes into a pair of overalls he'd wear to the mine tomorrow. He was counting the days until he'd see Eugenie again. Now only one week remained before he would climb onto the coal train with Peter on Sunday morning, June 7, for the ride to Salt Lake City.

"Personal reasons," Tommy had answered when Peter asked him why he wanted to make the trip.

"You're meeting someone?" Peter had asked. "A girl?"

"Uh-huh." But he hadn't told Peter which girl, or where the meeting would take place, and Peter hadn't pried.

The next hurdle would be to tell his mother, who would definitely pry. But he had an idea how to handle that. He'd take his guitar with him, explaining to Fiona that the tuning screws were getting loose in the headstock, and he needed a professional guitar man to fix them. If he used that as an excuse, it meant he'd have to lug the guitar around all day Sunday, but he was so used to it that he rarely noticed the weight at the end of his arm.

Now, walking the streets of Castle Gate, he ignored the looming mountains, keeping his eyes on stones he kicked to the side of the road. He was wrestling with a much bigger problem. Money. He didn't have any. Or at least not much.

The train wouldn't cost anything because Peter knew the engineer. Anyway, it wasn't a passenger train, it was a coal train; they'd ride in the locomotive. But everything else would cost, and right now the Quinlans were short on cash.

During May his mother had hired two girls to help with the laundry—one named Velma, the other Verna. Velma and Verna happened to be Dorothy's younger sisters. Though they were still in school, they came to the house every afternoon to work the washing machine and hang the clothes out on the line while Fiona concentrated on mending and alterations. She paid them each a dollar a week—good wages, compared with what Dorothy earned for much longer hours. Yet even that extra two dollars had stretched the Quinlans' budget, since the increase in cost hadn't been matched by an increase in income. And as always Fiona insisted on making her payments right on time to Peter for the washing machine.

Tommy had saved more than five dollars in a pipe tobacco tin he kept underneath his bed. Just taking Eugenie to eat in a nice restaurant might wipe out most of that. If he met her at ten in the morning and they spent two hours with each other, that would bring them up to noon. What could he do then, except invite her to lunch?

"Why are you bringing the guitar?" Peter asked him at six forty-five on Sunday morning. "You planning to sing on street corners for nickels?"

That was something Tommy hadn't even considered, but an idea took root in his mind. Not street corners, but . . . "Are the saloons open in Salt Lake City on Sundays?" he asked.

"Depends on where you're going," Peter answered.

"Uh . . . to Saint Mark's Episcopal Cathedral."

Peter burst out laughing. "To get there from the railroad station, you'll be walking past the Mormon Temple and Tabernacle, and near to the Catholic Cathedral of the Madeleine, plus a few other churches in between. I'd say your chances aren't too good of finding an open saloon in that neighborhood."

They were waiting in the railroad yards in Helper rather than at Castle Gate. The town had been named that because it was where the extra "helper" engines—three of them—got added to coal trains for the long haul up the mountain. "Better get on board now," Mort called out to them, Mort being the engineer of the locomotive they'd ride to Salt Lake City.

"He'll probably ask you to throw some shovels of coal into the firebox," Peter warned Tommy. "As a bit of pay-back for the free ride, you know."

Tommy nodded. He'd had more sense than to wear his cream-colored linen suit. Summer or not, he had on his dark suit, which wouldn't show the grime much. To protect his white collar, he'd tied a red bandanna around his neck—which he'd better remember to take off before he met Eugenie.

"Come on, boys, let's get this blacksnake crawlin' up that mountain," Mort called out again.

It was Tommy's first ride in a locomotive, and he liked it, in spite of the noise and steam. He hung out the side window, enjoying the breeze stirred by the moving train.

Mort wore the striped overalls and engineer's cap that set him apart from the lower echelons of railway workers. Pulling out his big railroad watch, he commented, "We were twenty-seven seconds late leaving Helper. Not bad. We'll make that up going downhill past Thistle."

"Do you want the boy to shovel some coal?" Peter asked him.

"I'd rather have the boy sing for me," Mort answered. "I see he has his gee-tar there. And I heard he's good at makin' up songs."

"That he is," Peter agreed. "What do you say, Tommy? Can you concoct a song for this occasion?"

"Sure." He'd rather sing than shovel coal, any day. After flipping up the clips on the case, he took out the guitar, not bothering to tune it. With all the noise the locomotive made, who would notice if he was out of tune? "Have you heard the song 'The Rocky Road to Dublin'?" Tommy asked them. Peter had, but Mort hadn't, since Mort was a Scotsman, not Irish.

"Then here's a new version," Tommy announced, and sang,

"On the train to Salt Lake City
We'll be travelin' along, we'll be singin' a song.
On the train to Salt Lake City,
Tom with Peter by his side,
Peter goes there each Sunday morn
and won't come home till late.
Tommy's riding with him today,
they hopped aboard a freight—"

"How do you *do* that?" Peter asked, incredulous. "I mean, you just made that up right here on the spot, didn't you? Right out of your head."

"Yeah, sure," Tommy said. "I dunno—it just comes to me."

"It's a gift," Mort announced solemnly.

"You're so right," Peter agreed. "Tommy does it just like Joe Hill does. I wonder—could we fix it so Tommy could meet Joe Hill?"

"He's in jail," Mort reminded them. Even though Mort held the exalted job of train engineer, he was sympathetic to the union cause. That was why he let Peter ride in the coal-train locomotive every Sunday morning. Several people besides Mort knew that Peter spent his Sundays talking and arguing with other union organizers in Salt Lake City, men who worked in the copper mines and nearby silver mines. But they all kept quiet about it. If Mr. Farnham found out how heavily involved Peter was with the unions, Peter would be fired on the spot.

"Tonight at eight thirty," Mort told them when they got off the train in the depot at Salt Lake City. "If you're late, I'll leave without you."

"Have I ever been late?" Peter asked.

"No, not you. The warning was for your young pal there," Mort said, pointing to Tommy.

As they walked through the depot Peter asked Tommy, "How long do you think you'll be visiting with this . . . girl?"

"I'm not sure," Tommy answered. "It's up to her."

"Well, we can do two things, you and I. We can meet here at the depot this evening, or if you get finished with her early, you can come to this address." He handed Tommy a piece of paper and told him, "This is where I'll be. It's in Murray, to the south. Catch a streetcar—ask the motorman where to get off. The place is only a block from the streetcar tracks."

"Thanks, Peter," Tommy said. "Now, how do I get to Saint Mark's Cathedral?"

It was only a six-block walk, but in Salt Lake City the

blocks were long, laid out by Brigham Young when the Mormons first came to Utah. Tommy wished he owned a watch to tell him what time it was, but his uncle Jim's Ingersoll watch had vanished when Jim was murdered, and Fiona could never afford to replace it. So Tommy hurried, breaking into a sweat because the day was warm and his wool suit felt too hot for the weather.

He passed the Mormon Temple, with its golden, trumpet-blowing angel balanced on the spire. Higher up on a hill stood the round-domed State Capitol. He could see the massive Catholic Cathedral of the Madeleine up ahead, but he didn't pass it, because he had to turn off a block south of it to reach Saint Mark's.

Although at a quarter to ten the sun was already hot, Tommy found plenty of shade to wait in, and as he waited he thought about Eugenie. She must like him, at least somewhat. He searched his brain for any other possible explanation of why she would invite him to Salt Lake City, and came up with nothing. That a girl like Eugenie could have even the smallest interest in a coal-mining laborer was amazing—and unsettling. He'd have to be very careful to act gentlemanly, to remember every bit of manners his mother had taught him. Should he bow when he met her? He didn't have a hat to tip.

It wasn't long before he saw a one-horse carriage pull up. Eugenie was in it—with another girl! Tommy's heart sank.

"You can get out by yourselfs," the cranky driver told them, but Tommy rushed to help them step out of the carriage.

A bit anxiously Eugenie said, "Thomas Quinlan, I'd like you to meet my friend Isobel Cardin."

"How do," Tommy murmured, trying to be civil as his disappointment turned to resentment. Why would Eugenie invite him to meet her if she'd planned to bring a friend?

Impertinent, or maybe worse than that—maybe down-right snooty—Isobel looked Tommy over from hair to shoes, as if checking his qualifications. He must have passed, because she smiled then, showing deep dimples, and told Eugenie, "Be sure to be back on time. I can't cover for you if you miss the ride." And to Tommy's enormous relief, Isobel turned and walked into the cathedral—alone.

The first thing Tommy asked was, "When do you have to be back?"

"In two hours," she answered. "Services will be over at noon. If I'm not here by then, well, you heard what Isobel said. The nuns make sure there are two of us attending Saint Mark's every Sunday, because no girl is allowed to go any-where alone. If I don't return with Isobel, I'll be in trouble."

"Where shall we go?" he asked. "I don't know anything about Salt Lake City."

"Let's just walk."

When you were with a lady, his mother had told him, you always walked on the outside of the sidewalk next to the street. That was to keep her from getting splashed by any passing horses or automobiles. "*You'll* be the one to get splashed," Fiona had said, "but the lady won't, and that's as it should be."

That Sunday morning happened to be beautiful, dry, and summery, with no puddles in the streets for anything to splash through, but rules were rules. Each time they crossed a street, Tommy had to maneuver himself to the outside of the sidewalk, which meant he juggled his guitar case, chang-ing it back and forth from arm to arm.

Eugenie was much more sensibly dressed for the weather than he was. This time her dress was blue, with thin stripes of darker blue running from top to bottom, with a navy blue belt and, again, a square neck and short sleeves. He paid particular attention to the length, since that had seemed important to his mother. Eugenie's dress ended a good four inches above her ankles. Her nice, silk-stocking-clad ankles. And her high-heeled, soft-leather navy blue shoes.

He'd have been able to describe the whole outfit to his mother this time, but of course he wouldn't. Anyway, he didn't like the hat Eugenie wore—not because it wasn't pretty, but because the wide brim hid her face from him. He was so much taller that when they walked side by side, all he could see when he looked down was the top of her hat and the frilly stuff that decorated it.

"There's a little green square up ahead with some benches," she told him. "Want to stop there for a while?"

"Sure." It would give him a chance to put down his stupid guitar case, which he was sorry he'd ever brought, and maybe to ask her to take off her hat.

He didn't have to. She took it off without being asked. He'd never before seen her in full daylight, and he was startled that her skin looked so radiant, that her eyes were so green, that in the dappled sunlight her hair shone golden.

"What are you looking at?" she asked, laughing.

"You."

"Do you approve?"

"Completely."

He pulled off his suit coat, not having to be ashamed of his white shirt, because it had been laundered just as carefully as the ones Eugenie's father wore. They talked easily. She told him she was staying at the academy for the summer, studying piano, because her mother had sailed to England to get Glenn settled at Oxford. Then Mrs. Farnham would make a long-awaited trip to Paris, where she'd live in a hotel across from the Louvre.

"Mother will be in heaven," Eugenie said. "I'm really happy for her, because she's never been to England or France and she's always wanted to go there. She's hoping to get a glimpse of Empress Eugénie."

"What? Empress Eugénie is dead, isn't she?"

"No, she's still alive, but she's really old, almost ninety. So I hope Mother gets to see her. Mother asked if I'd like to go with her—I think she had this fantasy of presenting me to Empress Eugénie—but I thought I should stay home to check on Dad, at least on weekends. He's had a lot of worries lately."

Tommy wondered why a successful man like Ellis Farnham, who owned at least half of Castle Gate Mine, should have any worries. But he didn't ask.

A large clock across the street had been striking each quarter hour, reminding Tommy how much precious time was seeping away. "What is that big building?" he asked. "The one with the chime clock?"

"That's the Salt Lake City and County Building," she told him. "Where your friend Joe Hill will go on trial."

"He's not my friend," Tommy protested. "I never even met the man. I just think he writes funny parodies."

"And you write lovely valentines."

Tommy smiled. "That was just a parody too, Eugenie. But it's nice of you to call it . . . uh . . . lovely." It was such an unmasculine word that he stumbled over it. Once more the clock struck. A quarter to noon.

"Tommy," Eugenie said, "we'll have to start walking back in just a minute. But I wanted to tell you—I think I'll come home next Sunday."

"To Castle Gate?" His heart started to beat faster.

"Lately my father has been working weekends at his mine office," she said. "If I'm there, I can make sure he gets something to eat when he comes home on Sunday evening."

She didn't have to say any more; Tommy could fill it in. Mrs. Farnham and Glenn happened to be on a ship sailing for England. Dorothy, the hired girl, went home every Saturday night and didn't return till Monday morning. If Mr. Farnham stayed in his office until evening, then . . .

Sitting ladylike on the park bench, Eugenie waited for Tommy's next words.

"Eugenie," he said, "may I call on you at your home next Sunday?"

"That would be very nice, Tommy," she answered just as formally. "About noon? And please bring your guitar. We can play music together."

As they walked back along the broad sidewalks Tommy could just as easily have leaped across the roofs of the stately mansions that lined the streets—he was that buoyed up. He craned his head to see the turrets, the bay windows, and here and there a gargoyle grinning back at him.

"If you think these homes are nice," Eugenie told him, "you should see the ones on South Temple Street. That's where the millionaires live. And you know what, Tommy? Some of them started out as miners."

But not as coal miners, he knew. The richest ones got that way because they'd discovered gold or silver in the nearby mountains to the east, or because they hired impoverished foreign laborers to dig low-grade copper ore out of a mountain to the west.

When they got back to Saint Mark's, the carriage was waiting, with Isobel seated in it, pouting. "You'll have to tip the driver," she told Eugenie. "He got here early today, and I've had to listen to him grumble because you weren't here. If you don't want him to complain to Sister Superior, you better tip him good."

Isobel's annoyance was the only small blemish on those perfect two hours—not important enough to sully anything. They
had no time for good-byes, but next Sunday would come, with
its promise of—what? Tommy wasn't sure, but his anticipation
grew with each wave of his hand as the carriage rolled away.

While he walked back toward the depot, his thoughts
were so filled with Eugenie that he noticed nothing, not even
that he hadn't eaten for more than six hours. "Do you want
me to pack you a lunch?" his mother had asked him, but
he'd said no. The last thing he wanted was to arrive in Salt
Lake carrying food in a paper bag. Bad enough he had to
carry the guitar.

Tommy handed the address to the streetcar motorman,
who said, "You that kid with Peter Connolly? He was on my
car this morning. Said if you was to show up, I should tell
you where to get off the streetcar." After a half-hour ride in
the open car, with its bell clanging and its overhead trolley
sparking noisily, the motorman gestured to Tommy.

"Down one block, turn left, you'll see McClure's Saloon."

"Where do I go from there?" Tommy asked.

"Nowhere. That's it. McClure's Saloon."

When Tommy pushed through the front doors of the
saloon, he heard loud, raucous voices of men—and a few
women—all raised at once in argument or laughter or hilarity.
It sounded as if the whole gang of them had been drinking all
morning. The smoke was so thick he couldn't see much, but
he felt a smack on his shoulder as Peter yelled, "Tommy, my
boy, so you made it here! You said you wanted a saloon that
was open on Sundays, and this is it. And there are only about
twenty more in the next couple of blocks. What would you
like? Do you want a beer?"

"Sure." Tommy wasn't all that eager for a beer, but he was suddenly starved enough to crave the hard-boiled eggs and sliced ham set out on the bar as free lunch. But to get the free lunch, you had to buy drinks. He reached into his pocket for some change.

"No, no, it's on me," Peter insisted. "Come with me. There's some fellows I want you to meet."

"Mind if I eat first?" Tommy asked.

"Bring the food with you." He steered Tommy toward a table in the corner surrounded by men, all kinds of men: some with hats, some without; some wearing neckties hooked to stained celluloid collars, some in collarless shirts; half with thick, long mustaches and half—mostly the younger ones— with no mustache but with a few days' stubble on their chin.

"Here's the lad I've been telling you about," Peter shouted, to be heard above the rumble of voices. "Tommy, I want you to meet Frank Liebowitz, Zemo Roselli, Fred Koltar, Joe Kenyon, Emil Simchak . . ." Peter went on, reeling off a list of names that Tommy would never be able to remember.

"The kid who plays like Joe Hill," one of the men remarked.

"This is the one!" Peter said, and to Tommy, "These men think Joe Hill is a hero. He was with them at the Tucker strike." And turning back to the men, "Want to hear him play?"

"Sure!" they roared.

"Can I eat first?" Tommy asked Peter.

"Give us a minute," Peter told the men. "Now listen, Tommy," he said, leading Tommy back toward the bar. "Grab some grub, then ask the bartender for an empty bowl, the kind he puts pretzels in. Set it up on a chair next to you while you sing. You'll see what happens. All the fellows in here will want union songs, like those ones in *The Little Red Songbook*. Did you learn them?"

"I learned a lot of them," Tommy answered. "Not all."

"Well, sing as many as you know," Peter advised. "Forget the Irish songs today—you could swing a pool cue all around this crowd without hitting a single Irishman. Except me."

Tommy did just what Peter told him to. If he didn't know the songs all that well, the people in the saloon did. All he had to do was give them a couple of chords, and their voices shouted out,

"Oh, workers, do unite,
  To crush the tyrants' might,
  The one big union banner is unfurled,
  Come slaves from every land,
  Come join this fighting band,
  It's called Industrial Workers of the World."

As the singing heated up, men began to pound the tables with their fists and beer mugs, slopping beer onto the table-tops, slapping each other on the shoulders and throwing their arms around one another in camaraderie. They demanded one union song after another; if Tommy didn't know the songs, they sang them anyway, and he was able to fake the chords.

The men—and women—grew more and more fervent, leaping to their feet and standing at attention as they bellowed,

"It is we who plowed the prairies,
  Built the cities where they trade,
  Dug the mines and built the workshops,

Endless miles of railroad laid,
Now we stand, outcast and starving,
'Midst the wonders we have made,
But the Union makes us strong!"

They cheered loudly enough to shake the rafters, their fists raised toward those same rafters. Although in the past couple of years Tommy had played for a lot of gatherings, he'd never before heard such passion in the voices. Yet as consciously as he tried to satisfy their revolutionary zeal, he couldn't stop himself from glancing often at the bowl on the chair beside him, which he emptied every hour.

By the time he and Peter left that saloon, and the three others down the street they visited during the afternoon and evening, the pockets of Tommy's pants and suit coat were so full of change they slapped against him as he ran for the streetcar.

Not till he got onto the locomotive with Mort did he count the change. He'd made fourteen dollars and thirty-seven cents.

# CHAPTER ELEVEN
## June 14, 1914

Once again Tommy hesitated at the Farnhams' front gate. This time he wasn't worried about which door to use— he just wondered whether he should set down his guitar case and get it dusty, thereby perhaps dirtying the Farnhams' floor once he got inside, or if it would be safe to shift the case to his left hand while he opened the gate, even though his left hand held a bouquet of fresh flowers wrapped in butcher paper.

A couple of Polish women who were fine gardeners sold their cut roses and lilies to the manager of the company store, who then resold them for five times more than he paid the women. With all that Tommy had earned playing in the saloons last Sunday, he figured he could afford flowers for his girl.

"They're beautiful," Eugenie exclaimed when he handed them to her at the front door. She buried her face in the bouquet to inhale its fragrance. "Let me get a vase. Dorothy isn't here today."

As if Tommy didn't know that. He went directly to the library, and since Eugenie was not in the room to distract him by her presence, this time he paid some attention to the room itself. The top of the grand piano had been opened, exposing the strings inside. Tommy reached down to pluck the shortest strings; their *plinks* weren't that different from his guitar's.

Like the room where he'd entertained the Farnhams' guests, this room also had a fireplace, thoroughly cleaned of ashes now that it was summer. A few tables covered with fringed shawls held vases or lamps. Moving along the walls, Tommy scanned the rows of books on built-in shelves. There were Mrs. Farnham's French novels, all in a row, and other sets of books with matching leather covers: a complete collection of Shakespeare; another collection of the World's Best Literature, or so it claimed on the book's spines; a set of encyclopedias; and stacks of thick engineering books that looked well worn. Before he had time to read the titles on the dozen other shelves, Eugenie came in carrying the red roses and white lilies in a Chinese vase.

"I learned a new piece after I saw you last week," she told him, setting the vase on one of the tables. "Only, I had to practice it in secret so the nuns wouldn't hear me, so I'm not very good at it yet."

She sat on the piano stool, tucking her skirt beneath her. It wasn't a fancy skirt—just a plain navy blue, and today she wore a white shirtwaist with a sailor collar. Tommy had on his linen dead-man's suit; he'd pressed the pants himself.

"Do you want to take off your coat?" she asked him. "I opened the windows, but it's still warm in here."

He did, hanging it over the back of a chair. The room really was warm; he ran a finger around the neck of his high celluloid collar to wipe up a ring of sweat.

Then she began to play—ragtime! "It's called 'Twelfth Street Rag,'" she said, while Tommy bent over the piano, watching her fingers.

She was good! The music took him back to that day in Boise when the colored man in the hotel had played ragtime just for Tommy. The man's fingers were longer and stronger than Eugenie's, so he'd played better—but more than that, he'd had a feel for the music that went deeper than hers. Still, Eugenie was good.

"Great!" he cried, applauding her, and she seemed pleased. He took out his guitar then, and they went through a lot of songs that both of them knew. Suddenly she looked up and said, "I'm a terrible hostess. I never asked you if you were hungry."

Even though his height seemed to have finally topped off at six feet three, he was so lean that his mother joked he had to stand in the same place twice to cast a shadow. No matter how much he ate, he didn't gain weight, and he usually felt hungry. Seeing him hesitate out of politeness, Eugenie said, "Come on, let's go out to the kitchen and see if Dorothy's left anything for us."

"For us?" Tommy asked. "Did she know I'd be here?"

"No. Nobody knows, unless the neighbors were snooping."

The Farnhams' icebox was much larger than the small one in Tommy's house. "How much ice do you buy from the iceman every week?" he asked her.

"I have no idea. My mother and the hired help take care of things like that." Her careless answer made him uncomfortable, since his mother could be considered the Farnhams' "hired help" too.

"Mmm, this is nice," she said, taking out one dish after another. "There's ham and roast beef and . . . quail, it looks like."

Quail? To eat? The lower parts of the surrounding mountains were full of quail, but it had never occurred to Tommy that they could be eaten. Their legs were so little and skinny! Hardly a mouthful.

Eugenie pulled out a tin bread box and rummaged through it. "Here's some rye—do you like ham on rye?"

"Anything," he answered.

Clumsily she fixed him a sandwich that fell apart when he tried to pick it up. Just as clumsily he pushed it back together and took a big bite, terribly self-conscious about chewing in front of her. "Milk? Lemonade?" she asked. Since his mouth was full, he just nodded, so she poured both.

Afterward, as they moved back toward the library, he was surprised that she'd left all the food out on the kitchen table, not bothering to put any of it away. His mother would have had a fit, scolding that food left out in a warm room would spoil, or else the flies would get it. But maybe rich people didn't have flies in their houses.

Eugenie hesitated in the middle of the room, then turned to face him and asked, "Want to know what my friend Isobel said about you?"

"I don't know if I do," he answered. "Is it good or bad?"

"You can decide. She said you were the handsomest boy she'd ever seen, with your dark, wavy hair and your blue, blue eyes. But she said you ought to wear a hat."

"If she likes my 'dark, wavy hair'"—Tommy lowered his voice to show he didn't take it seriously—"why does she want me to wear a hat?"

"She says it isn't fashionable for a young man to go hatless."

Tommy knew that, but it hadn't mattered much to him. "And what do you say, Eugenie?" he asked.

"Well . . . maybe I agree with Isobel." Kneeling, she reached beneath one of the tables and pulled out a round black hatbox tied with a cord. "And maybe you'll think it's too forward of me, but I went and bought you a hat."

"What!"

She held out the box to him. A bit anxiously she asked, "Would you open it, please? You can set the box on the tabletop while you untie the string."

A picture on the side of the box showed a dapper gentleman wearing a high silk hat and an opera cloak. He was smiling—or was it leering?—and stroking his thin black mustache. The lid fit so snugly that Tommy had to pull to get it off. Lying inside was a hat unlike any he'd seen before—not a straw boater, not a felt fedora, but a hat of thick fabric patterned in small checks, woven tightly enough to keep its shape.

"Glenn has one exactly like it that he's taken to Oxford with him," Eugenie said, rushing the words. "That's how I knew what to buy. It's the latest style for well-dressed young men."

"I don't know . . . ," Tommy began. He felt uncomfortable, and a little embarrassed, taking a gift from a girl. No one else had ever given him a gift, except his mother, or maybe he could count Peter too, who often brought him sheet music from Salt Lake City. But sheet music cost only ten cents a copy, and the hat would have cost a whole lot more.

"Please, try it on," Eugenie urged, taking it from the box. "See, the brim stays up in the back but tilts forward in the front. May I?" she asked, and reached up to put it on his head. "Oh, Tommy! You look so elegant. There's a mirror over there on the wall. Look at yourself. Now Isobel will really say you're the handsomest boy she's ever met."

He had to bend a bit to see himself in the mirror. Tilting down the brim in front as she'd instructed him to, he frowned—it certainly didn't look like any hat he'd ever seen anyone wear in Castle Gate.

"Glenn says all the young gentlemen on the English country estates are wearing hats like this."

But none of the fellows around Castle Gate, where they all wore bowlers, boaters, or peaked cloth caps. But if Eugenie said it was the latest fashion, maybe he could get away with it in Salt Lake City. He still didn't know whether he should accept the gift, but before he could dwell on it any further, she asked, "Why don't you move a chair closer so you can sit next to me at the piano? Can you read music?" When Tommy said that he could, she asked him to turn the pages for her.

"I'm going to take the hat off now," he said, and set it on the same chair that held his coat.

After they'd played and sung a few more songs, she faced him and mentioned, "It's so much fun to play music with you and not have anyone scolding me about 'darky music' or 'songs unbecoming to a young lady.' But you know what I'd like? If you'd do it for me. Would you sing my valentine? I've read it a hundred times, but I want to hear you sing it." Placing a hand on his chair, she leaned toward him, looking up appealingly into his eyes. Her hair brushed his cheek, sending chills through him. At that point he'd have done anything she wanted—wear a checkered hat, or hand her his heart.

"Can you play it on the piano?" he asked her.

She fingered an introduction, then waited expectantly as he took a breath, closed his eyes, and began, "I dream of Genie with the light brown hair." He was surprised that his voice held steady through the whole song, since her nearness was making him tremble. When he finished the song, he put his arms around her. Without hesitation she turned toward him and let him kiss her.

It was the first time he'd kissed a girl. He must have been doing it right, because Eugenie's arms rose around his neck and he felt her trembling too. Then she kissed him back, her lips warm against his—

At that moment they heard the click of the front door opening. "My father!" Eugenie gasped.

Tommy didn't know he could move so fast. He picked up the chair he'd been sitting on and slid it back to the table where it belonged, in the same sweep picking up his suit coat and shooting his arms through the sleeves. He threw his guitar into its case so fast it twanged on contact, then slammed the lid just as Mr. Farnham appeared in the doorway.

"Daddy!" Eugenia exclaimed. "You're home! Do you remember Thomas Quinlan? He stopped by to pick up some sheet music he left here two weeks ago." Eugenie was fast too; she'd already bundled several pieces of sheet music together and was handing them to Tommy.

Mr. Farnham stared straight at Tommy, saying, "Well, I might as well tell you right now, Thomas—don't bother showing up for work tomorrow morning."

"Daddy!" Eugenie cried.

Tommy was so startled he didn't know what to say at first, but very quickly the words built up in his throat— words of disbelief, indignation, anger. He was just about to demand, "Do you mean you're firing me because I came to see your daughter?" But luckily he noticed the expression on Mr. Farnham's face.

The man looked pained, too miserable to care the least bit about who was in the room with his daughter, too defeated to notice how flushed both Tommy and Eugenie must have appeared. It was Eugenie who understood immediately; she ran to him, threw her arms around him, and asked, "Daddy, what happened?"

His voice breaking, he said, "I've got to lay off half the mine workers tomorrow. Maybe more than half, Empress. The market's in a terrible slump, much worse than the usual summer slowdown for coal. I went over the books all day today, and—"

"It's not your fault, Daddy," she cried. "Don't think it is."

"Maybe I could have managed things better." He was speaking as though Tommy weren't even in the room. "You know how I hate laying off the workers. Their families— they suffer . . ."

"I better go," Tommy murmured. Mr. Farnham barely nodded when Tommy picked up his guitar and left. He'd reached the door before he heard Eugenie call, "Wait, you forgot your hat."

Then she was beside him, pressing the hat into his hand. "I've got to take care of him," she whispered. "Layoffs like this really bother him." Rising on her toes, she quickly kissed Tommy's cheek and asked, "Next Sunday, Saint Mark's, ten o'clock?"

"I'll be there," he promised.

The day looked just as pretty as it had when he'd arrived at the Farnhams'. Sun shone, flowers bloomed, the mountains rose every bit as majestically, but everything had changed. Tommy was out of work. He walked down to the river and found a big boulder to sit on, first spreading his handkerchief on the rock to protect his good suit and setting the hat on top of his guitar case.

The river bubbled vocally, full enough of runoff from mountain snow to look like a real river, not like the nearly dried-up streambed it would become by September. Tommy picked up a willow whip and smacked it against the ground. He was out of work! By tomorrow half the town would be out of work.

That meant no income for him, and he was smart enough to figure out that his mother's laundry business would take a dive. Out-of-work miners didn't need any coal-blackened overalls laundered. And unfortunately this layoff had happened just as Mrs. Farnham and Glenn were out of the country, which meant Mr. Farnham usually stayed late at his office and had supper delivered there, so no more seven big white Farnham tablecloths to be washed and ironed every week. His mother would have to let Verna and Velma go.

So it was up to Tommy. And sitting there, he thought of a way out. Last Sunday had proved to him that he could sing for tips in saloons, and Lord only knew there were plenty of saloons in Castle Valley. With so many men out of work, the tips wouldn't be all that great, but he should be able to earn a couple of bucks a night. His mother might not like it, but on the other hand, she might. At least the layoff would get him out of the coal mine.

Throwing the willow switch into the water, he stood up, brushed off his pants, and picked up his guitar case. Peter kept telling him he ought to either fix that case or buy a new one, but Tommy rather liked the looks of the bullet hole.

As he trudged home he thought about Eugenie, but for once she wasn't uppermost in his thoughts. Work was. He'd have to stay up past midnight most nights, singing in saloons so full of cigar and pipe smoke that his throat would grow raw. He'd be a possible target for belligerent drunks who swung fists at anyone they took a dislike to, and he might get caught in the cross fire when Greeks and Italians fought it out with so-called Americans, meaning the miners who spoke English. At least he had a way to make a few dollars. Most of the laid-off miners would curse their bad luck, drink up the few pennies they had left, then go home and fight with their wives.

He stayed in the back alley on his way home because he didn't want to meet any Castle Gate miners, knowing what fate awaited them when they hadn't yet heard about it, and perhaps even more because he didn't want anyone to notice the hat, no matter how stylish it was supposed to be. As he walked around the side of his house he glanced through the window—and stopped dead.

His mother was sitting on Peter's lap, her arms wrapped around him, kissing him. Peter's hand was tangled in Fiona's hair, which had come all undone.

Tommy backed up fast. He didn't want to see what he'd just seen. But the window was open, and their voices carried clearly.

"Of course I love you," Fiona was saying. "Haven't I told you a thousand times?"

"Then marry me."

"And I've told you no a thousand times too."

Tommy heard the chair scrape as his mother got to her feet.

"It's more than just about you being a miner," she said. "I've got a little business here that I'm trying to build, and I wouldn't want any more children, although I'm not too old to have them, you understand."

"We wouldn't need to have children."

"How would we stop it?" she asked, giving a little laugh. "Look at us now. We can barely keep our hands off each other. What do you think it would be like if we shared a bed?"

"Like my dreams," Peter answered. "Like heaven. Like the leprechaun's pot of gold at the end of the rainbow—no, like the rainbow itself, pouring all its beautiful colors into my thirsty soul. Do you want me to go on, Fiona?"

"No, that's enough." Again she laughed. "You've got an Irish poet's tongue in your head, for sure, Peter Connolly."

Hoping he was giving his mother enough time to get her hair pinned up again, Tommy made extra noise stomping across the wooden porch. He wished he could stamp out the disastrous news he was about to spread through Castle Gate, which would begin when he told his mother and Peter about the layoffs.

His mother and Peter. He shook his head. Why didn't they just get married?

# CHAPTER TWELVE
## June 21, 1914

When Tommy met her at Saint Mark's, Eugenie was dressed all in white, almost like a bride. At seventeen a lot of girls in Utah were already married, especially the Mormon girls. But they married older men. Tommy had never known any man his own age—seventeen and a half (and a month younger than Eugenie)—who had actually gotten married. He'd been thinking about marriage a lot lately, ever since he'd seen his mother and Peter kissing. He shook his head. Remembering it made him feel uneasy, as if he'd been spying on them, so he pushed it out of his mind.

"That's a handsome hat you're wearing," Eugenie told him.

"Thank you." He was glad she couldn't know he'd carried it in a paper bag from Castle Gate all the way to Salt Lake City, not putting it on until after he'd said good-bye to Peter at the depot. Then he'd folded the paper bag into the smallest squares possible, hiding it in his pant pocket for the return trip. "I'm wearing the hat because you want me to, Eugenie. And I wish you *wouldn't* wear a hat."

"Why?" She had on another of those wide-brimmed, feathery, frilly things that hid her face.

"Because when we walk together like this and I look down, all I see is hat. I can't see Eugenie."

"But every well-bred young lady wears a hat," she teased. Their banter lasted until they reached the little park, where she took off her hat and set it on the bench beside her. "Better now?"

"Much."

"How have you been . . . getting along?" she asked, meaning how was he surviving the layoff.

"Managing. I'm playing tomorrow night at the Slovak Club, and at the Italian Lodge on Wednesday. Tuesday I'll just hit a couple of saloons and see if I can pick up some change."

"Is it awful?" she asked.

"What? Being a saloon singer? No, not too bad. The worst part is seeing my mother worry." Although Fiona wouldn't have any worries if she'd just marry Peter. Peter hadn't been laid off; he was one of the lucky ones who stayed in the mine to handle the small number of orders still coming in.

"My father's worried too. But he's keeping it from my mother. She's in Paris now, and he doesn't want to spoil it for her. Also, he doesn't want Glenn to hear about the financial problems, since at Oxford there's nothing he could do about it. So that leaves me. I'm the only one he can confide in."

Tommy looked away. His mother was worried because between the two of them they barely earned enough to put food on the table and keep soap in the washing machine. Mr. Farnham's concern was that his wife might buy a few too many Paris gowns. Or maybe he'd be a little late paying his son's university fees. That yawning chasm between the Quinlans and the Farnhams once again opened wide for Tommy.

Sensing his shifting mood, Eugenie covered his rough, callused hand with her soft one—not the best way to reassure him. "Let's not think about bad times," she said. "Not today. Not in these few minutes we have." As if to echo her thought, the clock across the street chimed ten forty-five.

Tentatively Tommy twined his fingers through hers. "Is that City and County Building, the place with the clock, open on Sundays?" he asked. "Would anyone be in there?"

"It might be open. Maybe there's a janitor inside, but I doubt if anyone else—"

"Let's go!" He pulled her up from the bench and they ran, holding hands, across Second South Street.

Beyond the big, carved doors everything seemed so quiet that Eugenie dropped her voice to a whisper. "The courtroom is upstairs. They brought us here on a school tour once to show us the system of justice or something."

After climbing the wide staircase, they tiptoed down the hall and tried the door to the courtroom. It was unlocked; they slipped inside. A flood of memories came back to Tommy: It was as if the same smell of prisoners, lawyers, jurors, and judges hung over this room as he remembered from the courtroom in Boise. The same sunlight poured through the windows; same brightly polished railings, tables, and judge's bench; and twelve jurors' chairs, all lined up side by side. Seven years had passed since he'd witnessed the last day of the Haywood trial, but he felt like a child of ten again, scared, wretched, the unintentional instrument of his uncle's death.

"What is it, Tommy?" Eugenie asked.

"What?"

"Your face changed. All of a sudden you looked . . . stricken."

He turned away and spoke low. "Something bad happened when I was a kid. I'd rather not talk about it."

But Eugenie wouldn't let him brush her away like that. "You can tell me. No matter what it was."

He shook his head, angry with himself because his troublesome memories from so long ago might spoil this day he'd looked forward to all week. All those nights in the saloons, when he'd been ashamed to accept the coins of out-of-work miners whose wives were waiting with hungry children; all those moments when maudlin drunks had cried all over him and begged him for songs of the old country; all that time in the stifling atmosphere of smoke and vomit and sour bodies, he'd thought of Eugenie, anticipating this day.

He felt her fingers touch his cheek, felt her arms encircle his neck. "It's all right, whatever it is," she said. "I'm here for you." Then she kissed him, and it really was all right.

After a long time in which no one bothered them, she pulled a little mirror from her tiny beaded handbag. Glancing in it, she said, "We've got to find some cold water."

"Why?"

"Look at my lips. And the skin all the way around my lips—everything's chafed red.

"But I shaved!" he said.

She smiled. "You can't help it—whiskers grow. But I can't go back to Saint Mark's like this. Isobel's such a wise guy, she'll make fun of me, first, and then she'll tell everyone at school that you and I were spooning on a Sunday when I should have been in church." She handed him the mirror. "Your mouth is a little swollen too."

Tommy didn't care—no one was going to be inspecting

him. The clock outside struck eleven thirty, its chimes booming through the building. "How long will it take the swelling to go away?" he asked, holding on to her, unwilling to let her go.

"I don't know," she whispered. "I've never done this before. I've never had a sweetheart before."

Sweetheart? She was calling him her sweetheart? He couldn't believe it. This miraculous revelation—that Eugenie considered him her sweetheart—drove the last of the bad memories away, at least for now. He raised her face and kissed her again, gently, to go easy on her sensitive lips.

"Hurry. We're really late," she said as they clattered down the staircase, not caring whether anyone heard them.

When they reached the street, they saw a man with a pushcart selling lemonade. "Ice!" Tommy yelled. "Mister, can I buy ice from you?" He began to pull change from his pocket.

"You no wanna lemonade?" the pushcart man asked, quieting the little bell he rang to let people know he was coming.

"Just ice. Is a dime enough?"

"Shu!" The man laughed, showing white teeth beneath his long black mustache curled at the ends. "Da lady, she no wanna lemonade?"

Tommy shook his head, laughing along with the man. "The lady only wants *ice!* Honest!"

Tommy wrapped the ice in his handkerchief and gave it to Eugenie, who pressed it against her lips. Neither of them could stop laughing as they handed the ice back and forth, from one to the other. By the time they reached the waiting carriage, their lips were tinged blue rather than chafed red.

Isobel looked at them suspiciously, which made them laugh all the harder. But Isobel didn't say anything.

"When?" Tommy whispered as he helped Eugenie into the carriage.

"Next Sunday?"

"Too long to wait, and we're never together long enough," he told her.

"I know. Maybe I can come to Castle Gate."

Before Tommy let go her hand, the driver smacked his whip over the horse's rump, and the carriage lurched forward, with Tommy running alongside it. Isobel mouthed the words, "*Big* tip," spreading her hands wide to show how much it would cost to buy the driver's silence this time. Then they reached South Temple Street and were gone.

He supposed he should walk back to the depot and catch a streetcar to McClure's Saloon. Peter was waiting for him there with Tommy's guitar; he'd taken it that morning, saying, "You don't want to lug this thing around with you when you're meeting a lady, do you?" Tommy had been grateful for that, yet he'd brought the guitar to Salt Lake City because he knew he could make more money in the saloons there than in Castle Valley.

He started in the direction of the saloon, but his steps slowed, then stopped. He walked back toward the courthouse and climbed the steps again.

Once inside the courtroom, he stood next to the lawyers' table, leaning on it, his knuckles pressed hard against the polished top, allowing himself to remember everything—the train ride; the frightening aloneness in the train depot, waiting for Uncle Jim to come; the night under the tree on the courthouse lawn. And the murder trial, where Big Bill Haywood was acquitted.

No one, not even Peter, who believed so strongly in the miners' unions, had ever come out and stated absolutely that Bill Haywood had nothing to do with that murder. Whenever Tommy asked Peter about it, Peter was evasive.

Head lowered, Tommy let himself think about these things for once, without trying to drive the thoughts away. Uncle Jim had been sent to Boise with bribe money for the jailers because everyone expected Bill Haywood to be found guilty. Through all the years between then and now Tommy had wondered, deep in a part of his mind where he didn't want to go, whether someone had already bribed those Boise jurors before he and Uncle Jim got there. Because against all expectations that jury had voted Bill Haywood *not* guilty.

If that's what had happened, then Uncle Jim had given his life for nothing.

So many strands of this terrible affair were woven together in Tommy's mind, like the nest of rattlesnakes he'd once stumbled across in the hills around Castle Gate, all twined together, with first one head and then another shooting out from the hissing knot of them, the tails rattling so threateningly that Tommy had run faster than ever before to save his life.

Now another union man, Joe Hill, was being tried for murder. All the way to Salt Lake City that morning Peter and Mort had talked about the Joe Hill trial. Joe Hill, named Joel Hagglund in Sweden before he emigrated to America, then called Joseph Hillstrom, and finally Joe Hill. Accused of murdering a grocer and his son in Murray, Utah, not far from the location of McClure's Saloon.

There was no evidence to tie him to the murders, Peter insisted, except a bullet wound Hill claimed he'd gotten in a fight over a woman. The police believed the wound had come from a shot fired by the grocer. Since the case against Joe Hill had been flimsy from the start, he probably would have been released—but then the police found out he was a Wobbly. Not only was Joe Hill a member of the Industrial Workers of the World, he was their poet, their songwriter. In the eyes of most Utahns, who believed all Wobblies were anarchists and saboteurs, that was enough to convict him on the spot. But this time Peter believed completely and vehemently in the man's innocence.

Joe Hill's murder trial had begun a few days earlier, in the same courtroom where Tommy was now standing. It would resume tomorrow. Suddenly Tommy wanted to be there. If he could become convinced that the American system of justice worked, that a jury of twelve honest men could actually penetrate all the bluster and posturing of the lawyers to get to the core of truth, that Bill Haywood's jury had been right when they voted him innocent—why, it might help Tommy wash away a little of the self-reproach he always carried inside him.

Part of his burden had already been lightened when Eugenie called him her sweetheart. Here in this very courtroom. Amazing! Astonishing! If someone like Eugenie could care for someone like Tommy, perhaps he was worth more than he thought.

He wondered whether she'd go to the trial with him. On Monday, Tuesday, and Wednesday he had singing jobs. Thursday he could help his mother by chopping wood, piling up enough coal for the stove, and delivering whatever laundry she needed delivered. By Friday the trial should still be going on, most likely, and he would go to it; he could even stay in Salt Lake City until it was over. His mother could turn to Peter for help if she needed any. Slowly descending the stairs from the courtroom, he walked toward the depot, stopping first in the lobby of the Hotel Utah. "May I have a sheet of paper and an envelope?" he asked the desk clerk.

"Yes, sir," the clerk said, handing them to him.

"How much?"

"No charge, sir. The pens are over there on the desks."

No charge, in a fancy hotel like this. And in the company store a piece of paper and an envelope cost thirty-five cents. That was another union grievance: Everything cost way too much in the company-owned stores, but the miners had to buy there because they got paid in scrip that was good only in stores owned and managed by the coal companies.

*Dear Eugenie,* he wrote. *Can you meet me under the clock tower at the City and County Building on Friday morning, June 26, at ten in the morning? If you aren't there, I'll know it was too hard for you to leave school, and I'll understand.*

For a long time he held the pen poised, wondering what else to write. *Love?* Someone might see it. Anyway, she knew he loved her.

He signed *Tommy,* sealed the envelope, and asked the desk clerk to mail it.

*He couldn't sleep. He'd never seen this part of the country before. His destination—Chicago—was called the Midwest, but it was a lot nearer to the East than to the West. The land outside the train window kept changing as the train drew closer to Des Moines.*

*He thought about bringing down his guitar from the rack to work on the song he was writing for the funeral, but the other passengers might not like it. Or they might like it. Either way it would call attention to Tommy, and he didn't need that. To create a song, he needed to be alone inside his head.*

*He'd already gone over all the songs in* The Little Red Songbook. *Now he wanted to write his own song, the whole thing—words and music—by Thomas Quinlan. A song of love and death, of separation and heartbreak, of murder and maiming. Of men who die and women who cry for them.*

*"Des Moines!" the conductor called out. "Des Moines, Iowa. Transfer here for Kansas City, Saint Louis, and all points south."*

*How good it would be to catch a different train and go to Saint Louis, to walk the streets where those blues came from. The memory of "Saint Louis Blues" took him back to his first real meeting with Eugenie, when she sat at the piano and sang in her husky voice, "Oh, I hate to see de ev'nin' sun go down, 'Cause ma baby, he done lef' dis town."*

*Poor Eugenie. His heart ached for her.*

# CHAPTER THIRTEEN
June 26–27, 1914

"What do you mean you'll be in Salt Lake City tomorrow?" Fiona demanded.

"I mean I'm going to Salt Lake City on the early train," Tommy said curtly. He was in no mood for a confrontation. He'd just come home from playing music in the saloons, he was tired, and since it was after midnight, he'd been unpleasantly surprised to find his mother still awake and sitting in the kitchen.

"Why in the world would you be doing that?" she asked him, putting down her mending.

"I want to get to the Joe Hill trial before it's over."

Fiona frowned. "I'm still not understanding this. Why should you want to go to a murder trial?"

How could he explain it to his mother when he'd never told her about his part in Uncle Jim's murder? "I just want to," he said.

"Well, I don't want you to," Fiona declared.

Ignoring that, Tommy emptied his pockets onto the table,

dumping quarters and nickels and dimes that rolled around until he scraped them into a pile. "Here's six dollars and eighty cents. It ought to be enough for you till I get back Saturday night."

"Saturday night! This is only Thursday. Well, it's Friday now, I guess, since it's past midnight, but where do you plan to spend Friday night, if I may ask?"

"At the YMCA. If the trial doesn't end by evening, I'll stay in Salt Lake City all night."

"And what if it doesn't end that day or the day after? Or the day after that?"

"Then I'll stay till it does. Anyway, it's easier to earn money in Salt Lake City than here."

"Absolutely not!" She rose to her feet, leaning forward with her roughened fingers splayed upon the tabletop. "No seventeen-year-old son of mine is spending nights in a strange city with who knows what kind of riffraff."

"Seventeen! You just said it yourself—I'm seventeen!" he shouted, his voice harsh. "I've been earning our bread for six years now, starting when I was eleven, and ever since I got laid off two weeks ago, I've been working nights in the saloons to keep things going here at home." He pushed the money toward her. "I'm leaving for Salt Lake City on the early train, Mom, and I'll come home when I'm damn well ready!"

If she cried, he'd cave in, he knew he would, because he'd never before yelled at his mother, not that way anyhow. Through lowered eyelids he watched her and saw a strange, mocking smile twist her lips.

"Well, well. So it's a grown-up man we have here, is it? Making up his own mind regardless of his mother's wishes."

She shrugged, then said, "All right, Tommy, go if you must, but I don't want you visiting any bawdy houses up there in the big city."

"Mom!" Not only did her words shock him, he found them offensive. Yet he felt the blood rush guiltily to his cheeks, as though he'd actually been planning a trip to a brothel. "I can't believe you'd even *say* such a thing!" he rebuked her.

"Well, considering those low-life union men you hang around when you're with Peter, I couldn't be too sure, you know."

"They're not lowlifes," he shot back. "Your brother Jim was a union man."

"And look what it got him! Beaten to death!"

Tommy's head pounded from fatigue and from the argument, and even more from the image her words stirred in his memory—of his uncle Jim, beaten so bloody by the Pinkertons that his coffin had to be kept closed. "That's enough," he told Fiona. "I'm going to bed now." Turning his back on her, he hurried into his room and slammed the door behind him.

In the morning he moved quietly, hoping to get out of the house before she awoke, but of course she was waiting for him in the kitchen. "You're not riding in the coal freight wearing that good linen suit, are you?" she asked.

"Why else would I have it on?" Then he softened. Time to declare a truce. "No, for this once I'm going to buy a ticket and ride in the passenger train," he explained.

She mumbled something he couldn't quite catch, something about wasting good money, then she said, "I've fixed you oatmeal and eggs and ham for breakfast. If you get filled up now, you won't need to spend as much on lunch. I'd have packed you a lunch, but I figured you wouldn't want to take it."

"You figured right," he answered, and sat down to eat as quickly as he could. Through a mouthful of oatmeal he told her, "You can find out when the trial ends by checking the newspaper in the company store. I'll come home after it's over."

She nodded, accepting it. She was still in her nightgown, her hair in a long braid that hung down to the middle of her back. When he was little, Tommy used to ask her why she braided her hair to go to bed. She'd told him that it prevented her hair from getting all tangled up when she tossed and turned because she couldn't sleep. At the time he hadn't questioned why anyone should toss and turn and spend sleepless hours in the dark. Now that he was older, he wondered if it was loneliness that kept his mother awake nights. "Sorry about our fight," he told her, putting his arms around her to wish her good-bye.

"So am I." She kissed his cheek, then said, "Just be careful. You're all I have."

Again Tommy was surprised that this courtroom should smell exactly the same as the one in Boise—furniture polish, stale cigar smoke, sweaty jurors. Women spectators seated behind the railing waved paper fans, trying to move the torpid air. Beside Tommy, Eugenie dabbed at her forehead with a lace handkerchief, then smiled wryly at him and whispered, "You're the only man in the place still wearing his suit coat. You don't have to be *that* refined, Tommy."

It wasn't refinement; he'd been so absorbed in the proceedings that he'd hardly noticed the heat. As he shrugged out of his coat and folded it over his arm he felt her fingers slip into his, beneath the cover of the folded linen jacket. He gave her hand a quick squeeze, then turned his attention back to the prosecuting attorney, who was summing up his case.

"We must enforce the majesty of the law as framed by the people of this great state of Utah," the prosecutor orated, sweeping his arms in wide, dramatic gestures like a stage actor. "Enforce it so that anarchy and murder and crime shall be pushed back beyond the pale of civilization. . . ."

*Anarchy again,* Tommy thought. That seemed to be a favorite word of prosecutors, a word they trumpeted loudly, intending to strike fear into the hearts of listeners.

"So that you and your sons and all upright men shall walk the earth free from the danger of those parasites on society who murder and rob rather than make an honest living."

"What about daughters?" Eugenie whispered. "Shouldn't upright women be free from parasites too?" She giggled, not taking this seriously, but it was no laughing matter to Tommy. A man was on trial for his life in this room.

Whipping around, the prosecutor pointed an accusing finger at Joe Hill, who sat calmly, almost motionless, in the prisoner's docket. "If you were an innocent man, Joseph Hillstrom," the prosecutor thundered, using one of Joe Hill's aliases, "you would tell where and how you were wounded. And if the story could be corroborated, you would be freed. *Why,* in God's name," he demanded, his voice growing higher and louder, "did you not tell the story and clear your name from the stain upon it?"

To answer his own question, the prosecutor came closer, his eyes boring like drills into Joe Hill's. "Because you do not dare, Joe Hillstrom. Because you are a guilty man, that's why! Guilty of murder!"

Tommy had been trying to get a good look at Joe Hill, but

the prisoner sat facing the wrong direction, and people's heads kept blocking Tommy's view. From the glimpses he got he saw a man who was tall and thin, with thick brown hair, prominent cheekbones, and sunken cheeks. Joe Hill never seemed to change his expression, enduring all the terrible things the prosecutor said about him as though his attention were somewhere else, as though those words being spoken were not about him.

Turning to the jury, the prosecutor leaned over the railing to declare in a sinister voice, "I am asking you, gentlemen of the jury, to bring in your verdict, to find *this man*"—again the accusing finger pointed at Joe Hill—"guilty of murder in the first degree!"

Tommy let out the breath he'd been holding. That was it. That was all. Now it would be up to the jury.

By the time the twelve men had filed out of the courtroom to go to their jury quarters, it was late afternoon. "No sense hanging around," Tommy told Eugenie, leading her into the hall.

"Don't you want to wait here? What if they come back? I thought you wanted to hear the verdict."

"I have a real strong feeling about this," he admitted as they walked down the steps to the sidewalk. He didn't tell her that the whole drama seemed to be an uncanny reenactment of what had happened in Boise; didn't say he felt positive the jury would be out all night and would return in the morning to pronounce Joe Hill not guilty, just as it had happened with Big Bill Haywood in Boise. Instead he suggested, "Why don't I take you to dinner now? What time do you have to go back to school?"

"I don't," Eugenie told him. When he looked at her inquiringly, she explained, "I told the nuns I was going home to Castle Gate and wouldn't be back at school till Monday."

Tommy stopped dead on the sidewalk, unsure what this was leading to. "Then . . . your father's expecting you tonight?"

"No. I didn't tell *him* I was coming home. I just told the *school* that." She smiled up at him. "Don't look so worried, Tommy. I have a friend who lives here in town. She said I could sleep at her house tonight."

"Isobel?"

"No, another girl, named Mary Therese. She's in my music class."

"Well . . . well . . ." He was stammering, and he hated that because he sounded so bumbling, so inept. "Does that mean we can spend the whole evening together? I mean . . . not just dinner, but after?" His heart began to pump harder.

"That's what it means," she agreed.

"So . . . where would you like to go?"

"That's easy," she cried, grabbing his hand. "To Saltair."

"I don't know what that is."

"I'll show you." Eugenie led him to the Union Pacific station, where they managed to catch a train just leaving for Saltair, which turned out to be a resort on the shores of the Great Salt Lake.

Tommy, who'd hardly seen anything outside the towering stone cliffs of Castle Valley, was astonished by Saltair. What first caught his eye was the enormous building with turrets topped by cupolas on the four corners, like a Turkish castle. Boardwalks led across sand from the train stop all the way to the resort, and those boardwalks were packed with people who all seemed to be enjoying themselves. Beyond the buildings lay the waters of the Great Salt Lake.

He heard music; it sounded like a combination of organ and accordion music, but tinny. "It's the merry-go-round," Eugenie told him. "Let's try that first."

Pulling him across the boardwalk, snaking through the throngs, she jumped onto the moving merry-go-round. Clumsily he followed her, almost losing his balance until he grabbed a wooden horse that was rising up and dipping down in time to the music. "Climb aboard the horse," she told him. She was already seated on the back of another moving horse, one whose nostrils flared like a savage cavalry charger.

"Don't we have to pay for this?" Tommy asked.

From her pocket she pulled an accordion-pleated strip of tickets. "I had these left over from the last time I was here."

They rode the merry-go-round four times, then the roller coaster—another first for Tommy, whose necktie fluttered behind him in the wind as the cars raced downhill at heart-thudding speed. In the cars ahead of him he noticed young men with their arms around girls who screamed and squealed when the coaster dropped fast. Taking a cue from them, Tommy put his arms around Eugenie, who never screamed, but laughed out loud, crashing against him on the fast turns.

Saltair had a movie theater showing a film called *Tillie's Punctured Romance,* but they decided against watching it because Eugenie had seen the movie the week before in Salt Lake City. "It has a brand-new comedian who's really funny, though," she told Tommy. "A little Englishman named Charlie Chaplin."

He'd planned to take her to a nice restaurant for dinner; instead they ate hot dogs along the boardwalk. "The best part hasn't even started yet," she told him. "It's the dancing."

"I'm not much of a dancer," he admitted.

"You have to be. For anyone as musical as you, dancing has to come naturally."

She was right. By the time the sun had set, casting brilliant orange and red medallions across the low waves of the Great Salt Lake, she'd led him onto the enormous dance floor, where two separate bands performed. Holding her in his arms, Tommy felt he could do anything—dance, fly, walk on water if needed. He'd never been happier in his whole life, moving and swaying to the rhythm of the music while Eugenie swayed close to him.

She knew most of the songs, and she sang along with them in her husky voice. "You made me love you, I didn't wanna do it, I didn't wanna do it. You made me love you, and all the time you knew it, I guess you always knew it. . . ."

Since he was a good eight inches taller than she was, he kept his head bent because he couldn't take his eyes off her eyes, looking up at him. "Give me, give me, what I cry for, You know you've got the brand of kisses that I die for. . . ."

They danced for hours, taking time out to sip a lemonade now and again, and then she'd hear a song she particularly liked, and they'd head back to the dance floor.

Outside it grew dark. And darker, with a moonless sky full of stars. Tommy didn't want the evening to end, but he felt responsible for her. "Shouldn't we be getting back to Salt Lake City?" he asked.

"Oh, let's wait for just a little longer. Let's go out on the deck and watch the moon rise over the Great Salt Lake—it's such a beautiful sight. I was here once with my parents when we saw it, and I'd love to watch it again with you."

At the back of the building a wide veranda spanned the whole width of the Salt Palace. A long row of wooden deck chairs, tilted backward at an angle, faced the lake; Eugenie told Tommy they were like the deck chairs on an ocean liner.

The Great Salt Lake was so vast it really did look like an ocean to Tommy, who'd only seen pictures of oceans in magazines.

They waited in vain for the moon to rise. After a while Eugenie asked, "Do you know what time it is? I'm not sure when the last train leaves for Salt Lake City."

"I don't have a watch," he told her. "Maybe we'd better go and check."

They reached the tiny station in time to see the train chugging away, far enough ahead of them that they couldn't run to catch up. "Was that the last one?" Tommy asked the stationmaster, who was hanging a wooden shutter across the ticket booth. "Last one till tomorrow," he answered.

"What are we going to do?" Tommy asked Eugenie.

"First we'll have to find a telephone so I can call my friend Mary Therese—otherwise she'll call the school, and I'll be in real trouble."

"Isn't it kind of late to be calling somebody?"

"I'm sure she's been waiting up for me, so she'll grab the phone as soon as it rings, and that way her parents won't hear."

After the phone call was made, Tommy asked, "Now what?" Men were sweeping refuse from the boardwalk, but other than that, no one was around, and all the concession stands had been closed.

"I guess we spend the night on the deck chairs and wait for morning," Eugenie answered. "I'm really sorry, Tommy. I know you wanted to be at the trial early to hear the jury's verdict. Well, at least we'll get to see the moon rise, I guess."

They sat side by side on the deck chairs, holding hands. After a while Eugenie left her chair to sit in his lap, and soon they didn't care whether the moon would ever rise again, or the sun, either, or whether the earth fell right off the edge of the universe. They'd kissed before, but never before had Tommy felt the full, delicious weight of her body on his. He grew almost drunk from excitement.

As it always does at the end of June, the sun came up early, stabbing the surface of the lake with a shaft of gold, fluttering Tommy's eyelids with the sting of its rays. He didn't know how long they'd been asleep, but his arm was numb where Eugenie's head rested upon it. For a long time he watched her, saw the thin mist of moisture form on her upper lip as the sun bathed her face with gold, and hungered to kiss away that mist. But he didn't want to wake her.

Sometime in the middle of the night, when the air had cooled, he'd covered her with his suit coat. Now, in the sunlight, she stirred from the warmth, pushing back the coat so that it slid to the deck. That woke her.

She smiled up at him. "I love you," she said.

Was she awake enough to know what she'd just said? Tommy was afraid to ask, because he wanted so much for it to be true.

They took off their shoes and walked along the shore of the lake, Tommy with his pant legs rolled up, Eugenie lifting her skirts to her knees as they ventured a little way into the briny water, where, she told him, swimmers always bobbed like corks. There were no swimmers that early in the morning. They were alone.

"Do you remember the valentine I wrote for you?" Tommy asked.

"What a question! Of course I remember it. Every word."

"The last lines were 'Yet in my dreams we walk together at dawn; Then when I awaken, sweet Eugenie is gone.' But here we are, walking together at dawn, and you're still here. So am I dreaming?"

"If you are, then I am too. You're such a fine poet, Tommy."

"Poet!" he scoffed. "I write parodies, Genie."

"But you could be a serious poet. You have the talent."

"I don't think so. And anyway, I wouldn't want to be." The sun climbed higher over the edge of the lake, quickly growing hot, waking the brine flies, which started stinging their bare ankles. "Uh, don't you think—" Tommy began.

"That we need to go back? Yes," she answered. "Things that are perfect, like this, can't last anyway, you know."

"Why not? We can do it again, often."

"It will never be this perfect again. Nothing ever will. When I'm very old, I'll still remember this, but you won't. Men don't."

"How do you know what men do or don't remember?" He didn't want to be drawn into a futile discussion, because he was anxious to get back to the courtroom. Any minute now the jurors might be coming in.

She sighed. "All right. We'll leave."

When they reached Salt Lake City, Tommy felt obliged to be gentlemanly and offer Eugenie breakfast. Since he'd hardly spent any money on her except for lemonade and train fare, it was the least he could do. At the Hotel Utah, after both of them had washed up in the restrooms, he positioned himself so he could watch the clock at one end of the dining room. To her credit, Eugenie didn't dawdle. She ordered quickly and ate her breakfast quickly, then stood up and said, "It won't take us long to walk to the courtroom. Come on."

They walked so fast they almost broke into a run, and arrived just as the jury was filing into the room. The courtroom clock pointed at seven minutes to ten.

Weeks before, when the jurymen had been selected, Tommy had read about them in the newspaper, paying attention to the kind of work each man did. Of the twelve men good and true, eight of them had the kind of job that required hard labor, sweat, and long hours. Tommy thought that would be a good thing for Joe Hill. Those eight men were likely to sympathize with a hardworking miner like Joe, who sat stoically in the prisoner's box, his face betraying nothing.

"Gentlemen of the jury, have you reached your verdict?" the judge asked.

"We have, Your Honor," the foreman answered.

Tommy and Eugenie had just barely squeezed into a seat. Since Tommy was removing his hat and trying to hold it so it wouldn't get crushed by the elbows of the man next to him, he wasn't completely focused on what was happening in the front of the courtroom.

"How do you find the defendant, Joseph Hillstrom?"

The foreman took a folded paper from his pocket. "We the jurors impaneled in this case find the defendant, Joseph Hillstrom, guilty of the crime of murder in the first degree."

Something was wrong. Those were the wrong words. Startled, Tommy sat upright and dropped the hat.

Joe Hill didn't as much as flicker an eyelid, not when the verdict was read, not when a phalanx of nine guards surrounded him to lead him out of the courtroom. Only at the door did he jerk backward to announce loudly, "I am innocent of that killing, and I will prove it before I get through."

"Come on, Tommy," Eugenie said, taking his hand. "It's over."

It couldn't be, he thought. All week long he'd been waiting to get a good feel for America's system of justice, to find out whether it could be trusted. And here the trial was over—before he'd even had a chance to figure out anything!

Outside Eugenie told him, "There's no way you and I

can salvage the rest of this day. You're too upset. Go back to Castle Gate, Tommy, and I'll go to my friend's house. Next weekend I'll be home for the Fourth of July." When he nodded, she said, "Come to my house that evening so we can watch fireworks together."

"Yes." He couldn't think of anything more to say.

As he walked slowly toward the train station Tommy stopped every half block or so, trying to get a grasp of what had just happened. He'd believed Joe Hill would be acquitted, because Peter was so certain the man was innocent. In some complicated, connected way Tommy felt he'd traveled in a circle from the Boise murder trial to this one. Whatever happened today was supposed to set things straight. Was supposed to change things for him. And it hadn't.

What he couldn't know was that the whole world was about to change.

# CHAPTER FOURTEEN
## The Great War

Tommy was so tired that he slept past the time for early mass, but his mother woke him to get ready for eleven o'clock mass. "I've already been to church," she told him. "I won't make your ham and eggs now—I'll wait till you get back, so you won't break your fast if you want to receive Communion."

Did he? He knew he'd have to go to confession first. From catechism class he remembered something about "carnal desires," but he'd been pretty young and he was hazy on the details. That night at Saltair he and Eugenie had not done what married couples do—Tommy would never compromise her that way—but all that kissing and touching had given him feelings that undoubtedly qualified as carnal. It would be embarrassing to confess all that to Father Mike; Eugenie was lucky she wasn't Catholic. But maybe she hadn't felt the same way Tommy did. Maybe girls didn't get all that carnal. He was too inexperienced to know.

On the street in front of the church, Black Edo Cvetek and a crowd of other Slovenians stood shouting in their native language, obviously agitated. "What's going on, Edo?" Tommy asked him.

"We wait for newspapers from Denver," Edo answered. "Is terrible news."

"Yeah, I know. I was there yesterday when the jury said Joe Hill was guilty."

"What? What you talk?" Black Edo demanded. "This not anyting about Joe Hill. Who care about Joe Hill? We got telegrams from Slovenia, from our families. Archduke Franz Ferdinand get shot in Bosnia today. Killed dead."

Tommy asked, "Who's Franz Ferdinand?"

Black Edo just shook his head, astonished that Tommy had to ask such a thing. Another Slovenian who spoke better English came up to tell Tommy, "Eleven o'clock this morning a crazy Bosnian boy assassinated the archduke and his wife in Sarajevo."

"Eleven o'clock? It's only eleven o'clock right now," Tommy pointed out.

The Slovenian gave Tommy an odd look, half pitying and half exasperated. "In Bosnia is now seven o'clock in the evening, June twenty-eighth, 1914. Archduke Franz Ferdinand got shot eight hours ago."

"Oh." Tommy left them to their chattering and went inside the church. What did it matter if some foreign duke or other was assassinated? What really mattered was that Joe Hill had been declared guilty when he was innocent. Or most likely innocent. Even some of the Salt Lake City newspapers admitted that the trial hadn't been fair. There would be an appeal, another chance for justice to be done. But for now, Tommy had other things on his mind. Like the Fourth of July coming up.

Monday night, and every night that week, he sang in the

saloons, going from one to the other in Castle Gate, Helper, and Price. As the mine layoffs continued and the men ran out of money, Tommy's tips got fewer and leaner. Men who still had a quarter or a dollar wanted to spend it on hard liquor, not on tips for a saloon singer.

On Friday night at the Red Rock Saloon the bartender handed him an envelope. "What's this?" Tommy asked.

The bartender answered, "Some kid dropped it off here about an hour ago. Said to give it to the singer. You're the only singer we got, Tommy, so it must be for you."

The envelope was sealed with real sealing wax, not candle drippings. He carried it outside, opening it in the light from a globe that hung over the door with RED ROCK painted on the glass.

9:30 P.M., SATURDAY, it said. GROVE OF QUAKING ASPENS AT THE FAR END OF OUR YARD.

Eugenie. So few words, but the message was clear enough: *Don't come to the front door, Tommy. Meet me in secret so my father won't know.*

Well, if that's how it had to be, he'd do as she asked. He didn't feel good about it, though—sneaking around in the backyard. Why couldn't he come calling on her the way young men were supposed to call on young ladies: all dressed up, bearing flowers, ringing the front doorbell?

He got there first, setting off the barking of a dozen dogs in the quiet neighborhood. Elsewhere the valley was raucous with shouts and clattered with the shallow bangs of fire-crackers as everyone, men and women and children, cele-brated the nation's 138th birthday.

Surrounded by tall, thin trees, the grove at the back of the Farnhams' yard looked dark and secluded. Several marble benches had been placed in a cleared-out center circle; pale in the shadows, they seemed romantic and inviting. He sat on one of the benches to wait for Eugenie. When she arrived, carrying a folded blanket, she shyly asked him to help her spread it on the ground.

"We can lie on it and look straight up to see the fireworks," she said. "That's what I used to do when I was little, with my parents and Glenn. It's probably the best view in the valley." Just as she told him that, they heard a boom, and a fountain of gold sparks exploded over their heads in the night sky. "Good! They've started," she said.

He helped her arrange herself on the blanket, then sat beside her. "No, don't sit," she told him. "You have to lie flat to stare up at the sky. It will feel like you're inside the fireworks, that they're falling right on top of you."

Hard as it was for him, with Eugenie so close and the sky filled with glorious color, Tommy kept his emotions under control, but he still didn't feel completely at ease. "I got your note," he said.

"I can see that you must have, since you're here." She turned to face him in the dark.

"Why did you want us to meet out here?" he asked.

"I told you. It's the best place to watch fireworks in the whole valley."

He wanted to ask if her father knew where she was, and if he knew she was with Tommy, but then she moved a little closer to him and it didn't matter. The fireworks exploded overhead, one after the other, their booms echoing off the sandstone cliffs. Leaves of the quaking aspens shimmied above them; the breeze cooled their overheated faces. He loved her. He loved that she chose her own path, did what she wanted. If they had to meet secretly because she knew her father would disapprove, he was proud that she had the daring to do that.

But why shouldn't she be daring? She'd never had to struggle for anything in her life.

"I have a secret to tell you," she whispered against his cheek. "I know it will make you happy."

"What is it?"

"You're the first in the valley to know. My father is reopening the mine next week. You and all the other men will be called back to work."

"Really!" He sat up, accidentally catching her hair beneath the heel of his hand, so that she gave a little shriek. "Oh, did I hurt you?" he asked.

"Yes, but you can kiss it and make it well." As he kissed her lips she laughed, "I mean my hair."

A little later he asked, "Why is your father calling the men back to work right now? Do you know?"

This time it was Eugenie who sat up, smoothing her dress. "He's pretty sure there's going to be a war, and that will create a big demand for coal to supply the steel mills and metal smelters. He wants to get his coal stockpiled now because the price will go way up, he says."

"A war? He really thinks there'll be a war?"

"Because of the assassination of Franz Ferdinand, the archduke of the Austro-Hungarian Empire. You know about that, don't you?"

"Sure," he replied, mentally thanking Black Edo.

"My father says the Germans will retaliate against the Serbs, and the Russians will rush—" She laughed a little. "That sounds funny—Russians rushing. Anyway, they'll rush to defend the Serbs, and then Germany will attack Russia, and France will attack Germany, and all Europe will be involved, my father says. You know all about how tangled those political alliances are in Europe, Tommy."

*All* about them! He didn't know *anything* about them.

"My dad telegraphed my mother to come home on the first ship where she can book passage." Eugenie was no longer laughing. "Dad wants Glenn to come home too, but Glenn says he'll stay at Oxford. And that," she said, "changes everything for me. They'd planned to send me back East to college, but now Dad says he wants me closer to home, since Glenn is staying so far away in these dangerous times."

"College?" Tommy asked. "You're going to college?"

She seemed surprised that he would ask. "Yes, and now it seems I'll be attending the University of Utah. With most of the girls gone home for vacation, my piano teacher has lots of extra hours to work with me, so I'm hoping I can make it into the music program at the U of U."

Tommy moved a bit farther away from her. "You didn't tell me you were going to college."

"I guess it never came up."

The fireworks had ended. Both of them were sitting on the blanket now, facing each other; in the darkness he couldn't read her expression. "Why do you have to go to college? If your father wants you close by, why can't you just stay here in Castle Gate?"

She gave a little shrug. "It's what girls like me are expected to do. Go to college. To go hunting."

Bewildered, Tommy asked, "Hunting? Hunting for what?"

Her voice took on an edge as she answered, "The hunting would be better in an Eastern college, but as I told you, my father wants me near." She leaned forward and took his hands. "Why do families send their daughters to college, Tommy? To hunt for husbands. It's like a trophy if a girl lands a nice, young, college-educated man with a future."

He felt as though cold lead had been poured inside him all the way down to his gut, solidifying in his throat so that no words could force their way out. He pulled away his hands, those labor-roughened hands that shoveled coal in the mine, those hands with fingertips callused from picking at guitar strings for nickels in smelly saloons.

"Have I shocked you?" she asked.

He got to his feet.

"Tommy, where are you going?" she cried.

"Home."

"Don't go, Tommy. Please!"

He couldn't answer her. His misery would soon turn to rage; that cold lead inside him would melt and churn into a boiling volcano of fury and self-loathing, and he wanted out of there before that happened. He turned and ran. All the way across the Farnhams' manicured lawn he could hear her voice calling to him, "Tommy, please come back!" But he kept running—through the neighborhood, through the town, down to the river.

Now that spring runoff had ended and the days were hot, the Price River's level was lower, but it wasn't as shallow as it would become in September. Tommy sat on the bank, savagely hurling stones into the water.

What had made him think he could mean anything to Eugenie? She'd said she loved him, but how could she? He was nothing! He was worthless, and he'd known that since he was ten. Inside his head the list of his inadequacies exploded like the firecrackers he could still hear in the distance: He was seventeen years old and he'd never made a telephone call, never sent a telegram, never ridden in an automobile, never seen a play in a real theater (the vaudeville troupes that came through Price and Helper didn't count), never heard a symphony orchestra, never even bought a suit from a men's clothing store. He wore dead-men's clothes because he was as good as dead, stuck in a mine in a one-horse town with no hope of ever getting out. As for those tangled political alliances in Europe that Eugenie had talked about, he couldn't name one-fourth of the countries in Europe. He was an uneducated, ignorant, pitiful, pathetic clod.

He hurled rocks until his arm hurt, not caring that the moon had finally come up above him. He was too agitated to go home and sleep—he would stay on the riverbank until the sky lightened. Since the mountain peaks were so high, the sun never became visible above them until long after light bathed the opposite side of the valley. Each time despair threatened to send tears to his eyes, Tommy called up his rage—at himself, mostly; but also at the Farnhams; and at his uncle Jim for taking the two of them on that trip to Boise; and at his mother for not marrying Peter Connolly, so Peter could have supported them all these years and Tommy could have gone back to school before it was too late. None of the rage, though, spilled over to Eugenie; only pain. He still heard her voice calling him back.

Toward morning he slept a little. Sun on his face woke him, as it had on the deck at Saltair, when Eugenie had opened her eyes and told him, "I love you."

When he remembered that, he threw himself face-down on the bank, deliberately scraping his knuckles against the rocks. Then he thought about what else she'd told him last night—that the men would be called back to work on Monday. Monday was tomorrow.

How could a shot fired by a Bosnian man only two years older than Tommy, half a world away, affect a coal mine in

Castle Gate, Utah? Was that assassination the real meaning of *anarchy*, the word people liked to throw around so loosely? Tommy thought it might be. Maybe if he weren't so ignorant, he could figure it out.

He got up to work the kinks out of his muscles. The company store ought to be open by now. Last night's edition of the *Denver Post* would be on the shelves. If he read about the situation in Europe, maybe he could start piecing together the mysterious political causes and effects that Eugenie thought he already knew.

For the rest of the day he stayed home, his expression as black as his thoughts. Fiona was certainly happy when he told her he was going back to work. "Not because I like you being in the coal mine, mind you, Tommy," she assured him, "but because the unmarried men will need their dirty overalls laundered again, and the married women can pay for the mending I've been doing for them on credit."

Monday came, and just as Eugenie had said, the men were called back. Tommy was glad to be in the mine again, glad to thrust his shovel into piles of coal as though gutting one of those clean-skinned college men who had a future. Each evening after work he bought a newspaper and read it. Each day during the dinner break in the coal mine he asked Black Edo to explain about his homeland.

"Dis boy who pull the trigger—his name Gavrilo Princip—he was Bosnian, but he want Serbia to grow more powerful," Edo said. At first when Edo talked about Bosnia and Herzegovina, Montenegro and Macedonia, Austria and Hungary, the Serbs, Croats, Magyars, Bulgars, Slovakians, and Slovenians, Tommy was hopelessly confused. Day after day, as Black Edo explained it all, Tommy was able to sort things out, because Edo was a knowledgeable and patient teacher. Never again would Tommy remain silent when other miners spouted off about ignorant Hunky foreigners, the offscourings of southern Europe. Those immigrants knew plenty.

One evening toward the end of July, when Tommy stopped after work to buy a newspaper at the company store, the manager handed him an envelope, saying, "Some kid brought it in here. It has your name on it."

From Eugenie. Outside, in the early-evening light, he read her words: ASPEN GROVE, NINE O'CLOCK, JULY 25. PLEASE! He folded the paper into smaller and smaller squares and put it into his shirt pocket. He'd have to remember to take it out before his mother washed the shirt, or she'd find it and ask questions.

July 25 was a Saturday. It came and went. Tommy stayed home to read in the *Denver Post* that a war in Europe seemed imminent, although the words swam before his eyes as he pictured Eugenie waiting alone in the aspen grove. How long would she wait before she realized he wasn't coming? Never again would he sneak around to meet her on the sly. Never again would he go to the Farnhams', unless he could march up to the front door and knock, say good evening to Mr. and Mrs. Farnham, inquire about their son, Glenn, chat about the weather, and spend the evening in the music room with Eugenie. All up front and open. He might be a worthless human being, but he was a human being, not a dog to be shut outside in the dark.

Which meant that he'd probably never see Eugenie again.

One item in that newspaper did catch his attention: JOE HILL'S ATTORNEYS FILE MOTION FOR NEW TRIAL. A brief paragraph beneath the headline said that Hill's lawyers claimed the state of Utah had failed to establish, beyond a reasonable doubt, the identification of Joe Hill as the murderer of the grocer.

That night Tommy slept fitfully, dreaming of Eugenie asking him to sing "I Dream of Genie with the Light Brown Hair," hearing her call out to him, "Please come to me! Tommy, please come back!" Early in the morning he was awakened by a knocking on the kitchen door.

A young Slovenian girl stood there—Jana Zagar, the daughter of the woman who ran the boardinghouse where Black Edo lived. "Please come," she said, and for a few seconds Tommy wondered if he was still dreaming.

"Come where?"

"To our house. It's Edo Cvetek—he's gone crazy," she said in a rush. "He's yelling and screaming and smashing things. He says he hates America, and you're the only decent American he knows. My mother is frightened. She asked me to fetch you before Edo wrecks the whole house."

Luckily Tommy had pulled on his pants before he opened the door. "Let me get my shoes," he told Jana.

They ran through the streets of Castle Gate, where a few churchgoers were on their way to the earliest mass. The Zagar boardinghouse lay on the outskirts of town; when they reached it, Mrs. Zagar was standing at the door. Gesturing rapidly and dabbing her eyes with her apron, she spoke a long stream of Slovenian aimed at Tommy. "What is she saying?" he asked Jana.

"She says Edo is lying on his bed now, but she's still afraid. She begs you to come inside and reason with him."

Following Mrs. Zagar, Tommy walked through a dark, cramped hallway covered with pictures of the Virgin Mary. The farther he went, the louder the moans were that came from a room at the end of the hall, where Edo lay sobbing on his bed. Two liquor bottles, one empty and the other half empty, lay on the floor beside him.

"Edo," Tommy said, shaking his shoulder. "Look at me. It's Tommy. Tell me what's wrong."

Edo rolled over, staring up through bleary eyes to make sure who it really was, then threw his arms around Tommy and bawled all the louder. Awkwardly Tommy peeled away the man's arms and knelt beside the bed. "Tell me, Edo."

From a stream of broken English, Tommy was able to piece it together. Edo had finished paying for the dowries of all six of his sisters, and preparations had been made for his own bride to come to America. Now, with war ready to break out, his bride could not leave Slovenia. All the ships had been commandeered to prepare for war.

"That's terrible, Edo," Tommy said, still patting the man's shoulder. "But maybe there won't be a war. And if there is, it'll end soon, and then your bride will be able to come."

"She no come, she no come," Edo cried, slamming his fist into the wall until the plaster crumbled. "Nobody comin' no more from Europe—is end of ships bring people."

"If that's true, Edo," Tommy said, desperate to soothe the man, "then you can get yourself another bride. One from America. I mean, you never even met this girl you were supposed to marry. Your family picked her out, didn't they? So now you can choose someone yourself, a Slovenian girl that's already here."

Edo raised himself up on his elbows to glare balefully at Tommy. "Looka dis face," he said. "Black Edo. What girl gonna marry me if her family don't make her?"

Tommy had to drop his eyes. Edo's face was a terrible mess. The black coal dust that had been blown through his skin was mottled with red splotches from his drinking; his eyes were bloodshot; his nose dripped.

"Come on, get up," Tommy said, hoisting the man to his feet. "We'll go to mass and light a candle." He didn't know how that would help, but it seemed to mollify Edo, who staggered to his feet, hanging on to Tommy. "Wash your face first," Tommy told him, and to Mrs. Zagar, hovering in the doorway, he said, "Get some coffee."

Half dragging Edo through the streets, Tommy took him into the church, where they lit a candle beneath the picture of the Virgin Mary. Before mass was halfway over, Edo was asleep, stretched out in the back pew. Tommy explained to the priest what had happened, and Father Mike, a forgiving sort, agreed to let Edo stay there until he'd slept it off.

When Tommy got back home, he found Peter Connolly in the kitchen finishing breakfast while Fiona dressed to go to the next mass with him.

"I haven't been here all night," Peter said, "if that's what you're thinking. I just came to take your mother to church."

"I'm not thinking anything," Tommy said, "except . . . it looks like a war is really going to happen. Edo told me no more Slovenians can leave Europe now. Spaces on the ships are being given to Americans trying to get back home, but not to immigrants."

"So?" Only half interested, Peter mopped up the last of his eggs with a piece of bread.

"So it won't mean only Slovenians can't come here to the U.S. It'll mean other Slavs and Italians and Poles and Greeks—"

"So what's your point?"

"Mr. Farnham thinks"—just saying the name gave Tommy a pang in his chest—"a war will cause a huge demand for coal.

To make steel and other metals for armaments. That means the coal mines will be working full blast."

Tommy pulled up a kitchen chair and straddled it, back to front. "Every time the union has gone on strike for higher wages, the owners have brought in immigrants from Europe as strikebreakers. So the strikes usually failed."

Peter began to look interested.

"When the war starts, immigrant laborers won't be able to get here. For as long as the war lasts, all ocean shipping will be just for the military. That means, if the union goes on strike—"

"The mine owners will be stuck," Peter finished. "No strikebreakers. Good thinking, Tommy. I'm glad to see you taking an interest in union matters."

Why not, Tommy thought. Ellis Farnham and the other mine owners were the enemy now.

"I'll go talk it up to some of the other men," Peter was saying. "But maybe there won't be a war."

"From what I've been reading in the newspapers," Tommy said, "there's going to be."

There was. Two days later Austria declared war on Serbia. Four days after that, Germany declared war on Russia. Within the next three days England, France, and Belgium had joined the conflict, and the price of Castle Gate coal began to climb.

# PART FOUR

# Murderer or Martyr

# CHAPTER FIFTEEN
## 1915

Tommy's world had changed, all right. No more eight-hour days. Because the war machine in Europe needed American steel, and steel mills needed coal, he'd begun to work ten and twelve hours a day. Miners' wages had risen without even the threat of a strike. His mother had bought another washing machine and hired another girl. Tommy had quit singing in saloons, and even at parties. He was too tired, he didn't need the money, and his heart was no longer in his music. As his muscles hardened from the intensive labor his heart was hardening too.

Over the Christmas weekend Black Edo had invited him to a dance at the Slovenian Hall. All evening long Tommy had danced with Jana Zagar. She was pretty, she was sweet, pleasant, and a good dancer, and she seemed to like him. When the evening ended, Tommy had been glad to leave the hall—alone. Nice as she was, he had no interest in Jana Zagar or any other girl.

On New Year's Day Tommy opened the door to find Eugenie standing on his doorstep, her hair and eyelashes speckled with flakes of falling snow. For a long moment they looked at each other, saying nothing, until Fiona called out, "Who is it, Tommy?"

"It's Eugenie Farnham, Mom."

"Well, for heaven's sake invite her in and close the door. You're chilling the whole house." Fiona came forward, all smiles, offering her rough, chapped hands to Eugenie's gloved ones. "How nice to see you, Miss Farnham. Please take off your wraps and warm yourself at the stove. Would you have a cup of tea? You will, won't you?"

"I can't stay. I just brought this book for Tommy," Eugenie answered, handing him a package wrapped in brown paper. Her cheeks were flushed from the cold, and her eyes looked too bright as she unwound a scarf from around her head. "My brother Glenn sent it for you, Tommy," she told him.

Awkwardly he took it from her hands and undid the wrapping. Inside was a beautiful volume with gilt edges on the pages. *The Oxford Book of English Verse.* "Why—?" he began, but Eugenie broke in, speaking to Fiona, "Glenn sent all his books home. He wanted that one especially to go to Tommy, because he thinks Tommy is so clever as a writer of lyrics, and lyrics are very much like poetry." The way she was speaking to Fiona, she didn't sound at all like Eugenie, but like some stiff, elegant parody of the girl Tommy knew. "You see, Mrs. Quinlan, my brother has left Oxford to join the British army."

"Oh, my dear," Fiona said, sounding unlike herself too. The two women were behaving as if they were characters on a stage, very properly reciting the lines expected of them. "That must worry your poor mother a great deal."

For a moment Eugenie's guard slipped. "Yes, it does," she said, her voice low. Then she smiled, held out her hand again, and said, "I must be going."

"Tommy!" Fiona ordered. "Put on your coat and muffler and walk Miss Farnham home."

"That won't be necessary," Eugenie said.

"Of course it is! It's dark out there. Tommy, hurry! Don't make Miss Farnham wait."

Eugenie kept her eyes cast down as Tommy shrugged into his overcoat. "Take Miss Farnham's arm," Fiona instructed him. "There's snow on the porch and it might be slippery. Good night, Miss Farnham. When you write your brother, please thank him for his thoughtfulness."

As soon as they got into the street, Tommy dropped Eugenie's arm. Both of them stared straight ahead as they walked. In a low voice Eugenie asked, "Why didn't you come that night last summer? Why haven't you written? Or telephoned? I'd have met you wherever you said."

His jaw worked before he answered, "The empress Eugenie should find herself a prince, at least. Not a serf who burrows underground shoveling coal."

She stopped dead. "Oh, Tommy, that's cruel. I don't deserve that."

"So, what made Glenn send me that book? Don't try to kid me that he thinks I'm a poet. That's your idea, isn't it, to turn me into something respectable?"

"Tommy!"

"Face it—*I* don't deserve *you*, Eugenie. The price of coal keeps going up, so you're a lot richer now than you were just last summer. For sure you'll require some college-educated man with a future."

"I knew that was what it was!" she cried, her voice rising. "If only you'd listened, I said that was what my parents wanted for me, not what I wanted!"

"Eugenie, I don't think we should talk about this. I've had six months to get over you—"

"Have you?" she asked.

"Gotten over you? Yes," he lied. "How about you? How's college? Have you met any nice young men with bright futures?" He couldn't keep the bitterness out of his voice.

For a long time she stayed silent. Then she said, "I don't know you anymore, Tommy. Don't bother walking the rest of the way with me."

As he watched her disappear into the darkness, all the anguish he'd suppressed for all those months mutinied, mounting the barricades to break out in the first tears he'd cried in years. "Eugenie," he whispered. "I'm sorry." He stood rooted to the spot until the snow covered his boots up to the ankles. Then he went home to lie in bed with *The Oxford Book of English Verse* pressed against his cheek because her hands had touched it.

Everything in Tommy's world was black. He worked in the blackness of the mines from the hours before dawn to the hours after sunset and emerged into the blackness of the night, even when the days grew longer at the vernal equinox. If there was a sun, it never shone on him. Winter faded into Easter Week, which was winter still, with a fresh fall of snow in the high mountains.

Working so many hours of overtime meant bigger pay-days, yet each week Tommy handed the money to his mother without counting it. He had no use for it. At night he trudged home, shoulders and back aching, interested in nothing except a bath, supper, and the latest edition of the *Denver Post*. He read that the Germans had pushed back the British and French at a town in Belgium called Ypres. How the devil did you pronounce a word like *Ypres*? he wondered. *Why-press*? *Yippers*? Eugenie would know. Anyway, according to the paper, at Ypres the Germans were using a deadly new weapon called chlorine gas against the British and French troops. As soon as they breathed the gas, the paper said, the soldiers died and turned black.

Tommy shuddered. Maybe some things were worse than being eighteen years old and shoveling coal for long hours in a mine—like being eighteen years old and dying from poison gas in a place you couldn't pronounce. At least when Tommy turned black from coal dust, it washed off.

The day after Easter he worked with Peter at the dark end of a tunnel that led to a seam nearly mined out. More and more Peter had trained Tommy to do the job of a real miner, not just a laborer. There were certain things, though, that Peter did himself, things that could be dangerous if done incorrectly, like tapping the roof of the seam with the pick handle, listening closely to the sound it made to make sure the roof was solid. On that Easter Monday he let Tommy undercut the coal, which meant Tommy used a pick to take out a long slice at the bottom of the seam so the coal would break clean when the dynamite blew it off.

"You can drill the hole too, if you want," Peter told him.

Using the long pole with a drill at the end, Tommy reamed deep into the coal seam, then scraped out the dust from the hole he'd made. Meanwhile, Peter had rolled a piece of newspaper around a two-inch-thick rod to make a cylinder. While Tommy finished the hole, Peter bent one end of the paper tube to close it tight and then pulled out the rod. Covering the bottom of the cylinder with black powder he poured from a keg, Peter put in a long fuse, filled the tube the rest of the way with more black powder, and tamped this handmade stick of dynamite into the hole Tommy had drilled.

"All right, get out of the way. I'm going to light it," Peter said.

It was the same routine they followed every day: undercut the seam, fill a paper tube with black powder and a fuse, tamp it into the drill hole, and light the fuse. Blasting was always done at the end of the shift so that the coal dust could clear away by the following morning.

The blast seemed ordinary—it knocked maybe half a ton of coal off the walls of the seam and down to the tunnel floor. Suddenly Tommy heard a sound that scared him—a sharp *crack* unlike the normal crash of falling coal, followed by a roar. Everything went dark except for the carbide lamp on Tommy's miner's cap. The tunnel's electric lights had gone out.

"What happened?" he yelled, but he knew. A rockfall! Part of the roof had broken loose and collapsed, filling the tunnel with tons of heavy sandstone from the ground above the coal seam.

At first he couldn't tell how bad it was, because dust from the coal blast had already filled the tunnel before the rockfall sent more dust billowing all around. He choked and gasped for breath. The dim light from his miner's cap wasn't anywhere near powerful enough to penetrate the dust. "Peter, are all you all right?" he shouted, but there was no answer.

"Peter, where are you?"

In the silence he could hear smaller rocks and pebbles still dropping, settling onto the floor of the tunnel.

"Peter! Can you hear me?"

After the coal dust and rock dust began to settle, he could

see Peter—or the part of him that wasn't buried. "Peter," he yelled, "talk to me!"

No response. From the chest down Peter lay buried under huge chunks of rock. Was he dead? Crying, "God, God, God, God, God," Tommy began pulling away the chunks of rock from Peter's chest because he knew a weight like that could crush a man's lungs. Black Edo rushed up then, and both of them frantically yanked away as many rocks as they could lift with their bare hands, pulling them off Peter's chest first because the massive chunks of debris on his legs were too huge to worry about until later. Lungs and heart first—that mattered most.

Bending close to check whether any breath was coming from Peter's open lips, Tommy cried, "Peter, can you hear me?" Still no answer, but at least Peter was breathing, although so shallowly it frightened Tommy into furious action.

To free Peter, he grabbed a pick and swung it against the rocks pinning Peter's legs. The only way to remove slabs that size was to break them up. Starting with the massive chunks heaped on Peter's left leg, knowing he had to be careful not to impale Peter with the point of the pick, Tommy swung with all his strength again and again until the huge slabs began to crack and crumble. "I help you," Edo said, but Tommy shouted, "No, I'll do this. You go for the doctor. And send in an empty coal car so we can get him out."

In a frenzy Tommy smashed rocks with his pick until he was able to clear enough debris to free the lower part of Peter's body. Peter's left leg lay twisted, flattened, and so bloody that Tommy couldn't bear to look at it. He told himself it might not seem as bad under better light. But by then other miners had arrived, carrying carbide lanterns, and when *they* got a look at Peter's mangled leg, they shook their heads.

The company doctor hurried toward them. Taking one brief glance, he told them, "We've got to bring him out fast and get him to the hospital." Once the men had loaded Peter into one of the coal cars, they pushed and pulled together to roll it to the mine portal, where the company ambulance was waiting.

"I'm going with him," Tommy insisted after they laid Peter, still unconscious, into the back of the ambulance. As the motor started, Tommy was ashamed of himself for thinking that he was finally getting a ride—maybe not in a real automobile, but in something pretty close to it.

Bad news spread fast in a coal town. By the time they reached the hospital, Fiona was there waiting. She rushed to Peter and would have taken his cold hand, but the doctor pushed her away. "Let me do my job," he said, and wheeled the stretcher into the room where he performed operations.

"Are *you* all right?" Fiona asked Tommy.

"I wasn't that close to the rockfall," he told her. "It was Peter who was right underneath it. I don't know what happened, Mom! He tested the roof for sound like he always does. I heard it myself. It sounded solid. You never know, though—the men said no one can be sure how rock-solid surfaces might get split from freezing and thawing. They said things like that just happen, and there's no way to know when or why. . . ." He was babbling, trying to assure himself that he wasn't in any way responsible for the rockfall that hurt Peter. Trying not to imagine what was going on inside the operating room.

Hours passed before they were allowed to see Peter. Almost as pale as the sheets, he lay on the narrow hospital bed with his left leg—what remained of it—propped on pillows beneath the bedspread. Barely conscious, fighting the effects of the chloroform the doctor had used on him, he raised his hand. Fiona grasped it in hers.

"One thing is lucky, Peter," she murmured to him.

"What?" His lips shaped the word, hardly audible.

"Easter was yesterday, which means Lent is over."

"So?" Even in his drugged state Peter realized he'd missed her meaning.

"So we won't have to wait six whole weeks to get married."

"Married?" It was Tommy who spoke it aloud.

"My leg . . . ," Peter said. "Gone."

"Just below the knee, love," Fiona told him. "Just enough to keep you from working in the coal mine. I said I would never marry another miner, and now you'll never be a miner again. So I'll marry you. If you still want me."

Overhearing that, the doctor took Fiona aside. "Can you stay beside him tonight?" he asked. "So much of his tissue was crushed that he may go into shock. If he lives through the night, we still have to worry about infection. But I've seen many a man pull through a crisis when the woman he loves is beside him."

"I'll stay," she said.

Not just that night, but every night, Fiona sat at Peter's bedside, holding his hand and talking to him. "I've asked the priest to announce the bans of matrimony on the next three Sundays," she told him. "After that we can be married at once. So you need to hurry and get well, Peter."

It was one of the times when Tommy was visiting that Peter muttered, "All these years when I was a whole man, Fiona, you wouldn't have me. And now that I'm crippled, you want to marry me. Out of pity, is it?"

"You're still a whole man, Peter," she told him. "Missing a left foot—that's nothing! Everything that matters is still there." Glancing up at Tommy, blushing a little, she said, "I meant his kind heart. That's what really matters."

On another evening Black Edo came to the hospital to visit. After frowning at the flat part of the sheets where Peter's left leg and foot should have been, Edo began, "That day . . . I get so scared, Peter, I dunno what to do. But Tommy—you shoulda seen that Tommy. He grab a pick and bust them rocks, you shoulda seen—*bam, bam, bam*—bust 'em all up, what a rockbuster! I never seen anyting like him. Bust all them damn rocks—"

Peter smiled. "He's a real champ. And we're going to be related now, this rockbuster and me. Right, Tom?"

Tommy gave Peter a gentle, affirmative tap on the shoulder, wondering what he'd be expected to call him now. Dad? No. Not after all these years. He'd still be Peter.

On one of the rare occasions when Tommy was alone with Peter in the hospital, he built up his courage to ask, "Peter, was that rockfall my fault?"

"*Your* fault! How could it be?"

"When I drilled the hole for the dynamite . . ."

"You did everything right, Tommy. It was just one of those freak accidents that happen in mining."

Tommy said, "I figured I'd done something wrong. If you'd died, Peter, then I would have . . . I would have . . ."

"You'd have what?"

"I would have been guilty of two murders."

Peter raised himself on one elbow and then, grimacing with pain, fell back again against the pillows. "You'd better explain that, Tommy."

Haltingly, stopping every few words because it was so hard to talk about, Tommy told Peter how he'd betrayed Uncle Jim on the train to Boise. "I said, 'He's not Jimmy Mack. He's my uncle, James McInerny.' So then they knew."

"Tommy, Tommy . . ." Peter reached to take his hand. "It didn't matter what you said. Those Pinkertons already knew. Jim's picture was on file in every Pinkerton office across the country. Why do you think he came to Castle Gate?"

Tommy answered, "To take care of me and my mother."

"That, sure, but there was more to it. Jim was on the lam because of some . . . uh . . . unpleasant business in the Pennsylvania coalfields. They called him Jimmy Mack back then, but all the Pinkertons knew his real name was James McInerny. They didn't need you to tell them that. They'd already recognized him from his picture."

"Are you sure?" Tommy asked, almost reluctant to believe Peter.

"You bet I'm sure. You didn't betray Jim—you've got to get any crazy ideas like that out of your head. I'd kick them out of you myself, except I won't be doing much kicking anymore. However"—Peter grinned—"even if I'm not alive and *kicking,* I'm *alive!* And that's all due to you, rockbuster. You're a hero."

Tommy gripped Peter's hand hard. "That's not really true."

"It's true, all right. You started being a hero when you were ten. Think what you did, Tommy! All alone, in a strange town, you managed to find Bill Haywood and deliver that cash. Any other kid would have crumpled up and fallen apart. But you—you were amazing! You've got great stuff inside you."

Tommy had to bite his lip hard. He still didn't believe Peter, but the praise came at a time when he was tormented with self-doubt over Eugenie.

Even so, it took a while for the guilt to wear away, since it had been so much a part of him for so long. At home he kept checking himself in the mirror to see if he looked any different. Outwardly he was the same Tommy, but inside, the soul-draining darkness began to lessen. He stood a little taller, talked a little oftener to the other workers in the mine, smiled a little more.

When Peter was discharged from the hospital, Fiona wanted to bring him straight home with her, but to make things proper, they stopped at the church on the way. The wedding mass was kept brief because Peter couldn't manage to stand and then kneel on his new artificial leg. It would take time, the doctor said, for him to learn to use it.

Afterward friends crowded the Quinlans' kitchen, bringing food and good wishes. Though now that Fiona was no longer a Quinlan, Tommy supposed it should be called the Connollys' kitchen. Peter's good union buddies came, and of course Tommy couldn't say no when Peter asked him to sing and play union songs. It was the first time he'd picked up his guitar in months. "Let's raise a glass to Joe Hill, rotting in the Utah State Pen," Peter cried. "Sing some Joe Hill songs, Tommy."

Too many changes were hitting him at once: Peter's insistence that Tommy was blameless in Jim's death; Peter's presence in the house twenty-four hours a day; Fiona's radiance—she sang while she was peeling potatoes and washing clothes; and the still unexpected sound of two voices and muffled laughter coming from his mother's bedroom. Tommy had to get used to hearing Peter thump around at night on his crutches because the phantom pain in his missing limb kept him awake. And each morning Peter was up and dressed and sitting at the breakfast table before Tommy left for work. Tommy couldn't have been fonder of Peter, yet he was beginning to feel like a stranger in his own mother's house.

About that time Peter's horse, Johnny Bull, went lame and had to be put out to pasture. Peter gave a rancher his sleigh and the cart in return for providing pasture for the horse.

"Funny thing about me and old Johnny Bull," Peter mused. "All those years we were a team. Then I went gimpy in the leg, and he did too. Same leg, left hindquarter. Think he did it on purpose, out of sympathy?"

"Could have. Now maybe he'll find himself a filly, like you did," Fiona answered, laughing.

"I only hope he's that lucky," Peter replied.

One evening in June, when Tommy returned home before the sun had set, he found Peter sitting on the porch. Peter looked up at him, smiled, and said, "Sit down for a minute, Tommy. I've got news for you."

*Oh, God, no,* Tommy thought. He remembered that conversation he'd overheard a year ago, when Fiona had said she didn't want another baby. What if the news was that she was pregnant? For sure Tommy would move out of the house then. Cautiously he asked, "What news?"

"Fella from the IWW came to see me today. It was you he really wanted to talk to, but I told him you'd probably be working late like you usually do, and he had to get back to Salt Lake City to Wobbly headquarters."

"He wanted me?" Tommy was surprised. "What did he want me for?"

"He said Joe Hill is asking to see you."

"*What!*" There had to be some mistake. Joe Hill didn't even know Tommy existed.

"That's the message," Peter said. "On your next day off you're supposed to go to the Utah State Penitentiary to visit Joe Hill."

"Why?"

"Dunno. The fella didn't tell me that. I guess you'll find out when you get there."

# CHAPTER SIXTEEN
## July 4, 1915

Because of stepped-up production in the mine Tommy didn't get a day off until the Fourth of July, a day when he was anxious to get out of Castle Gate. Memories of last year's Fourth of July still pained him.

There was no need to dress up to visit a prisoner in the penitentiary, he figured. Dark pants and a white shirt with rolled-up sleeves ought to be good enough. After arriving at Salt Lake City's Union Pacific station, he took a streetcar to the section of town called Sugarhouse, an ironic name for the location of a penitentiary.

Following a guard down the long corridor in the cell block, Tommy glanced from side to side into the different cells he passed. Men with cold, angry eyes, or with desperate, pleading eyes, or with deadened eyes that showed no spark of curiosity about him, watched him pass. Joe Hill's cell was at the end of the row.

It was small and austere—nothing but a narrow bunk, a stand holding a pitcher and a washbasin, and a writing table covered with papers and stubs of pencils. The guard unlocked the cell door and then locked it again behind Tommy.

There he was. Joe Hill. Standing only two feet in front of Tommy. Whether or not the trial had been a fair one, this was a man convicted of murder.

"I'm Thomas Quinlan," he said. "I heard you wanted me to come here."

"Oh, yeah. You're the singing coal miner, right?" Joe Hill's eyes, the most intense and piercing blue eyes Tommy had ever seen in a man, looked him over. "Have a seat. They haven't given me a lot of furniture in this suite, but you can have the chair and I'll sit on the bunk. Did you bring your guitar?"

"No. I didn't know I was supposed to."

"Never mind. You can use mine. They let me keep it with me, and that's good, because I'm writing new music."

What all this was leading up to, Tommy couldn't imagine. The wooden chair scraped on the concrete floor as he sat down, stiff as the chair itself. Joe Hill kept staring at him, and Tommy glanced back, finally getting a good look at this famous criminal—or victim, whichever a person believed him to be.

He was thinner than Tommy remembered, but then, Tommy hadn't been able to see him too clearly on that last day of the trial. The clothes Joe Hill wore were rough and not too clean, the shirt unbuttoned at the collar, the pants baggy, the shoes splitting on one of the soles. A bluish shadow of unshaven stubble lined his jaw, which in another man would have been called firm, but in Joe Hill's face seemed overpowered by the broad, prominent cheekbones. Or maybe the cheekbones looked so pronounced because the cheeks beneath were sunken. Sunken and sallow—he'd lived in a cell for a year and a half now. But it was the eyes, those penetrating eyes, that commanded attention.

The voice was surprisingly mild. "I saw you at my trial the day they said I was guilty. You surprised I'm still alive?"

"No. I've been following it in the newspaper." The appeal to the Utah Supreme Court for a new trial had taken up a lot of time, but in the end it was denied.

Now the voice became more forceful. "I'm not afraid of death, but I'd like to be in the fight a little longer. Pretty soon the lawyers are going to ask the board of pardons to change my sentence to life imprisonment. I suppose if I beg real nice, they'll give me life. But I'll tell you what, Tommy, I'd rather be buried dead than buried alive in this smelly little cell. I don't want my death sentence commuted if it means I have to stay in prison. What I really want is a new, fair trial."

Tommy tried to speak, but the presence of this man who so calmly faced death by firing squad disconcerted him. He had to clear his throat and begin again. "Why am I here? Why did you want to see me?"

"Because I want you to take my place."

It sounded so preposterous that Tommy didn't know how to answer.

"Look," Joe Hill said, leaning forward, his arms resting on his knees. "They said they'll let me go if I tell them who shot me. Well, I'm not going to tell. So they're not going to let me go. I'll be stood up in front of the firing squad, and that's all right, as long as they don't bury me in this state. I wouldn't want to be caught dead here." He laughed a little.

How could a man joke like that about his own death? Tommy squirmed, feeling the uncomfortable chair press against his backbone.

"I've been useful to the IWW," Joe continued. "You know, Tommy, an awful lot of our members don't speak or understand English, but they sure learn to sing my songs. You ought to hear 'em at a rally. They sing loud, they sing proud, and they're unified! And I make that happen. With my songs!"

Songs! Tommy began to get a glimmer of a connection.

"I'm gonna be executed, I don't kid myself about that. After I'm dead, the One Big Union will need someone who can do what I do. You, Tommy. You're young, you're handsome, you're a miner and a musician. Lots of fellows told me how you make up parodies that sound almost as good as mine. Here"—he walked a few steps to where his guitar leaned against the cell wall—"give us a sample."

"I—I don't sing much anymore," Tommy stammered.

"Why not? Too busy working? Or could it be woman trouble?"

Why would Joe Hill ask that—about woman trouble? When Tommy hesitated, Joe chuckled and said, "Handsome fella like you, I figured there might be a woman behind it. There's nothin' that'll dry up a man's vocal chords quicker'n a woman. In fact, as you probably know, it was woman trouble that landed me here in the slammer."

Joe leaned forward to stare at Tommy with those disconcerting blue eyes. "But Tommy, you got something a lot more important to think about than women. You got working men and women who need songs to sing—not just here in the U.S., but all over the world. Do you know they sing my songs in South America? Australia too. Plus all of Europe and especially Russia."

"I don't think I can do . . . what you want me to do." How could Tommy tell this man who was probably going to be executed, that to Tommy the union just didn't matter all that much?

"Sure you can. Go ahead and sing for me, Tommy. Oh, yeah, we'll change your name. See, my real name is Joel Hagglund, but it got, uh . . . transmuted to Joseph Hillstrom, and then Joe Hill. Joe Hill—short and snappy, a name people remember. They tell me you're nephew to Jimmy Mack, the union man the Pinkertons butchered. So your new name will be Tommy Mack. Short, snappy, easy to remember. Now, sing for me, Tommy Mack. Make up a song."

Tommy felt as if he were the one being backed against a wall in front of a firing squad. He fingered Joe Hill's guitar; it was in tune. His mind raced, trying to think of something to sing about. Looking around the cell, he began,

"In Salt Lake City there's no salt of the earth;
   There's nothing sweet about the Sugarhouse Jail.
   Tears will taste bitter, and salty, not sweet,
   If the struggle to save Joe Hill should fail—"

"No, no, no," Joe interrupted. "That sounds like a dirge. A song's gotta have punch! Gotta make a man want to get up and march. March with all the other workers. Gimme that thing."

He took back the guitar and strummed a few chords. "This is one of mine. The workers love it.

"Join the union, fellow workers,
   Men and women side by side;
   We will crush the greedy shirkers
   Like a sweeping, surging tide;

> For united we are standing
> But divided we will fall;
> Let this be our understanding—
> 'All for one and one for all.'"

"You get it, Tommy? Punchy! Lots of heart and soul. Now, make up another parody for me. Write fresh words, but use a song people already know, like 'The Old Gray Mare.'"

"Look, uh . . ." Tommy wanted out of there. He didn't enjoy being railroaded into something he wasn't sure he believed in, didn't like this condemned man demanding Tommy's life to replace his own. But he wasn't sure how to say no. He muttered, "I need to go somewhere and get something to eat, so I can think better."

"Yeah, well, I'd offer you prison food, but all we get is beans. Eat enough of those, you get what I call beanisitis."

Those piercing blue eyes cut right into Tommy, peeled him apart all the way down to his unspoken refusal.

"Hey, I'll come back," Tommy promised. "Maybe not today . . . because I have to think. . . ."

"Take your time," Joe said. "I'm not due to be executed for a couple of weeks at least."

Tommy banged on the cell door. It seemed to take forever for the guard to come and let him out. It wasn't true that he wanted to eat; in fact, his stomach felt so queasy he was afraid he might vomit. The smells; the terrible clanking as the cell door closed, freeing Tommy but keeping Joe Hill locked up; the hostile stares of the other prisoners; the contemptuous look of the guard—when Tommy got outside, he gulped air to try to get the imagined pestilence out of his lungs.

On the streetcar going back toward the center of the city

he saw happy families waving American flags, kids running around throwing firecrackers into the bushes, dogs yelping and cowering away from each minor explosion, little girls giggling and running away from the little boys. It was a beautiful day, the second Fourth of July in a row that had turned into misery for Tommy.

And it was a Sunday. He was too late to find a Mass being said in any Catholic church, but maybe he could at least slip into the Cathedral of the Madeleine and kneel for a while, since his thoughts were too disturbed for prayer.

Into his life had come yet another person pushing Tommy to be something he didn't want to be. Tommy just couldn't get worked up over union causes—never had. Maybe it was because for years he'd heard his mother ranting against the union, which she blamed for Jim's death.

Funny, during those same years Tommy had been blaming himself for Jim's death. Now he was starting to see that if anyone deserved blame for the death, it was Jim himself. Not only had he been reckless with his own life, he'd taken a ten-year-old on a way too dangerous venture.

Tommy stood in the gloom at the back of the cathedral, letting his eyes adjust to the colored light streaming through the stained-glass windows. Not more then a dozen people knelt in the pews; they were scattered here and there throughout the vastness of the cathedral. Above, in the choir loft, an organist played music Tommy didn't know—not happy music, but a . . . dirge. He guessed that was the right word for it, since it was the word Joe Hill had used.

Moving to the emptiest part of the church, he knelt with his elbows on the pew in front of him, his bowed head in his hands. Every inch of him opposed what Joe Hill wanted him to do, yet was it right to refuse a man who was about to be shot for a crime he swore he didn't commit? The doleful organ music swelled, matching Tommy's unease.

With his eyes tightly shut, he was unaware that someone had slipped in beside him in the pew. Until she spoke. "I come here every Sunday to hear the music. He's playing Mozart's Requiem."

For a long moment Tommy lacked the will to raise his head. When he did, it was to say, "How could this happen, Eugenie? That we'd meet, here, today—"

"The Fourth of July," she finished. "One year afterward."

"Why aren't you home with your parents?"

"They're in Washington. Trying to influence the British ambassador to have Glenn pulled back from Ypres into a safer job with the war ministry."

*EE-pra.* So that was how it was pronounced. Except he'd never be able to say the *R* the way she did.

"I'm taking summer makeup classes because I'm not studying music anymore."

He slid back into the pew, turning to face her. "I don't play music anymore either. But I like what's coming from that organ. It matches the way I feel right now." The requiem had grown louder, foreboding.

"I stopped studying music because I've decided to become a social worker, to work with poor children."

"Oh." As the Mozart swelled, Tommy asked her without anger, "Have you found the right kind of man yet?"

"No." She looked down at her twisted fingers. "I can't. I keep remembering you, Tommy. And when I remember you, the university students all seem like they're made of cardboard. You're the only man who's real to me."

"Oh, God," he whispered, and it was a prayer of thanksgiving. In awe he studied her. Dressed in a pale cotton blouse and skirt, her hair piled high beneath a summer straw hat, she looked more beautiful than ever. No longer girlish, but womanly. Without thought, operating only on emotion, Tommy pulled her by the hand out of the pew and into the aisle. Still holding her hand, he crossed the church to a confessional, where he opened the door and drew her inside, closing the door behind them.

The confession box was so narrow they were crushed together. Arms wrapped around each other, bodies melting, their hungry kisses mingled with their tears, mingled with their whispers—"I'm sorry . . . never again . . . my fault . . . love you so much . . ."—until the words became so intertwined they hardly knew which one spoke them.

Suddenly the door of the confessional was flung open by a startled assistant pastor, whose astonishment immediately turned to outrage. "Shameful!" he hissed. "This is God's house."

Hand in hand Tommy and Eugenie ran the length of the aisle, bursting through the heavy doors and into the sunshine, skipping down the stone steps, where they broke into gales of laughter. "Thank heavens he doesn't know who you are," Eugenie gasped. "You'd be excommunicated!"

They went to their favorite spot, the small green park across from the City and County Building, where they talked for hours, their words punctuated by the chimes of the big clock across the street. After spilling out to each other everything that had happened to them during the past year, they suddenly realized they were hungry.

With all the overtime he'd been working, Tommy could afford to take his girl to dinner in a good hotel. Over a nice meal at the Hotel Utah—where the maître d' insisted on lending him a jacket and a necktie—Tommy told Eugenie about his visit to Joe Hill, and what Joe wanted of him. Eugenie listened intently but said nothing.

After dinner, while the western sky flooded with the gaudy colors of a mountain sunset, they walked the thirteen city blocks to the University of Utah. "I live in a sorority house," Eugenie explained. "Hardly any of the girls are there now because it's summer vacation, but the housemother's still with us. And no men are allowed past the front door."

They lingered on the sidewalk, not willing to say good night. "What about the front porch?" Tommy asked. "Are men allowed on the front-porch swing?"

"Let's find out," Eugenie answered.

For a while they rocked on the swing, until Eugenie murmured, "It's getting dark. I've never seen fireworks in Salt Lake City, but I bet they're better than Castle Gate's."

"We won't be able to see much from this porch," Tommy told her. The street was lined with tall houses, side by side, with gables and dormer windows shadowing black against the growing darkness, and with full-blown maple trees in a row along the curb.

"We could walk up into the hills behind the university," she suggested. "The view there should be wonderful. Wait right here."

In a moment she was back with a blanket folded over her arm. "Good thing the housemother didn't see me," she whispered, "or she'd have asked what I was up to. Come on. Let's go."

The climb up a narrow footpath was steep, but the higher they went, the greater the view they had of the Salt Lake valley beneath them. Streetlights came on. The windows of houses blinked with paler light, and far to the northwest they could see the lights of Saltair. Tommy had been carrying the blanket; he spread it on the ground just as the first of the fireworks exploded over their heads.

Both of them were quiet, both remembering the night exactly a year ago that had started just like this but had ended so badly. "Nothing has really changed, has it?" Tommy murmured. "Except that we're a year older. You're still the mine owner's daughter, I'm still a coal miner."

"This much has changed—I never want to lose you again," Eugenie told him.

"Remember that time your father came home and found me with you? And you lied. You told him I'd just come to pick up some sheet music."

"I remember."

"You were afraid—or ashamed—to tell him I'd come to see you. Would it be any different now? Could I come calling on you in your home? Or would I still be unwelcome?"

She was silent for a long time. Then she answered, "I don't know. I don't know what would happen. We could try, if you want to."

"But wait a minute," Tommy said, pressing the issue. "What if I do what Joe Hill wants me to and become a singing, song-writing troubadour for the Industrial Workers of the World? If I decided to do that, and I came to your house to see you—what then?"

Eugenie just shook her head.

"Your father would throw me out bodily, wouldn't he, if I wrote songs for the union. And then maybe he'd throw my mother out of her house—she owns the house, but the coal company owns the land it's on."

Hotly, Eugenie answered, "My father wouldn't do that!

He's a decent man, and he's always fair. You're making him sound like some kind of tyrant, and he's not!"

Gently pulling her down beside him on the blanket, Tommy said, "I just want you to realize that nothing's been solved. We're really no different than we were last Fourth of July. Nothing has improved for us in this whole awful year."

"But something *did* happen today," Eugenie said. "Joe Hill asked you to write songs for the union, Tommy. He sees the same talent in you that I see." She traced her fingers across his roughened hand and asked, "Why can't you use that talent to write poetry instead?"

"Eugenie—"

"No, wait. In literature class we studied Carl Sandburg. He writes wonderful poems about the common people, the working class. You could do that. You know what it's like to work with these hands of yours, to labor in the mines."

Tommy rolled over and sighed. "Joe Hill wants me to be Tommy Mack, the songwriter. Peter wants me to be Tommy Quinlan, the union man. You want me to be Thomas Quinlan, the poet."

In a soft voice she asked, "And who do you want to be?"

"My own man." He didn't even have to think about the answer. "Tom Quinlan—rockbuster."

# CHAPTER SEVENTEEN
## Labor Day, 1915

"I got a message from IWW headquarters," Peter mentioned. "Joe Hill's wondering why he hasn't heard from you."

"Oh, Lord." Tommy was soaking in the tin bathtub he dragged into the kitchen every night after work. "When did I have time to get up there? I'm working every day."

"Well, Labor Day will be here in a few days," Peter said. "You'll have time off then."

Tommy sighed. "All right. I'll go."

Labor Day was sacred to the workingman. No matter how desperately the nation's industries needed coal to fuel the war machines, Labor Day belonged to the miners. And to the steelworkers, to the men who laid track for the railroads, to the women who ran machines in the factories, to the dockworkers who hoisted heavy cargoes onto transport ships heading for war, and to every other man and woman who toiled and sweated for wages.

It was a day they stayed away from work to honor their

own worth. But it didn't feel like a holiday to Tommy, obliged as he was to go and see Joe Hill.

This time when he walked down that long corridor in the cell block, he kept his eyes straight ahead. No looking at the other prisoners—that was too unsettling. When the cell door closed behind Tommy, Joe Hill glanced up at him and remarked, "You sure took a long time to get lunch. What was it—two months?"

"Sorry," Tommy muttered.

"Well, pull up the chair. As you can see, I'm still alive, but probably not for long. Now I'm scheduled to be executed on October first. But there's to be another hearing—before the board of pardons this time. In about ten more days."

Tommy expected to be asked whether he'd decided to be the new Wobbly songsmith, but Joe seemed in no hurry to bring it up. "You know, Tommy," he said, "from all over the world people are rallying to my cause. Thirty thousand union members in Australia got a boycott going against American products, and they'll keep it up till I'm released. Mail's pouring in, from every state and nation, to the Utah governor, begging, threatening, ranting—hell, some of the letters are even polite. They're all asking the governor to let me go. Even the Episcopal bishop of Salt Lake City sent a letter. I got a copy." Joe rifled through a stack of papers on his desk, found the letter, and announced, "From Bishop Paul Jones of Saint Mark's Episcopal Cathedral."

The church Eugenie went to. Tommy knew Saint Mark's, all right.

"Here's what the bish says. 'The infliction of the death penalty on Joseph Hillstrom'—blah, blah, blah—'will burden the conscience of Utah's administration of justice.'"

He threw back his head and gave a harsh laugh. "Conscience! What conscience? Justice! What a joke! I haven't seen a nickel's worth of justice since I hopped off the freight in this godforsaken city. The minute they found out I was a Wobbly, they figured I had to be guilty of *something*. And my lawyers!" His agitation growing, Joe stood up and began to pace the narrow cell: three strides toward the door, three strides back to the wall, which was as far as he could go in the confined space.

"My defense lawyers couldn't have defended a fish in a bait-swallowing trial. They were stupid. But the prosecutors were worse—they were vicious. Know what the head prosecutor said to the jury? He said I belong to the class of predator that would rather kill and rob than do honest work. Me! I've never killed anybody, and I've worked hard every day of my life since I was a boy!"

Collapsing onto the edge of the bunk, Joe shook his head at the injustice of it all. Tommy thought that either this man had to be innocent, or else he was a remarkable actor.

"I want you to hear what I'm going to say to that board of pardons next week, Tommy. You're a poet like me, so I'd like your opinion. I've written it down." Again he shuffled through the papers on the small table. Then in a clear, loud voice he read, "'I do not want my death sentence commuted to life imprisonment, and I am not clamoring for a pardon. I do, however, want a new trial—a fair trial. If I cannot have a new trial, I am willing to give my blood as a martyr so that others may be afforded fair trials.'" Joe fell back onto the bunk and stared up at the ceiling. "There, Tommy, what do you say? Think you could make up a song about that?"

How could Tommy answer? The words he'd just heard sounded obstinate, maybe self-pitying, and yet they were . . . noble! Joe Hill was ready to die to help the workers of the world. And Thomas Quinlan—what was *he* willing to do? Anything at all?

Joe rolled over then, lying on his side to face Tommy. "Last time you were here, you said you had woman trouble. And you're what—nineteen?"

"Eighteen."

"You got your whole life ahead of you, plenty of time to figure out women. Me, I've been a rolling stone that gathered no girls. But a woman named Elizabeth Gurley Flynn came to call on me in my cell a couple months ago. Like me, she's given her all to the union. If I'm allowed to live, I want to go find her. She's not only beautiful," Joe said, "she has the heart of a true union rebel." Sitting up again on the edge of the bed, he added, "After she left, I wrote a song about her."

He pulled out his guitar from under the bunk, tuned it for a little while, then began to pluck the strings and play chords. Instead of singing the lyrics, he recited them: "There are women of many descriptions; In this queer world, as everyone knows; Some are living in beautiful mansions; And are wearing the finest of clothes. . . ."

Tommy sucked in his breath.

"There are blue-blooded queens and princesses, . . ."

*Add empresses,* Tommy thought.

"Who have charms made of diamonds and pearl. But the only thoroughbred lady is . . . the Rebel Girl."

At the chorus, Joe began to sing:

"That's the Rebel Girl, that's the Rebel Girl,
To the Working class she's a precious pearl.

She brings courage, pride and joy
To the fighting Rebel Boy.
We've had girls before but we need some more
In the Industrial Workers of the World.
Yes it's great to fight for freedom
With a Rebel Girl."

When the song was over, Tommy commented, "Nice," in a low voice. He should have said more, but he couldn't find the right words, because the song had hit too close to home.

Joe Hill's sharp gaze cut into him. "So, how about your girl, Tommy? Is she a rebel?"

"In a lot of ways," he answered. But not all. Not enough. He and Eugenie had been meeting secretly on Saturday nights in the aspen grove behind the Farnhams' house. Not once had she suggested that Tommy come into her home to visit her. One evening when he'd cautiously brought it up, she'd said, "I can't cause my parents any more worry right now. They're tormented enough about Glenn being in the trenches near the river Marne. The Germans have started using mustard gas against the British troops, and that's a lot worse than chlorine gas."

"I thought your parents were getting him a desk job," Tommy said.

"They did. He wouldn't accept it."

After that, Tommy had never mentioned it again. Sneaking around to see Eugenie was better than never seeing her at all, he'd decided, but it still bothered him. It seemed that in a contest between what Tommy wanted and what Eugenie thought her father would want, her father always won. She kept telling Tommy she loved him, but she wouldn't stand up for him.

"You need to find a girl who's a true rebel, Tommy," Joe

told him. Just then the guard banged on the cell door. "Guess you gotta leave now," Joe said. "It's time for us jailbirds to eat our bean slop."

Tommy stood up to go, feeling both relief and reluctance. Nothing had been settled between him and Joe Hill. "I'll be back," he promised.

"In another two months?" Joe asked. "I won't be here."

"No. Before that. Next Sunday." If he was ordered to work overtime in the mine, he'd refuse.

Every day during the following week he put in extra hours. On Saturday night, after he'd finished his bath and put on his dark suit, getting ready to meet Eugenie, his mother told him, "You can't keep wearing that suit."

"Why not?"

"Look at it! It's too short for you. I can't let the pants down any farther, and the jacket is short too. Besides that, it's altogether out of style—it was the suit your father was supposed to be buried in back in 1900. Men's styles don't change as much as women's, but they do change over fifteen years, Tommy."

"You going to Salt Lake City tomorrow?" Peter asked him. "Here's twenty dollars. Go to a store and buy yourself a new, ready-made suit."

"I can't take your money," Tommy protested.

Peter and Fiona exchanged glances. His mother said, "Why don't you stay here for a few minutes and talk with us before you go out, Tommy? Wherever it is that you go on these Saturday evenings."

"He's a man now, Fiona," Peter said. "Don't pry."

"I didn't! I didn't pry," she cried, raising her hands as if to deny everything. "Anyway, can you sit down for a moment, Tommy? There's something we haven't told you. Peter, you do the telling."

Peter pushed his tea mug across the oilcloth, away from him, and settled his elbows on the table. "While I was still in the hospital," he began, "Mr. Farnham came to see me. In private. He said that because I'd lost a limb in the mines, I'd be given compensation."

"What could compensate a man for losing a leg?" Tommy asked, his bitterness over Ellis Farnham rising into his throat the way it always did.

"A year's wages, that's what," Peter answered. "Farnham got a record of what I'd earned in March, and multiplied it by twelve months. He gave me a check for the total."

Almost too stunned to speak, Tommy blurted, "Farnham did that? Of his own free will?"

"Well, I was in no condition to twist his arm," Peter answered. "Of course of his own free will."

"And out of the goodness of his heart," Fiona added.

Peter laughed a little. "Lucky thing your mother'd asked me to marry her before that, or I'd have figured she was marrying me for my money."

"Which he didn't tell me about until after the ceremony," Fiona added.

"Tommy, all this time when you've been handing over your pay to us, week after week," Peter said, "we've put most of it into the bank with that lump sum from Farnham. Trying to decide what to do. Expand the laundry business? Start some other business? Send you back to school?"

"I'm too old," Tommy muttered, still not believing that Ellis Farnham, the coldhearted capitalist, would donate a year's wages to an injured man.

"So since we've got a nice sum in the bank, and part of it's yours, I think all three of us can afford to buy you a new suit," Peter said. "One that fits."

"Will you go to a store tomorrow and find one?" Fiona asked.

Tommy considered. "I guess so." Eugenie never said anything about his too-short, out-of-style dead-man's suit, but if it ever happened that he could come calling on her at the Farnhams' house, it would be a point of pride for him to look decent.

Since it was owned by the Mormon Church, Salt Lake City's main department store, the Zion Co-operative Mercantile Institute, was not open on Sundays. But on a side street Tommy found a men's tailor shop that had a nice rack of suits.

"Tall fellow, aren't you?" the short, bald sales clerk commented. "A thirty-eight long will fit you, but when you get older, you'll probably gain a little weight. Most men do. Our suits are guaranteed to last for years, so you might want to take a forty long, and that'll give you growing room."

In Tommy's pocket was the twenty-dollar gold piece Peter had given him, plus an extra ten-dollar bill. The more he'd thought about Eugenie and her father, the more he'd wanted to own a really good-looking suit. *Someday*, he kept telling himself. *Someday I'll be invited into their house as a guest.*

"Try this one," the clerk said, holding up a dark gray suit coat with the barest suggestion of pinstripes. When Tommy caught his image in the mirror, he was startled.

This was the real Thomas Quinlan, not the ghost of any corpse. He looked good. He liked what he saw. What's more, he was starting to like the man he was finding inside himself, a man who was learning to think for himself and sort things out.

After that he tried on half a dozen other suits, but the clerk had a good eye—he'd picked the perfect one for Tommy on the first try. "Excellent fabric, excellent lines," the man said. "A steal at thirty dollars. Alterations free."

Tommy calculated. "How about if I take care of the alterations and you give me a good necktie instead." He'd worn the same necktie every time he needed one, and it belonged to Peter. Now he was ready to choose one for himself.

"You? You can do alterations?"

"No. My mother does."

"Is that right?" The clerk leaned back to stare up at Tommy. "Is she good at it?"

"The best."

"Would she like a job? Ask her to come in and talk to my boss. It's hard to find a good alterations person in Salt Lake City."

Tommy shook his head. "She lives in Castle Gate, and she has her own business there."

"Oh. Too bad."

Tommy made arrangements for the man to keep the suit until after he'd visited Joe Hill at the penitentiary. Walking back to Main Street, he caught sight of a departing streetcar and ran for it. The closer he got to Sugarhouse, the more he wrestled with what he was going to tell Joe Hill. He still hadn't decided.

If he promised to write songs for the Industrial Workers of the World—the One Big Union, as Joe called it—did that mean he was committed for the rest of his life? If he said yes, he'd undoubtedly lose his job as a coal miner. The mines meant hard work but the pay was pretty steady, while unions rarely rewarded the people who worked for them. Always broke, the unions were constantly raising money for one cause or another but never had enough to pay their officers.

Deep in his thoughts, Tommy didn't notice, at first, how crowded the streets had become around the penitentiary. When he got off the streetcar, he had to push his way through crowds of men and women waving placards. FREE JOE HILL, the placards read, and THE WORKERS' ARMY, and JUSTICE FOR LABORERS.

Then—he didn't know how or where it started—one of Joe Hill's songs broke out somewhere in the crowd, augmented by more and more voices until it rose in a full-throated anthem:

> "Arise, ye prisoners of starvation!
>   Fight for your own emancipation;
>   Arise, ye slaves of ev'ry nation,
>   In One Union Grand.
>   Our little ones for bread are crying;
>   And millions are from hunger dying;
>   The end the means is justifying,
>   'Tis . . . the final stand."

Caught in the crush of bodies, swept up in the human tide, Tommy felt electrified. He'd never heard anything like it—all those people, maybe a thousand of them in the street, singing together with such passion, waving their fists and shouting out the words. This was what Joe Hill had been trying to tell him! Music could move the masses. *Tommy's* music could move the masses, if he'd let it.

The song rose as if it had a life of its own. More than just words and music, this was conviction, yearning, dedication! Why hadn't Tommy learned the words to that song? He wanted to be a part of that spirited crowd, to feel a sense of brotherhood he'd never experienced before. It was powerful!

He hurried toward the towering walls of the penitentiary but stopped dead when he almost ran into a Pinkerton detective. He could tell it was a Pinkerton man; he could almost smell it. Other Pinkertons mingled in the crowd—so obvious Tommy didn't know how they could be called undercover agents.

As he got closer, he noticed armed soldiers cordoned around the penitentiary gate—men from the Utah National Guard, holding machine guns.

"I need to get inside," he told one of the guards. "I need to see Joe Hill."

"No one's allowed," answered the guard, who wasn't much older than Tommy. "Anyway, Joe Hill's in solitary confinement."

"Why?" Tommy asked, but the guard just said, "Get moving," and pushed Tommy with the stock of his machine gun.

A man standing nearby told Tommy, "You'll never get in to see Joe Hill."

"Who are you?"

"Sam Bowman, from the *Salt Lake Herald-Republican*. Didn't you notice what's happening in downtown Salt Lake? There're Pinkerton detectives and state militia on guard all around the Hotel Utah, the City and County Building, the State Capitol, and the Mormon Temple. The governor thinks the Wobblies are arriving here from all over. That part's true. But he's afraid they're going to break into jail and free Joe Hill, plus burn down the Mormon Temple or something. That won't happen, because Wobblies don't have any real leadership. They just kind of mill around and sing a lot."

The reporter sounded like he knew what he was talking about. "Anyway, I've got to get in there," Tommy said.

"Not a chance," the reporter answered. "I hear they've got guards all along the corridor outside Joe Hill's cell."

"Could I send him a note?"

"I tried that, but they're confiscating everything that goes through the door."

As Tommy moved away from the gate someone thrust a leaflet into his hands. THE PREAMBLE TO THE CONSTITUTION OF THE INDUSTRIAL WORKERS OF THE WORLD, it said. He began to read:

> The working class and the employing class have nothing in common. There can be no peace so long as hunger and want are found among millions of working people, and the few, who make up the employing class, have all the good things in life.
>
> Between these two classes a struggle must go on until the workers of the world organize as a class, take possession of the earth and the machinery of production, and abolish the wage system.

Agitated, Tommy dropped the leaflet, but the first line had burned itself into his brain: "The working class and the employing class have nothing in common." Rephrase it: "Tommy and Eugenie have nothing in common." *Give it up, stick with your own class, and help them the best you can,* the leaflet was saying.

*Dammit!* Tommy thought. *Why is it that the* workers *are the ones always harping about class?*

Unable to get to Joe Hill, he took the streetcar back to

the center of the city, picked up his new suit, and caught the train to Castle Gate.

From then on, on his way home from work each night he bought two newspapers, the *Denver Post* and the *Salt Lake Herald-Republican*. The reports went from bad to worse. Joe Hill raised a fuss at the hearing before the state board of pardons, claiming he'd be satisfied only with a new trial, where he was sure he'd be acquitted. Said he'd had lousy lawyers, so how could his trial have been fair? Said the whole justice system in Utah was a farce. He managed to antagonize everyone—lawyers, government officials, the members of the board of pardons. It was as though Joe courted execution; as though he were trying to become a martyr. Not surprisingly, the board turned down his appeal. His execution was still set for October 1.

"What's the matter with that man?" Peter asked. Even Peter, the staunch union supporter, couldn't figure out Joe Hill.

"I think he wants to die," Fiona said.

By then, tens of thousands worldwide were clamoring for Joe Hill's release. People sent telegrams to the Swedish ambassador, since Joe Hill was still a Swedish citizen. The ambassador contacted the president of the United States, Woodrow Wilson.

On September 30, one day before the execution, a death watch was placed over Joe Hill. Extra guards stood outside his cell. The prison blacksmith shop became hastily converted into quarters for the firing squad. And Joe Hill wrote his farewell letters.

As the hours of September 30 ticked away, Utah's governor received a telegram saying,

RESPECTFULLY ASK IF IT WOULD NOT BE POSSIBLE
TO POSTPONE EXECUTION OF JOSEPH HILLSTROM,
WHO I UNDERSTAND IS A SWEDISH SUBJECT, UNTIL THE
SWEDISH MINISTER HAS AN OPPORTUNITY TO PRESENT
HIS VIEW OF THE CASE TO YOUR EXCELLENCY THE
GOVERNOR.
WOODROW WILSON

That telegram, from President Wilson, won Joe Hill a reprieve until the board of pardons could consider the case once again. The next meeting of the board of pardons was set for October 16.

This roller coaster of fear and hope was having an effect on Tommy. The exhilaration he'd felt—those moments when the mob sang Joe Hill's song outside the penitentiary—had drained away, replaced by a growing resentment. Joe Hill was demanding that Tommy give up his own future, wanted him to fulfill an unfamiliar role Joe had created for him. To change his name, his good, honest name of Thomas Quinlan, and become Tommy Mack, someone Joe was trying to invent.

And yet Joe Hill wouldn't do anything to save his own skin.

The board of pardons had declared that if only Joe would admit who'd shot him on the night of the murders, and if his story could be proved, he'd be acquitted. Set free. But Joe refused to tell. "Why should I drag in a woman's name?" he asked. "Even if it would help, I have not the slightest intention or desire of going into that matter."

Tommy remembered the saints' stories he used to hear in catechism class, stories that were supposed to inspire little

Catholic boys and girls to lead good and holy lives. Too often, Tommy thought, the martyred saints had acted foolishly. Why didn't they save themselves, so they could keep on doing good in the world?

Why wouldn't Joe Hill save himself?

*This was the second time he'd ridden in a train with a corpse in a casket a few cars back in the baggage car. The first time was eight years earlier, when he'd brought Uncle Jim's body home from Idaho.*

*Death. Violent death. Mine explosions, beatings, executions. Plus wars and murders. But some people were lucky, like Peter, and escaped death. Like Tommy, who could have been under that same cave-in that cost Peter his leg, and maybe Tommy wouldn't have survived.*

*The saying was that not many miners grew old enough to have gray hair—they died from one thing or another before they reached middle age. Tommy wanted to live. He had the best reason in the world to live.*

*He took the telegram from the inside pocket of his suit and began writing lyrics on the back of it:* When fathers, sons, or brothers die . . .

# CHAPTER EIGHTEEN
### Firing Squad

Tommy could hardly wait to buy a newspaper after work on October 17. The headline read: HILLSTROM MUST DIE, PARDONS BOARD DECIDES; SWEDISH MINISTER'S APPEAL IS FRUITLESS. For the third time an execution date was set for Joe Hill. Now it was to be November 19.

"That man has more lives than a cat," Fiona declared that night. "I don't think he'll ever be executed."

Peter answered, "Even cats run out of lives sooner or later."

Tommy wasn't sure. As October turned into November the Joe Hill case stirred more and more controversy worldwide. Several lawyers across the U.S. volunteered to come to Salt Lake City to appeal for Joe Hill's life; Joe turned them down. A mammoth Joe Hill Protest Meeting was held in New York City. Even the famous blind and deaf woman Helen Keller sent a message to President Wilson, beseeching him "as official father of all the people, to use your great power and influence to save one of the nation's helpless sons."

Once again President Wilson telegrammed Utah's Governor

Spry, asking for "a thorough reconsideration of the case of Joseph Hillstrom." And once again Governor Spry refused, unless new "tangible facts" could be presented.

Tangible facts. Why didn't Joe tell where he'd gotten that wound? He just wouldn't. November wore away a day at a time, and now, it seemed, the cat really was running out of lives.

Although Tommy wanted to visit Joe Hill one last time, no visits to the condemned man were permitted. Somehow, on the night before the execution, Sam Bowman of the *Salt Lake Herald-Republican* managed to get inside the penitentiary to interview Joe. As Tommy read about it he could picture Sam Bowman, could almost hear Sam's voice describing it:

> "Hill stood and leaned against the door of his cell during the interview, resting his arms on one set of crossbars. A second set of crossbars, in front of the first, kept the visitor at a distance. Joe wore a dark blue shirt of coarse material, a coat made of overall material, dark blue pants and white canvas shoes. His hands, protruding through the bars, hung down in a relaxed manner." When Sam Bowman asked Joe why he didn't spill out the name of the man who'd shot him, or at least ask the man to come forward and tell the truth, Joe had answered, "I have never in my life asked anybody to help me, and I won't now."

After work on the night of November 18, just twelve hours before the scheduled execution, Tommy paced back and forth across the small kitchen, his head bowed and his hands clasped behind him. He had unfinished business with Joe Hill. Ever since that last time he visited Joe in his cell, there'd been no way to communicate with him. Tonight Joe's face kept coming up before Tommy, with those piercing blue eyes and that sad, stubborn look. . . .

Growing impatient, Fiona said, "Stop that pacing and sit down, Tommy. Peter and I need to talk to you."

"Can't it wait?" he asked.

"No, it can't."

He turned a chair backward and straddled it, his arms crossed on the chair back. That only made him think of Sam Bowman's description of Joe's arms resting on the prison bars.

"We've made a decision," Fiona announced, and Peter nodded. "Are you paying attention, Tommy?"

"Yes," he lied.

Suddenly his mother's words did shock him into attention: "Peter and I are planning to move to Salt Lake City. I'm going to open an alterations shop. We've already put a down payment on a small house with a shop in the front."

"You have?"

"Yep! As for me," Peter added, "I'll be working at IWW headquarters. A gimpy leg won't handicap me there. After hanging around here all these months, I really want to do something useful again."

Caught unaware, Tommy sputtered, "When did you two decide on this?"

Both of them answered, "A few days ago."

"And," Fiona continued, "we want you to quit the mine and come with us. You can find a safer job in the city and go to school—Peter says you could take evening classes to make up for the years you've lost. What does it matter if you finish high school a couple years late?"

"Or you could learn a trade," Peter said. "There's plenty more opportunity in a big city than here in this little coal-mining town. More for me, more for your mother, and definitely more for you, Tommy."

The two of them watched him, expectant. All he could think to say was, "Why did you have to bring this up now? Why tonight, of all nights?"

"Because you're part of our plans," Fiona answered. "What we do affects you, whether you want it to or not. We're going to sell this house—if you stay in Castle Gate, you'll have to find a boardinghouse, Tommy. But I don't want you to do that. I've always wanted you out of the coal mine—this is your chance."

Rubbing his forehead with his hand, Tommy told them, "I need to think." He went into his room to be alone.

All night long he tossed and turned, sleeping only in short snatches. While it was still dark, he got up, dressed, and walked to the telegraph station next to the railroad depot. He didn't know what he was hoping for—that someone in Salt Lake City might have sent the news by telegraph, perhaps, announcing whether Joe Hill had actually been executed or had magically escaped death once again? But no news came, and by 7 A.M. it was time to report to work.

All through the early morning he waited for news. If it didn't arrive at the telegraph office, there'd surely be extra editions of Salt Lake City newspapers delivered to Castle Gate by train. The news would have to filter, miner by miner, from the outside world through the tunnels, but that would happen fast.

Nine o'clock, nine thirty, and nothing. Then, like a collective sigh, the bad tidings blew through the mine tunnels. Joe Hill had been executed. He was dead.

That night the newspapers were full of nothing except Joe's last hours. He'd been led from his cell to the prison yard, where the firing squad, hidden behind a sheet of canvas, waited inside the converted blacksmith's shop. Five holes had been cut into the canvas for five rifle barrels to poke through. Four of the rifles had been loaded with real bullets; one had only a blank cartridge in the chamber. That way the men in the firing squad would never know which of them had *not* killed Joe Hill.

Twenty feet in front of the canvas, an empty chair waited. Led toward it, Joe exclaimed, "I will show you how to die." After he was strapped into the chair, and his eyes covered with a mask, he announced loudly, "I have a clear conscience."

A doctor used a stethoscope to check the exact location of Joe's heart. After he found it, a guard pinned a paper target over the spot.

Joe shouted, "I'm going now, boys. Good-bye!"

The deputy called out, "Ready, aim—"

"Fire! Go on and fire," Joe yelled.

Five rifles cracked. Joe slumped in the chair. Dead.

Afterward one of the members of the firing squad had told the reporter, "We fired. I wanted to close my eyes, but they stared at the white paper heart. It was scorched and torn by four lead bullets. Four blackened circles began to turn crimson. Then a spurt, and then the paper heart went all red."

When Tommy read those words, walking home through

the clean white skiff of snow falling on Castle Gate, he dropped to his knees and said a prayer for the dead.

"Have you thought about moving to Salt Lake City?" his mother asked him as soon as he got home.

No. He'd thought about nothing but Joe Hill. "Later," he told her.

The next day, around three in the afternoon, while Tommy was working a deep seam at the end of a long tunnel, Black Edo came running toward him. The whole length of the tunnel Edo kept shouting Tommy's name.

"What?" Tommy demanded when Edo came close.

"The boss Mr. Farnham wanna see you. You s'pose to go to his office quick. Awful quick."

"Why?"

"Dunno. Maybe he find out about you and Eugenie."

Tommy considered that possibility and then dismissed it. He'd seen Eugenie only three times in the past two months, and those meetings had been strained and unsatisfactory. Eugenie claimed to be working hard at the university, doubling up on her classes because, she said, she wanted to finish college early so she could get a job to support herself, without requiring help from her parents. And because of his own overtime hours Tommy'd had little chance to travel to Salt Lake City to see her.

As he trudged the length of the mine tunnels he wondered whether to go home and wash up before going to Mr. Farnham's office. But why should he? He was a laborer in a coal mine. Let Mr. Farnham see what eight hours' worth of coal dust looked like when it blackened a miner's skin.

"Go right inside," the male secretary told him, but his expression was odd—lips twitching with a tiny, suppressed glimmer of glee, like a schoolkid who'd just snitched on another kid and was waiting to hear the whack of the teacher's paddle.

Ellis Farnham sat behind his desk, his eyeglasses halfway down the bridge of his nose. When he stared up at Tommy, his flat blue eyes reminded Tommy of Joe Hill's—direct, but a little calculating. "Thomas Quinlan?" he asked.

"Yes, sir. I'm Thomas Quinlan." Didn't Farnham even remember him?

"Have you ever heard of Tommy Mack?" Mr. Farnham asked.

It was so unexpected that Tommy couldn't think how to answer.

"The reason I'm asking," Mr. Farnham went on, "is that one hour ago this telegram was delivered to Castle Gate. The telegraph operator brought it to my office because he didn't know any Tommy Mack, but he thought I'd be interested in the message." Again that flat, blue-eyed stare. "Would you happen to be Tommy Mack?"

"Uh . . . it's a name someone once suggested that I use."

Raising the yellow sheet of telegraph paper, Mr. Farnham said, "Thomas, I'm taking the liberty of reading this out loud to you. It says, 'Joe Hill wanted you to sing at his funeral. Am wiring fifty dollars to get you to Chicago. Come soon as possible.' And it's signed 'Bill Haywood, IWW.'"

*My God,* Tommy thought. Even from the dead, Joe Hill wasn't giving up on him.

Mr. Farnham leaned back in his chair, waiting for Tommy to respond. "I don't know anything about it," Tommy said stonily, trying to keep his wits about him, trying to figure out how to handle this.

Mr. Farnham pointed to a small layer of paper money on his desk. "That is the fifty dollars. Why would Big Bill Haywood wire you fifty dollars if you didn't know anything about it?"

Tommy just shook his head.

"You are the Thomas Quinlan who sings, correct? So if you have been invited by Bill Haywood to sing at Joe Hill's funeral, this cannot be a case of mistaken identity. Am I right? Do you know Big Bill Haywood? Did you know Joe Hill?"

"Yes, sir," Tommy admitted. "I've met both of them."

"And do you intend to go to Chicago as Bill Haywood instructs you in this telegram?"

"I . . . don't know," Tommy answered.

At that, some of the stiffness left Ellis Farnham. "Listen, Thomas," he said, "you don't want to get mixed up with these hard-core union men. They're bad types, especially the Wobblies, the IWW."

Tommy answered, "Not all of them."

Mr. Farnham got up then and walked around his desk to face Tommy. "Not only are they undesirables, they're ineffective. Let me tell you something, Thomas." More relaxed now, he sat on the edge of his desk. "I keep up with what the unions preach. Those men are always ranting that government and law are tools used by capitalists to control the masses. They blather about equality. When they're asked who their leaders are, the members say, 'We're all leaders. One Big Union, every man equal.' Do you know what that leads to, Thomas? Anarchy!"

There was that word again.

"Do you know why, Thomas? Why you can't have a

decent organization if every man thinks he's a leader? Because then no one leads at all. All they do is squabble, and the organization falls into disarray."

Sounding like a professor, Mr. Farnham continued, "Those Wobblies think they've come up with this noble ideal that will change the course of history. One Big Union for everyone, male or female, black or white or brown or yellow or immigrant. Mark my words, Thomas—notions like that, when they're thought up by dreamers who find themselves in power, cause nothing but catastrophe. Under Big Bill Haywood the IWW is going to collapse."

For a long moment Ellis Farnham stared at Tommy, while Tommy's mind whirled, trying to make sense of everything the man had said.

"So, Thomas, what are you going to do about this telegram?"

Clenching his jaw, Tommy stared at his blackened hands. Then he looked up and answered, "I can't see that it would hurt anything if I went to a funeral and sang."

Mr. Farnham gave a little laugh, as dry and unreadable as his eyes. "You planning to sing 'Amazing Grace,' or some song appropriate to a funeral? Don't be foolish, Thomas. They'll want you to sing rabble-rousing union songs. This funeral won't be a quiet and respectful memorial—it'll be a wild rally for the One Big Union."

"I . . . can't say if that's what will happen or not."

Mr. Farnham continued, "The songs they'll expect you to sing are the kind that get people all fired up so they stop thinking logically. Doesn't matter what kind of music it is— church music, patriotic songs, or union songs—when you get a bunch of people stomping and clapping, or marching together to the beat of a drum, their brains shut down. That's when the demagogues step in and lead the masses around like so many sheep."

No use arguing with that. Tommy remembered his own fervent reaction to the crowd singing and shouting in front of the penitentiary.

"Listen, Thomas." Mr. Farnham laid a hand on Tommy's shoulder. "You're a bright young fellow. Honest, too—your bosses have mentioned you to me. If you forget about this union business, I'll promote you to weighmaster. The miners will trust the weights you give them."

"And if I don't?" Tommy asked it so quietly, Mr. Farnham had to lean close to hear him repeat, "If I don't?"

"Then you won't have a job at all. Not here, not in any mine anywhere. Tomorrow's Sunday—take the day to think about it. If you're not here at work on Monday morning, you're fired."

Tommy started to leave. He was almost to the door when Mr. Farnham called out, "Come here and get the fifty dollars. It was sent to you. Whatever you do with it is your problem, not mine."

When Tommy turned around, Ellis Farnham said, "You'd better think carefully, Thomas. Don't allow your life to be defined by two murderers."

There was no point in going back to work that afternoon. Clutching the five ten-dollar bills, Tommy walked through the snow-lined streets to his home. This time it was Tommy who asked Fiona and Peter to sit down for a talk.

After he'd told them about the telegram and Mr. Farnham's ultimatum, Fiona asked, "So, what are you going to do?"

"I don't know."

"If Mr. Farnham thinks he's breaking your mother's

heart by threatening to fire you," she said, "he's got another think coming. Nothing would make me happier than having you leave the mine."

"What I don't understand," Tommy told Peter, "is about going to Chicago for the funeral. The funeral is in Salt Lake City. It says so in the newspaper."

"You didn't read far enough," Peter answered. "They're having two funerals. One's Sunday—that's tomorrow—in Salt Lake City, the second one's on Thursday in Chicago."

"Thursday's Thanksgiving," Fiona objected. "I don't want Tommy to be away from us on Thanksgiving Day."

"Fiona, there will be many Thanksgivings when we can all be together," Peter told her.

"Of course, and it was you who got him all involved in this union business in the first place," she complained.

"And it was you who wanted him out of the mine," Peter shot back. "Things have a way of turning out. Anyway, it's Tommy's decision. And he'll have to make it quick to reach Salt Lake tomorrow in time for the first funeral."

Looking up at Tommy, who now towered above his mother, Fiona asked, "So, Tommy, what's it to be?"

Maybe it was because she asked it so forthrightly. At that moment all his doubts dissolved. "I'm going," he answered.

# CHAPTER NINETEEN
### November 21, 1915

Peter went with Tommy, and that turned out to be a good thing. When they reached the O'Donnell Mortuary, several thousand people crowded the street outside. "We'll never get in to see the body," Tommy predicted, but then the crowd began to part to make way for Peter and his crutches.

"Follow right behind me," Peter advised him. Since Tommy had checked his guitar and a small suitcase—there was nothing in it except a clean shirt and underwear—into a locker at the Union Pacific station, he could easily slip behind Peter into the space people cleared. "Thank you, fellow workers," Peter kept saying as the mourners moved aside for him.

The room where Joe's body lay was crowded beyond capacity by people of all descriptions: women in worn cloth coats and women wearing furs around their necks; men trying to remove their heavy overcoats without bumping into other men who had no coats to wear; even a few children whose parents pushed them toward the coffin, telling them, "Take a good look. And remember him. He was a hero."

Again the crowd made way for the man on crutches. Tommy stayed near to Peter, not only because he wanted to approach the coffin, but because he really was afraid that Peter, awkward on the artificial leg, might trip over someone's feet and be hurt. When they got close enough to gaze right down into the open coffin, Peter said softly, "There he lies. Our Joe."

Cheekbones even more prominent in death, the pallor even more ashen than in prison, closed lids blocking that once intense blue-eyed stare, Joe looked almost like a statesman. Death had dignified him. The right lapel of his plain black suit bore an IWW pin; on the left lapel lay two roses, one red and one white.

*Forgive me, Joe,* Tommy told him silently. *I should have understood you better when you were alive. You said you only wanted justice. Now you'll have to settle for fame.*

Tommy searched for a kneeler so he could say a prayer for Joe, but there was none. "Let's step back," Peter murmured. The paleness around Peter's mouth worried Tommy —the two of them had done a lot of walking to get there, and Peter was evidently hurting. When a woman stood up to offer him her seat, Peter looked embarrassed, but he gratefully sank into it. Standing next to him, Tommy began to survey the crowd.

Almost all the men in the room, and a number of the women, wore red ribbons on their lapels. Many had red armbands. The lower part of Joe's coffin was swathed in red cloth.

"Why all the red?" Tommy whispered.

"Don't you know?" Peter asked.

Then Tommy understood. Since he studied the newspapers every night, he'd read plenty about the Socialist Party, whose radical members were despised by the owners and managers that ran the newspapers and the banks and the businesses. Red was the color of Socialism, and Socialists were the main supporters of the Industrial Workers of the World.

At three o'clock the funeral service began, different from any funeral Tommy had ever attended. No preacher, no priest, no man of the cloth of any description—just a lot of speakers who talked about justice, and the sad lack of it in Joe Hill's case.

"Guess we'll have to say our own prayers," Tommy whispered, and Peter nodded.

At least there was music: choral renderings by the Swedish Temperance Society Choir. The songs they sang were patriotic rather than religious. Tommy wondered whether the funeral in Chicago, the one where he'd been asked to sing, would be the same as this. Mr. Farnham had said Tommy would be expected to sing rousing union songs. He'd brought *The Little Red Songbook* with him so that during the long train ride he could memorize more of Joe's songs. All at once he understood why it was called *The Little Red Songbook*. He'd never thought of that before.

After the orations everyone was allowed to file past the casket for a final farewell, but Peter couldn't manage it. "Listen, if you can walk just a block or so," Tommy told him, "I'm sure I can find you a taxicab. There's no way a cab could make it all the way up to the door here with those thousands of people outside."

"I'll be fine," Peter said, but Tommy wasn't at all sure of that. Again people were kind and let him through, and then a policeman—a policeman! (Tommy didn't expect that, since Wobblies considered police the enemy)—flagged a taxi for them.

"Why don't you stay?" Peter suggested from inside the

cab. "I'll go straight to the YMCA and get a bed. You can be part of the funeral cortege, Tommy, and then go directly to the station to board the train for Chicago."

Even though he worried about Peter, Tommy was glad to stay behind with the thousands of mourners, since he didn't want to miss anything. So tall that he could see over most people's heads, he watched as Joe Hill's closed coffin, now all covered in red and piled high with flowers, got lifted into an open automobile hearse. Slowly the chauffeur drove the hearse through the streets, slow enough for the procession of mourners to follow on foot. Six women in white dresses with red sashes braved the cold to walk alongside the hearse all the way to the Union Pacific station. There the coffin and flowers were packed together in a traveling box, with a letter to Bill Haywood placed on top.

Tommy figured the train might depart a little late, but he wasn't taking any chances. He quickly bought a round-trip ticket to Chicago, retrieved his guitar and suitcase from the locker, and had just turned around when he saw—Eugenie! Not only Eugenie, but Mr. and Mrs. Farnham, not twenty feet away from him.

He froze, unsure what he should do. None of them glanced in his direction, because both Eugenie and her father were supporting Mrs. Farnham, who seemed about to collapse. It wasn't until after they'd led her to a bench and lowered her into it that Eugenie turned and saw him.

As she ran toward him he could see that her face was swollen from crying. Without even speaking his name, she threw herself into his arms. "Glenn's dead," she sobbed. "His troop train was bombed in Serbia."

"Serbia!" Tommy cried. "I thought he was in the trenches in Belgium."

"His unit got transported to fight the Bulgars—oh, Tommy, it's so awful! I can't believe my brother's dead!" Again she sobbed, clinging to him, her shoulders shaking with grief. Tommy felt at a loss—what could he possibly say to comfort Eugenie? Glenn—that smiling, happy young man who joked with his sister and thought Tommy was a poet— Glenn, dead in Serbia, where all the trouble had started.

"We're on our way to Washington to ask the ambassador to help bring back Glenn's body," she told him, still choking with tears.

Tommy wrapped his arms around her and held her tightly as she wept, with her face buried against his shirtfront.

"Eugenie, what is the meaning of this!" Ellis Farnham demanded, striding toward them.

Wearily she raised her head. "It's time you knew, Daddy. Tommy and I have been meeting each other for more than a year."

"Preposterous! Do you know where Thomas is going?" Mr. Farnham demanded. "To Chicago, to a Wobbly rally honoring the murderer Joe Hill. Get away from him! I forbid you to have anything to do with that . . . that . . . *anarchist!*"

Eugenie wiped her tears with a handkerchief, then slipped her arm through Tommy's. "I love him, Dad."

"You're a child, Eugenie!" her father shouted. "You don't even know the meaning of love. Now do as I say!"

Her voice softened. "Dad, you've just lost Glenn. Do you want to lose me too?"

Tommy would never forget the pitiful sight of Ellis Farnham, that imposing, dignified mine owner, breaking down in public, right there in front of everyone in the Union Pacific Railroad station. People turned their eyes away when Mr. Farnham sagged against a pillar and wept aloud, his head sunk in grief.

"I have to go to him," Eugenie told Tommy.

"Yes, you have to," Tommy agreed. He kissed her cheek and said, "You and I—we'll be all right. We'll be together."

He watched Eugenie take her father into her arms and lead him to the bench where Mrs. Farnham, too distraught to have noticed or cared what had gone on between Tommy and Eugenie and Mr. Farnham, sat looking pathetic and helpless. Eugenie and her parents would board a different train, traveling a more southern route, than the one Tommy would take.

"All aboard!" the conductor cried.

Clutching his suitcase and his guitar, Tommy hopped onto the train for Chicago. It wasn't decent for him to feel so happy—not when he was on his way to a funeral, and not right after hearing about Glenn's tragic death. But all he could think about was Eugenie, the way she'd stood up to her father and said, "I love him, Dad." It was what he'd wanted for so long: to have her declare that Tommy was her—he didn't know exactly which word to use. Her suitor? Her young man? Admirer? Beau? Whatever it was, the Farnhams now knew that their daughter loved Tommy. Eugenie—his own, true rebel girl! What they'd do now, he couldn't predict, but with Eugenie at the University of Utah, and Tommy possibly moving to Salt Lake City, it would be hard for Mr. Farnham to keep them apart.

As the train wheels clacked along the railroad tracks for the first hundred miles or so, Tommy couldn't stop smiling. Then he thought he'd better pull out *The Little Red Songbook* and get to work.

# CHAPTER TWENTY
### November 23 to Thanksgiving Day, 1915

Chicago! All Tommy's senses told him it was different from any place he'd ever been. It felt different, it smelled different, it even sounded different—pulsing with noisy life, with the rumble of industry, the footsteps of millions.

He stood on the train platform wondering where he should go—no one had given him any instructions. Farther along the platform he saw a man holding up a torn piece of a corrugated box; on the surface was painted TOMMY MACK. Drips of black paint had run from the bottoms of the letters to the edge of the cardboard.

"I guess you mean me," Tommy said when he reached the man.

"You're Tommy Mack?"

"Close enough."

"Follow me." Moving rapidly, the shabbily dressed man led Tommy through crowds denser than any he'd ever seen in Salt Lake's railroad depot, or anywhere else. Trying to maneuver his guitar case and suitcase to avoid hitting anyone, Tommy kept falling behind. Exasperated, the man would stop and wave his sign, urging Tommy to hurry.

As it turned out, there was no need to hurry. Mr. Haywood had just gone to bed, Tommy was told when he reached the funeral home near midnight on Tuesday evening. Tommy spent a long night sitting on an uncomfortable chair in one of the back rooms of the mortuary, along with half a dozen other people, all of them waiting to see Bill Haywood.

Around noon Wednesday, twelve hours after he'd arrived in Chicago and twenty-two hours before the funeral would begin, Tommy was summoned into the presence of Big Bill Haywood, the man who'd pinned fifty dollars inside Tommy's shirt so long ago. He wondered whether Haywood remembered. Becoming head of the IWW had greatly increased Haywood's power, that was true; yet, now that Tommy stood even taller than Big Bill, he wasn't sure why he'd been so terrified of the man eight years earlier. The blind eye was no longer frightening—Tommy'd seen worse mutilations than that from mining accidents.

The first thing Bill Haywood said to him was, "Where the hell did you get that tweed hat?"

Taken aback, Tommy answered, "My girl gave it to me. Why?"

"Get rid of it—you look like a fop. And what's with the fancy suit? You're supposed to be a singing coal miner, not a banker. Take off the suit coat, ditch the tie, and roll up your shirtsleeves before you go out on that stage."

Tommy nodded. "All right."

"So," Big Bill said. "Sing for me."

"Here? Now?" They were in a back room of the Florence Funeral Parlor, where Joe's body had been brought from the train. As in Salt Lake City, thousands of mourners filed past the coffin in another room, but these people had a different look—more foreign, more poorly dressed. Dark-haired girls placed small bouquets into the coffin, until it looked like a spring garden. Many of the flowers were red carnations.

"Yes, here and now," Haywood said. "I want this funeral to come off as smooth as the Ziegfeld Follies. No surprises. Let me hear which of Joe's songs you're going to sing."

Tommy fingered his guitar case. "Well, Mr. Haywood, Joe Hill wanted me to make up my own songs, so I did—I wrote one on the train coming here."

"Let's hear it," Haywood said. When Tommy tried to tune his guitar, Big Bill snapped, "Forget that monkey business. Don't waste time, just get to the song."

Tommy hoped he would remember all the words. The music wasn't a problem; once a song was in Tommy's head, it stayed forever. Words were different. Even if they were his own words, he sometimes forgot a few. He began,

> "When fathers, sons, or brothers die
>   From bullets, bombs, or bayonets,
>   Their loved ones' hearts are filled with grief and pain,
>   In mansions or in hovels,
>   Silver spoons or miners' shovels,
>   Both rich and poor will sorrow just the—"

"Wait a minute!" Big Bill yelled. "What the hell kind of a song is that? You're singing about . . . about . . ." he stammered, "rich people and poor people feeling the same kind of pain?"

"Yes," Tommy answered.

Haywood's face grew red. "This is a class struggle we're

in! Do you intend to tell the masses that rich people have hearts? Are you out of your mind? You used the word *bayonet* so you must be talking about the war. Don't you know that the war in Europe is being waged by capitalists? The rich get richer, and the poor do the fighting and get killed."

"That isn't true," Tommy said. Eugenie had told him that half of Glenn's class at Oxford, all of them from wealthy families, had enlisted to fight in the British army.

"I don't give a damn whether it's true or not," Haywood shouted. "And it don't make a bit of difference to me if rich people fall down and *drown* in their grief, that's not the union's message to the rank and file. Got it? Any questions?"

"Just one." The realization had hit Tommy that a man who didn't give a damn about truth wouldn't have any qualms about bribing a jury. He asked, "Did you give the order to murder Frank Steunenberg?"

The guitar flew out of Tommy's hands as Bill Haywood grabbed him around the neck and shoved him hard against a wall. "You little weasel!" Haywood exploded. "They said you're Jimmy Mack's nephew all grown up—hell, you're not even the shadow of the man Jimmy Mack was. What kind of a union man are you?"

Tommy muttered, "One that cares about truth."

The hand tightened around Tommy's neck. "I'd throttle you right now and throw you out on the street, except that Joe wanted you to sing at his funeral, and I respect the wishes of a dead man." Haywood's flushed face was so close that Tommy could see the veins in his one good eye.

"I respected Joe Hill too," Tommy gasped.

"Shut up!"

It would have been easy for Tommy to fight back. He

was young, strong, and hard-muscled from two years of shoveling heavy coal. Haywood, on the other hand, was middle-aged and paunchy; one good punch in the gut would knock the wind right out of him. But what was the point, Tommy thought. Why fight, when he'd come here to honor Joe Hill? His right hand shot up to grab Haywood's wrist in a powerful lock. It didn't take much pressure before Haywood buckled.

"All right!" Haywood took a step backward, pretending he'd intentionally let go of Tommy. Then he started to fish around in his vest pocket. He pulled out a folded telegram and growled, "Some reporter named Sam Bowman sent this to me. Said Joe gave it to a guard the night before he died, and the guard gave it to Bowman. It's Joe Hill's last will. Use *that* to make a song." Big Bill spat at Tommy's feet, threw the telegram on the floor, and stomped out of the room, muttering, "Sanctimonious little prig . . ."

Tommy massaged his neck, wondering if his vocal cords would still work. Then he picked up the telegram. He had less than a day to write the music and learn by heart these words he'd never seen before. But what words they were!

The funeral was held in Chicago's West Side Auditorium—after a night spent in a fleabag hotel, Tommy'd had a hard time reaching the place. Three thousand mourners crowded into the building, and outside it ten times that many packed the streets. With the other people on the program Tommy got hustled inside through a rear door. On his own he'd never have made it through the mob.

Since it was Thanksgiving and another organization would hold a party that night in the same hall, the decorations were a mixture of fruit and turkeys, funeral flowers piled high, and red flags propped upright in stands all over the room. A banner above the coffin in the center of the stage proclaimed, IN MEMORIAM, JOE HILL. WE NEVER FORGET. The same red shroud that had draped the coffin in Utah still covered it.

There were a couple of chairs on the stage; Tommy stowed his suit coat and tie under one of them, along with his overcoat. Good thing Haywood hadn't seen the overcoat—it had been Uncle Jim's, so the sleeves were too short and the cuffs were so frayed that Haywood would have wanted him to wear it onstage.

Before the services had even begun, without any prompting, the crowd started to sing Joe's songs. "Come on, play along with them," a pretty, young girl told Tommy.

"Who are you?" he asked.

"Jennie Wosczyuska. I'm supposed to sing 'The Rebel Girl.' Do you know that song? Can you play it?"

"Yes, I know it, but I don't think anyone will hear my guitar." To demonstrate, he plucked a few chords, which were drowned out by the thunderous singing of the people in the hall.

"When you and I are ready to sing, they'll be quiet," she assured him.

Promptly at 10:30 A.M. Bill Haywood strode to the center of the stage. His appearance was so commanding that the crowd immediately grew silent. In a voice that carried loudly enough that they could hear him at the back of the hall, Haywood announced, "I received a message from Joe Hill—it was delivered here with his body. This is what Joe wrote to me. 'Good-bye Bill: I die like a true rebel. Don't waste any time mourning—organize! It is a hundred miles from here to

Wyoming. Could you arrange to have my body hauled to the state line to be buried? I don't want to be found dead in Utah. Joe Hill.'"

Tommy felt his face flush. That message demeaned Utah, making it sound like a cruel, heartless place. Tommy had been born in Utah; his father was buried there; his mother and Peter lived there. Joe Hill's trial may have been unfair, but plenty of decent people lived in Utah. People like—Tommy had to admit it—Ellis Farnham, who might not want his daughter to be with Tommy, but who'd given Peter a year's wages after his accident, something he wasn't required to do. And what about all those sympathetic thousands who'd attended Joe Hill's funeral in Salt Lake City?

It got worse. Next Bill Haywood introduced the main speaker, O. N. Hilton, who spent most of two hours condemning Utah, saying that Utah's Governor Spry had turned down President Woodrow Wilson's "sacred request for a delay of Joe Hill's execution," and claiming that Joe Hill was "a martyr to the working class."

*Sure,* Tommy thought, *but Joe chose to be a martyr.* As Tommy listened to the long oration, he realized it was skewed with half-truths and distortions, dishing out prejudice against the wealthy class in the same way the wealthy class clung to their prejudices against the working class. The speaker kept demanding justice for the poor and revenge against the wealthy. But how could there be justice for the working class if justice didn't exist for everyone? Wouldn't that lead to *in*justice for all?

Then Tommy stopped paying attention, because he began to sort out what he believed. That all people deserved justice. That all people felt pain and grief and loss. And if they were lucky, all of them could feel love too, no matter where their families had come from, no matter what kind of work they did.

Before he'd left for Chicago, he'd said to his mother, "It seems everybody has a different idea of what I ought to become, Mom. So what do you want me to be?"

"Safe! Alive! Happy!" she'd cried. "That's all."

But it wasn't enough. He was eighteen years old, and he needed something to dedicate himself to. Not the union, because he could see both sides of the issues and the union could not. Not his music, because it didn't matter so much to him anymore.

But justice—that did matter. Justice depended on rules of law. Law, if it was to be fair, should guarantee justice. If Tommy wanted to believe in something, it was that fairness applied equally to everyone, could crumble away the rock walls that divided people.

Maybe he could get a job in Salt Lake City, go to night school, and—even if it took years of hard work—study law. Joe Hill had insisted that if he'd had the right lawyers, he'd have been a free man. Tommy had a way with words; maybe he could use those words in a courtroom to seek justice. For all.

"It's time for me to sing," Jennie Wosczyuska told him. Tommy stood up to accompany her, smiling to himself when she sang "Rebel Girl," because now he had his own rebel girl waiting for him.

"Here's Tommy Mack," Bill Haywood announced, "picked by Joe Hill himself to sing today. The music is by Tommy, the words by Joe Hill." Haywood threw a threatening glance in Tommy's direction.

Tommy made up his mind right then that this would be the first and only time he'd ever be called Tommy Mack. He was Thomas Quinlan. He began to sing.

"My will is easy to decide,
For there is nothing to divide.
My kin don't need to fuss and moan—
Moss does not cling to a rolling stone.

My body?—Oh—If I could choose,
I would to ashes it reduce,
And let the merry breezes blow
My dust to where some flowers grow.
Perhaps some fading flowers then
Would come to life and bloom again.
This is my last and final will.
Good luck to all of you,
Joe Hill."

*Good lord,* Tommy thought, feeling the tears in his own eyes. *I could never have taken Joe's place. I'm just not good enough.*

The large crowd began to file out of the hall then as a pianist played slow and mournful music. Jennie Wosczyuska asked Tommy, "Do you know what that music is? It's Chopin's Funeral March. Have you heard of Frédéric Chopin?"

"Yes," Tommy told her.

"I bet there's something you don't know about him."

"What? That he was Polish?"

Surprised, Jennie grinned up at him. "How did you know that?"

"My girl told me."

Tommy could hardly wait to get back to his girl. The funeral cortege would accompany Joe's coffin to the train station, where it would travel to a cemetery a few miles away for cremation. Tommy decided not to go to the cemetery. At the station he'd board the next train leaving for Salt Lake City, where his life was waiting for him.

"Good-bye, Joe," he said softly as he watched the coffin being carried onto the train. Cold wind blew around Tommy; after all, it was Thanksgiving Day.

He had a lot to be thankful for.

## Resources

For a thorough account of the Bill Haywood murder trial in Boise, Idaho, read *Big Trouble,* by J. Anthony Lucas, published in 1997 by Simon & Schuster, New York.

To learn more about Joe Hill, read *Joe Hill,* by Gibbs M. Smith, published in 1984 by Peregrine Smith Books, Salt Lake City, Utah; and *The Case of Joe Hill,* by Philip S. Foner, published in 1965 by International Publishers, New York.

Outstanding and informative Web sites include:

http://www.kued.org/joehill
http://www.kued.org/fire

Joe Hill's songs can be heard on the CD titled *Don't Mourn —Organize!* from Smithsonian/Folkways Records, Office of Folklife Programs, 955 L'Enfant Plaza, Suite 2600, Smithsonian Institute, Washington, D.C. 20560.

The following Web site plays original popular music that was actually recorded between 1908 and 1913:

http://www.besmark.com/popular.html

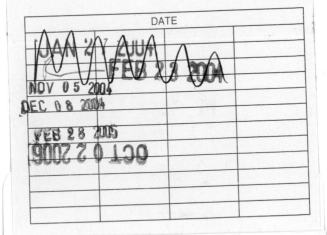

| DATE | | | |
|---|---|---|---|
| JAN 27 2004 | FEB 23 2004 | | |
| NOV 05 2004 | | | |
| DEC 08 2004 | | | |
| FEB 28 2005 | | | |
| OCT 02 2006 | | | |
| | | | |
| | | | |
| | | | |